LIMINAL

Also by Jordan Tannahill

Plays
Declarations
Botticelli in the Fire
Sunday in Sodom
Concord Floral
Late Company
Age of Minority: 3 Solo Plays

Books
Theatre of the Unimpressed: In Search of Vital Drama
The Videofag Book

LIMINAL

JORDAN TANNAHILL

ANANSI

Published in Canada in 2018 by House of Anansi Press Inc.
www.houseofanansi.com

House of Anansi Press is committed to protecting our natural environment.
As part of our efforts, the interior of this book is printed on paper that contains
100% post-consumer recycled fibres, is acid-free, and is processed chlorine-free.

22 21 20 19 18   1 2 3 4 5

Library and Archives Canada Cataloguing in Publication

Tannahill, Jordan, author
Liminal / Jordan Tannahill.

Issued in print and electronic formats.
ISBN 978-1-4870-0378-4 (softcover).— ISBN 978-1-4870-0379-1
(EPUB).— ISBN 978-1-4870-0380-7 (Kindle)

I. Title.

PS8639.A577L56 2018   C813'.6   C2017-904727-2
                   C2017-904728-0

Book design: Alysia Shewchuk

Canada Council   Conseil des Arts   ONTARIO ARTS COUNCIL
for the Arts   du Canada   CONSEIL DES ARTS DE L'ONTARIO
                                      an Ontario government agency
                                      un organisme du gouvernement de l'Ontario

*We acknowledge for their financial support of our publishing program
the Canada Council for the Arts, the Ontario Arts Council, and the Government of
Canada through the Canada Book Fund.*

Printed and bound in Canada

RECYCLED
Paper made from
recycled material
FSC
www.fsc.org   FSC® C103567

For my mother

AUTHOR'S NOTE

This is a work of fiction. And while I have drawn inspiration from real people I know, I can assure the reader that without exception the real people are better in every way.

"I" is merely one of the world's instantaneous spasms.
　　—Clarice Lispector, *The Passion According to G. H.*

When we speak the word "life," it must be understood
we are not referring to life as we know it from its surface
of fact, but to that fragile, fluctuating center which forms
never reach.
　　　　　—Antonin Artaud, *Theatre of Cruelty*

I

ON THE MORNING of Saturday January 21, 2017, you didn't wake up. Not at six thirty or seven, the time you were normally having your coffee and finishing your Sudoku. Or at eight or eight thirty, the time you'd wake after a dinner party with girlfriends, or even nine if you'd managed to get through a few bottles of wine together. By ten I managed to make myself think, *Good for her, she's having a lie-in.* You'd gone to bed early the night before. We were watching coverage of Donald Trump's inauguration when you began to complain of a headache. I joked you could expect to have one for the next four years. As the evening wore on it developed into a migraine, which of course worried us in light of your Transient Ischemic Attack. TIA. What your doctor had called "a warning stroke."

You said, "I'm going to turn in," and as you walked upstairs I called, "Make sure to keep your head propped up," for which I had absolutely no idea if there was any medical basis.

By ten thirty that morning I was sitting on my bed checking emails, waiting for the soft thud of your feet hitting the floor of your bedroom, the creak of the floorboards, the scraping of hangers in your closet. But the usual sounds didn't come. Not even a cough or the rustling of sheets. Only the occasional passing car punctuated the silence, the spitting of its tires on the asphalt suggesting the snow was melting to slush. I'd made plans to meet Ana downtown for the Women's March at noon; she was back in Ottawa visiting family as well. She sent me a photo of herself wearing her pink knitted Pussy Hat and a giant fabric banner she'd sewn declaring, *I'm So Angry I Stiched This Just So I Could Stab Something 3000 Times.* The text was laid out like a rainbow above a raised fist holding a large knitting needle.

"Purrrrrfection," I texted back, before pointing out that she'd forgotten the "t" in "stitched."

"Pretty sure Trump can't read anyway," she replied.

You'd mentioned wanting to join us but had to see how you were feeling. Should I wake you, then? To give you time to get ready? As it hit a quarter to eleven I jumped in the shower and was expecting to see your door open when I got out; to hear the clinking of your spoon against your cereal bowl in the kitchen. But as I walked into the hallway in my towel your door was still closed. I dressed, combed my hair, and packed my knapsack for the day. At eleven I peeled open a can of Whiskas for Chloe and let Al out into the yard to pee. And as I stood there watching him sniff about I fought an almost overwhelming urge to check on you. You'd been having restless sleeps all week. Maybe you'd had another bad night. You'd resent being woken. I was sure of it. But if I didn't it would gnaw at me the whole bus ride, at least until I got your text—"Sorry, I slept in. Send photos."—but what if that text didn't come? I'd be in the middle of the protest nauseous, ripped through with worry, noon, twelve thirty, one o'clock, Ana saying, "We can go home if you like," and yes, I'd have to come all the way back, an hour on the bus, always taking a goddamn eternity to get anywhere in Ottawa, calling the house over and over and if you didn't pick up what then, 911, the ambulance, the medics already outside the house when I arrived...

At three minutes and forty-five seconds past eleven I climbed the fifteen steps to the second floor, walked past the bathroom still humid from my shower towards your bedroom at the end of the hallway, placed my hand on the cool metal of the doorknob, and at four minutes past eleven turned it with the care of a minesweeper, extending my left arm slowly, taking a half-step into your darkened room and glancing towards your bed.

MY EYES FIND your body in the dark. And as your body comes into focus something inside me collapses. Caves in. You are still and unconscious. Eyes closed, mouth agape. Lips parted, like a cheesy perfume ad. I'm looking at your body and I cannot comprehend it. Why?

It is in-between. I cannot understand your body because it is caught between two distinct possibilities:

a) You are asleep.
b) You are dead.

I know you must be one or the other; that you are caught between these states is only my perception. And I know that it's impossible to know for certain, until I take the three steps towards the bed and touch your hand; until I place my ear to your lips and you startle awake, your head retreating into the pillow. Until I laugh and say, "I thought you were dead." "Dead?" "You looked dead." "What are you doing in my room?" "I'm sorry for waking you up. How're you feeling?" "What time is it?" "Eleven." "Are you serious?" And so on.

That you're asleep is definitely the more probable of the two possibilities. After all, every other time I've walked in on you in bed you've been alive, breathing, sleeping, dreaming, or sitting up reading, on the phone, crying, clipping your nails, or just lost in thought. Every other moment in my entire life you've been alive, an infinite number of living moments, why should this one be the exception? Eleven in the morning is not an hour for death. Death isn't a quiet thing to be happened upon like a bit of cat puke on the rug.

And yet something is different. It's undeniable. There is something about the room, the quality of the stillness, its breathlessness, the shape of your body, your face, the way it falls, that fills me with a terrible uncertainty. *Is this death?* Is this is what death looks like? Perhaps this is what death looks like in the light of late morning through beige curtains. What death looks like in the folds of your comforter, the wallpaper, the Moroccan rug, the wicker laundry hamper, your half-opened closet, the stack of historical novels on the floor, a copy of *National Geographic* on your bedside table, the Ikea floor lamp and its plastic shade. The absence of your life in every texture. The lack of that subtle scent, almost a warmth, of a sleeping body's breath in the room, a night's worth of exhalation.

As it comes into focus, your body is a thousand contradictions: the surest force I know and yet somehow almost immaterial; your face a kind of terrible death mask and yet beatific like a pre-Raphaelite Ophelia; the edges of your mouth tracing a smile and somehow a frown at the same time; your body weightless and yet leaden; suffused with light and yet dark.

AS I STAND here in the doorway in this second, less than a second, an instant between time, a synapse, I'm overcome, undone, suspended in a moment of what? Revelation? No. I hate the word. Anyone claiming revelation is usually a charlatan, ultra-religious, or insane — not that these three types are mutually exclusive. In fact, they rarely are. Perhaps this is a moment of "eureka," though the word feels burdened by the mythos of masculine scientific discovery, from Archimedes' fateful bath to Newton's gravity-weighted apple (why do I always imagine it hitting his head?). A "vision" is perhaps closer, but vision also carries religious undertones and the unfortunate limitations of its sensory association. A vision suggests something that is seen, either literally with one's eyes in a new way or within the mind's eye. As the ever-favoured child of the senses, sight seems to get undue credit for every discovery. If anything, like Proust and his madeleine, smell has always been the source of my strongest visions. But this moment of awareness is beyond sight, beyond any one sense. Even before my eyes have had time to fully adjust to the darkness, I am perceiving your body with every fibre of my own.

What I seek is a word that does not suggest a long sought-for answer, but rather a deluge of questions. A word for a kind of illumination that recalls a caver holding a torch up in an underground chamber and apprehending a few dashes of rock wall at a time, uncertain of how far the cavern extends into darkness. The first word in the Book of Revelation is *apokalypsis*, which in its original köine Greek means "unveiling" or "revelation." It's a word that seems to contain the possibility of discovery in the moment of destruction. Just as theatre is revealed in the instant of its disappearance. It exists in the temporal present between being and un-being, in what Plato calls the "something inserted between motion and rest…in no time at all." I like the almost preposterous gravity of *apokalypsis*, how its cataclysmic and eschatological associations mirror the way in which one world seems to end and another begins in a moment of newfound awareness.

But as your body comes into focus, "unveiling" somehow feels the most apt. An encounter, smell, sight, sensation that unveils an infinite system of questions and discoveries, which in turn spur more questions. Like a man in white gloves pulling a shroud off a painting, removing a covering that concealed what was there all along. Something which has been rendered ever more extraordinary by the very fact of its concealment. Not a divine conjuring, but a moment of discovery arising from matter-of-fact and mortal circumstances. A new way of experiencing something already in the world.

In this way the world is constantly unveiling itself. A stand of trees seen from a fresh angle, the laughter of a dog, a nameless colour, new patterns of movement, of light, of behaviour, patterns in fabric, in birds, in traffic, in music...In this way "revelation" is not something a bearded white man apprehends once an epoch, but rather a state of becoming that imbues all things at all times. Of course to be in a state of perpetual unveiling is exhausting and disorienting; it's essentially the way we moved through the world as babies, when everything was revealed and nothing was legible. Gradually, to make sense of the chaos, we fixed things in place, we fixed meaning, we fixed potential, we fixed objects and people and places as knowable and predictable entities and attempted to reduce the instances of unveiling because those upset the order by introducing new variables into the mix. Unveiling, by nature, un-fixes.

As I stand here at 11:04 a.m. on Saturday January 21, 2017, you in bed, me in the doorway in the moment of behold- ing, something—perhaps everything—is unveiled. And I become unfixed. But I do not yet understand. I am in the moment between awareness and comprehension. The inter- val between a hand touching boiling water and the pain of its scalding. Between sense and sensation.

II

MONICA. A name of North African origin. Santa Monica, mother of Saint Augustine. "Until the sun comes up over Santa Monica Boulevard" went the chorus of a song from my childhood. It was the name of a presidential intern-turned-mistress. A sitcom best friend. You hated it growing up. It didn't sound serious to you. And as a blond in the sixties, being taken seriously was a grail quest. Monica Tannahill. A young feminist in Trudeau's Canada. Now a fifty-eight-year-old feminist in another Trudeau's Canada. Single mother. Breast cancer survivor. Suburban jogger. Fitful yoga practitioner. Book club member (always loved a good multigenerational family saga). CBC Radio devotee. *Maclean's* magazine subscriber. Christian with new-age tendencies. Humanist. Card-carrying member of the Liberal Party. Gravitational force of a small galaxy of girlfriends. A self-proclaimed "hard-ass." You saw money and status as forms of emancipation. You saw female colleagues, close friends, ground down in the gears of public bureaucracies and chewed up in the lion's den of the private sector, and there was no way in hell you were going to succumb to that fate. You believed in getting your due. In tough love. In being a clear and confident boss, the kind that men got called "strong" and women got called "bitches" for being. Your millennial colleagues exasperated you. *Raise your voice once and they'll brim at the eyes; you wouldn't believe the amount of time I have to spend now just sorting through who said what to whom and what that made them feel; I mean, I'm there to run a lab, not a focus group.*

You worked full days in the lab at Carleton before coming home to cook dinner for me and sometimes for your friends, serving nice vintages and playing vaguely Celtic music on low, and on other nights driving me to soccer and T-ball and then increasingly to gymnastics and drama. You drove a mini-suv because you didn't want to feel pushed around and wanted traction whenever you needed it. After fighting for every goddamn thing in your life since the late fifties, you never wanted to be denied traction. Overworked, undervalued, burnt out, anxious. The holotype of the helicopter parent, amending school release forms in red pen and sealing pizza-day money in envelopes marked *Pizza Day*. Rocking up to school assemblies in intimidating shoulder pads in the early nineties, no-nonsense bob-cuts in the late nineties, and don't-fuck-with-me black thick-frame glasses in the aughts, arriving five minutes late but always in time to catch my cameo. You drank your coffee black, three cups in the morning and at regular intervals throughout the day.

It was a shock to see you felled by your own brain. The one thing you thought you could always rely on, the one thing that had always gotten you through. It had begun with your right hand. It was morning. You were in the kitchen. You had poured yourself a glass of water, but when you made to drink it you couldn't see the glass in your hand anymore. More specifically, you couldn't tell where the glass ended and your body began. You unclenched your fingers and heard the glass shatter on the floor. You looked down and saw the shards and spattered water.

Your Airbnb guest walked in, a young Spanish tourist. He found you on your hands and knees, cleaning up the mess.

You turned and looked up at him. "I couldn't see the glass." Except he couldn't understand what you were saying, and not because he was Spanish. He ran to the phone and called the ambulance.

During your TIA, you later told me, you felt like a piece of furniture. Like a couch or a chair. Immovable. Depersonalized. Detached. As if you were somehow outside observing the object of your own body. You said that feeling of detachment was likely due to the fact that the TIA had been localized in your left parietal lobe, the part of the brain that reconciles one's sense of self with the body. That confirms *you* are *your body*. That you are, in fact, human and not a table or a refrigerator. Or that your body is not mine. That when I touch your arm or your face you know where I stop and you begin.

I was in London when I got the call from the hospital. I landed in Ottawa Sunday night on what was probably the most expensive trans-Atlantic flight they could legally sell. They discharged you on Monday and you took the week off to rest. Your speech came back almost immediately, but you were tired. Depleted. You read, finished a book of Sudoku, ate a lot of fish as per the doctor's suggestion.

You liked to double down on anything you deemed productive, and because you believed in the power of regimes it became haddock for breakfast, tuna salad for lunch, and sole for dinner.

On Thursday you had a follow-up appointment in the middle of the afternoon.

"I hate this; it just cuts up the whole day," you said as you locked the front door of the house.

"Well, it's not like you have anything else planned."

"I do, actually, thank you. I have errands."

"Like what?"

"I need to pick up a birthday card for Carol's son Luke and a card for Javier from work. His wife just gave birth."

"Okay, well, we can stop at Dollarama on the way."

As we paced the wall of cards at Dollarama, I asked if you were Javier's boss.

You shook your head. "We're both project leaders."

"On NEST?"

You nodded. "NEST is just one of our projects though."

"And NEST is the artificial brain, right?"

You took in a deep breath, as if to say: *This is the last time I'm going to explain this to you so please fucking listen this time.* "It's an artificial neural network of about two billion nerve cells, which simulates just a fraction of the neurons in a human brain."

"Which is like—?"

"About eighty to a hundred billion."

"Right. Wow."

"About as many stars as there are in the Milky Way."

I recalled that was where our last conversation about your work ended up—with you trying to explain inconceivably large numbers to me with the aid of various cosmological analogies.

"So you're making an artificial brain."

"What we've made, it takes forty minutes to generate the equivalent of a second of an average human brain's processing time," you explained as you pulled your reading glasses out of your purse. "And that's with about eighty-three thousand processors. The simulation — each one eats up about a petabyte of system memory, which is one quad-rillion bytes."

"That sounds like a child making up a big number."

"So you know a terabyte?" I nodded. "It's a thousand of those."

"So then how much processing power does a human brain have?"

"Your question is flawed," you said, adjusting your glasses to read the inside of a card as if it were a legal document. "First of all, what is a human brain? You're presuming all human beings have the same brain."

"An average brain, then. Like, the median human brain."

"The other issue — we don't really have a good enough model for a single biological neuron, so it can only ever be an approximation given the neuron model we think is correct."

"Fine."

"A colleague of mine, not a close one, a fellow named Henry Markram — he got a ton of EU funding to basic-ally emulate the processing ability of cortical columns." You stopped and held up a card of a naked cowboy on a horse. "How's this one?"

"Mom."

"What? It's funny."

"That card's for gay men and middle-aged women."

"Well, I don't know, they have nothing here."

"The processing ability of cortical columns—"

"And um—"You flipped the card over a few more times as if not quite ready to put it back. "Markram theorizes the human brain has a processing rate of an exaflop, which is basically—"

"A what?"

"—about one million teraflops."

I shrugged and shook my head.

"A teraflop is a trillion operations per second. So it's a million times a trillion operations a second. What about this one?" You held up a card with a penguin wearing a birthday hat that said, *Well, waddle you know, it's your birthday.*

"How old is Luke?"

"Twenty-one."

"That card's for a five-year-old."

"I thought the penguin looked kind of sardonic." Which was true, it kind of did. I suggested a card with a Facebook thumbs-up that read, *Happy 24 Hours of Constant Notifications Day.*

"Really? A Facebook joke?"

We eventually settled on one that read, *If you were Jesus, today would be Christmas.* An appropriately wry millennial sentiment. The baby card was much easier to find. "They're all the same," you said, meaning either baby cards or babies.

As we waited in the checkout line I mentioned that I'd been reading about "the singularity"—the moment artificial intelligence would reach a critical mass of self-augmentation and exponentially supersede human intelligence. You nodded, nonplussed.

"This is, of course, presuming that computers will ever *think* as humans do," you said. "That computers can be people."

"And will they?"

You scrunched up your mouth and shook your head. "Not as long as we're using digital computers."

I watched as you began fishing for your wallet in your purse. How did I still know so little about your work? Your life? Our conversation felt tinted with the colour of loss, the loss of detail and intimacy that comes with a couple of Skype calls a month. After years of trying to push myself away, I suddenly felt the distance I'd managed to put between us. The Atlantic ocean. Six time zones.

"Computers will never be people because they're not indeterminate," you said at last. "A computer uses switches that are either on or off. But the neurons in a brain, they excite, they light up in all kinds of different ways because they're constantly getting information from other cells through synaptic contacts." You smiled at the cashier and handed her a five-dollar bill and said, "Keep the change," like a high roller.

As we walked back to the car you continued, "As long as we keep thinking of the brain as a computer we'll never replicate consciousness. People like Markram can increase data transfer rates till they're blue in the face, but that's not consciousness. Brains don't *store* and *retrieve* memories like computers. Brains don't operate like binary systems, ones and zeros. But unfortunately computer metaphors for the brain are so entrenched that even neuroscientists find it hard not to use them. I'm serious, talk to a neuroscientist about the brain, I deal with them all the time at the university and they're incapable of not using computer metaphors like *encode* and *process* when really these are describing computational functions." You were starting to get a bit worked up. The car blinked at us as you pressed the remote key—even though I was driving you had insisted on carrying the key in your purse while we were in the store. "We apply whatever technological metaphor is most current," you continued, opening the passenger-side door. "For thousands of years people believed the body worked like hydraulics, and science and medicine didn't progress for millennia." You climbed into your seat and then handed me the key. "A computer is like a really sophisticated filing system and it can sort numbers and images and videos and sound files at almost infinite speed, but I suspect it will never be able to truly *understand* what an image is, in a lived sense. The photograph of a loved one, say. What is that? Or understand that that sound file is a Chopin nocturne and be moved by it."

You latched your seat belt. I turned the key in the ignition and began navigating my way out of the parking lot.

"There's no…" you continued distractedly, pulling down the sun visor to check your eyes in the mirror for sleep. "What's missing is the very complex biochemical dialogue between the mind and body that we really have no idea how to replicate."

"But say if one day, like theoretically, we could reproduce that dialogue."

You were quiet for a moment as you studied your reflection. "I would still say consciousness is more than purely the—the replication of biological functions." You flipped the sun visor back up like a punctuation mark on your thought. You were avoiding the trap I was setting for you. I knew you thought the missing quotient was spiritual, the soul, but that you knew enough not to say it. That to say it would provoke me to further challenge you, and by that point you were getting tired and just wanted to get to the hospital. It struck me that there was a fundamental tension between your faith and your work. What aim were you pursuing if not to replicate consciousness? You always said you believed in artificial intelligence, but with marked emphasis on the *artificial*. Like the earliest of computer pioneers, Ada Lovelace, you said we were doomed once we began to mistake it as genuine intelligence. But to default to the soul, to the spirit, seemed like such a cop-out to me. And totally irreconcilable with the woman who valued exacting precision. Facts. Empirical evidence. Given that you were still recovering I should have let it lie, but for some reason I wanted to pursue you, chase you down this rabbit-hole of logic, and as I drove I tried to smoke you out of your hiding place to provoke a true tête-à-tête.

"Are we not just our brains, though, ultimately?" I pressed. We stopped at a traffic light and watched an old man walk a cluster of small white dogs through the intersection. "Like what do you make of that British guy — did you hear about this? — totally normal guy, married with kids, in his early fifties, develops this brain tumour and then all of a sudden can't stop himself from looking at child porn. He'd, like, never accessed it before in his life, then he got the brain tumour and became addicted to it, and then the tumour was removed and he no longer showed any inclination. By the time he went to trial, he was back to his old self and the court didn't know, you know—"

"Right."

"—was it even really him who had committed the crime? Could they try the tumour? The man he had been with the tumour?"

"I get it."

"Or your TIA. The way your brain made you feel like a couch or a chair. How you completely lost your sense of *you*."

I suddenly felt cruel, using your own experience in an argument against you. We drove in silence for a while, watching the nondescript vistas of a low-rise industrial park unfold before us. You turned on CBC Radio and we listened to the sound of a woman crying for eight seconds before you reached over and switched it back off, mumbling, "I can't deal with that right now."

As the hospital appeared in the distance, something inside you seemed to stiffen, almost imperceptibly. "Of course it's possible," you said, looking out the passenger-side window, "that quantum computing will change all this."

"Change what?"

"This conversation."

You said it was possible quantum computers would "crack" your research "wide open."

"You mean like actual thinking and feeling computers?"

"Well…at the very least allowing them to replicate the human mind's capacity for indeterminacy."

The key difference, as you explained it to me, was that unlike current digital computers which required data to be encoded into binary digits, each of which was always in one of two definitive states (one or zero, on or off, yes or no, stop or go), quantum computing made use of superposition to process data. The ability for things to exist between states or in more than one state simultaneously.

"A queering of the binary," I said with a smile, turning into the hospital parking lot.

"Um. Right. I'm not sure that's how Einstein would have characterized superposition but…sure."

IN 1935, Albert Einstein wrote an article about the strange nature of quantum superpositions. He posited that an atom or photon could, in a single instant, exist in multiple states on account of being tied, on a quantum level, to multiple possible outcomes. The prevailing theory suggested that this atom or photon remained in a state of superposition until it was observed, at which point the superposition would instantly collapse into one of the possible definite states. By extension, superposition, when applied to groups of atoms and to the objects that they comprised, meant that objects or even people could be in states of quantum indeterminacy. In a letter to Austrian physicist Erwin Schrödinger, Einstein wrote that an unstable keg of gunpowder will eventually contain a quantum superposition of both exploded and unexploded states. Schrödinger had some serious doubts about this. Namely, he wasn't sold on the idea that physical systems didn't have definitive properties until they were observed.

So that year he devised a thought experiment, which became known as "Schrödinger's cat," in order to illustrate the problem of quantum superposition as it is applied to everyday objects and living things. He came up with a scenario in which a superposition was created within a large-scale system by being tied to a superposition on a quantum level. The scenario centred around a cat that may have been simultaneously alive and dead given its entanglement with a subatomic event that may or may not have occurred.

You once described this experiment to me when I was eleven (seriously) after I asked what "quantum" meant. (I then proceeded to show off the next day in my grade six science class by bringing it up during a completely unrelated lesson on the water cycle.) Perhaps to make your explanation more graspable for me, you asked me to picture Chloe as Schrödinger's cat.

"Imagine Chloe is in a steel chamber."

I closed my eyes and nodded, imagining this terrible thing happening to our pudgy pet.

"Also inside the steel chamber is a device which contains a trace of radioactive material," you continued. "There is so little of the material that in the course of an hour there is an equal probability that one of its atoms will decay as will not. Are you with me so far?"

I nodded.

"If one of the atoms does decay, the device will trigger a hammer that will smash a small flask of hydrocyanic acid inside the steel chamber, which will kill Chloe. Sadly."

I opened my eyes and looked at our cat perched on the back of the chair in the living room.

"But if no atoms decay then Chloe will be fine. Well, she probably wouldn't like being in a steel box, but she will survive. According to quantum physics both possibilities remain equally in play until Chloe's body is observed. Until someone opens the steel chamber and looks inside. It's the moment of observation which pins Chloe's body to a fixed, perceived reality: dead or alive."

"That doesn't make sense," I said, crossing the room to

pet our cat, who seemed altogether unperturbed by the fate of her hypothetical self.

You nodded in agreement. "Quantum physics doesn't seem to make a lot of sense. But we know through math that it's true."

Schrödinger also thought this alive-and-dead cat was ridiculous. He reasoned there was no way Einstein's theory of quantum physics could apply to people and things in everyday life. If the chamber was lifted and the cat was found to be alive, it would have an unbroken memory of being alive. And it would certainly seem consistent with our perception of reality that we do not exist in multiple states in the same instant. Schrödinger's thought experiment also raised the question: When exactly did a quantum superposition collapse into becoming one reality or another? And did the cat itself not qualify as an observer of the situation, or did its existence in a single state require an external observer? Einstein was chastened by Schrödinger's provocations and wrote him a letter in 1950 basically saying: "Touché."

"Nobody really doubts that the presence or absence of the cat is something independent of the act of observation," he admitted, later adding: "Do you really believe the moon exists only when you look at it?"

You said that in the years since, quantum physicists had begun to say, "Yes, actually." Equation after equation, experiment after experiment kept indicating that subatomic quantum mechanics required macroscopic objects, even cats and people, to not always retain fixed states. A research team in Australia proved photons existed in multiple states until they were measured, which meant that if such a thing as an objective reality existed then so did objects in states of quantum indeterminacy. Another team in the U.S. successfully superposed molecules containing fifteen thousand protons, neutrons, and electrons. You said that somewhere in Europe researchers were trying to superpose a flu virus. It seems in the end that Schrödinger, in his effort to prove Einstein wrong, may have actually given us the most enduring vision for how Einstein was right. Or in other words, as I opened your bedroom door I opened the steel chamber, and as I stand here in this moment, in this gap in time on the threshold of your room, I look in. And I can see for myself.

The cat is both alive and dead.

WHEN YOU AND LYDIA were computer engineering students at Carleton University in the early eighties, you once pranked a sexist professor by keying in "1 divided by 0" into the lab's room-sized computer. *He said we were 'distracting the male students' by wearing skirts to class.* The computer chugged away all night trying to reconcile the impossible equation, filling the room with the smell of burning electronics until it overheated and shut down. It couldn't fathom divisions by zero, or infinity, or eternity, or any abstraction beyond the binary world.

In this moment I am that hulking computer, filling the room with my burning incomprehension, unable to reconcile the impossible equation of your body divided by oblivion. Perhaps you are between breaths. Perhaps you are in a deep sleep and I've just happened to find you in this moment traversing the valley between inhale and exhale, in which everything is suspended and airless. Or perhaps at this distance, in this dark, and under those comforters your breath is altogether hidden.

It then occurs to me that as long as I stand here you cannot be dead. You will, at the very least, be kept alive by being in-between, by being as much alive in uncertainty as you are dead. That even after this second passes I could continue to stand here for many seconds, perhaps even a full minute or several, savouring the possibility of your life. Of your being both one and zero.

III

GRANDPA LOU USED to joke: "I'm not afraid of death; I was dead for billions of years before I was born and it didn't bother me a damn." I later discovered he ripped that line off from Mark Twain. Maybe everyone, at some point in their lives, claims they're not afraid of death. For years my line was "There's nothing after death, so why fear nothing?" But in this moment I realize I am, of course I am, I'm fucking terrified and everyone is, particularly those who claim not to be, them more so than anyone. I'll never again believe anyone who says otherwise. I won't believe it from the religious or the irreligious, the old or the young. Of course the fear of death motivates everything—art, romance, capitalism, crime, social order, religion.

You've always said you want to be cremated (*quick and easy*) and kept in a place where your friends could visit you. A little niche, a marble wall, a brass plaque. Canada doesn't allow people to prepare the bodies of their loved ones for burial as humans did for millennia. It forces us to contract these services out to professionals, like a furnace repair. But if you're dead I want to touch your death with my hands. I want to understand your absence through the ritual of preparing your body. I wonder how long I could withhold your death from the state? Maybe I can buy just enough time to invite a couple of your girlfriends over, put on some Gloria Estefan and Annie Lennox, open a bottle of Cabernet Sauvignon, and lay your body down on the dining table. We'll wash your thinning hair and put some styling wax in it to give it volume. Lydia and Alice will drive out to Home Depot to buy some wood for the pyre. And as they build it in the backyard, I'll wash and moisturize your skin, anointing it with scented oils, running my hands over every part of your body without shame. I'll then dress you in a clean pair of underwear, a freshly laundered bra, your "funky" leather pants, black silk blouse, and the showpiece necklace of interconnected silver hoops you bought from a craft fair in Quebec City last summer. And finally we will carry you outside surrounded by your loved ones, and we will place you on the pyre built of fresh cedar and dried sage so that after we light it you won't smell like meat grilling on a barbecue. And just as the fallen seeds of a sequoia tree open only from the heat of a forest fire, the flames will release your soul through divine sublimation, from solid into vapour, from seen into the unseen, all within the confines of a modest backyard in suburban Ottawa.

The Torajan people of Indonesia don't believe biological death marks the departure of one's self from one's body. For them, a person isn't truly dead until a water buffalo, a soul's vehicle to the afterlife, has been sacrificed at their funeral. Until that time families will keep the deceased relative at home for weeks, months, even years. They preserve the bodies with a mixture of formaldehyde and water, ensuring the bodies do not putrefy. Family members dress the bodies every day and bring them breakfast, lunch, and dinner. Sometimes afternoon tea. Here I'm saying "bodies," even though they are still *persons*; in the subjective experience of their relatives, they are still living people. It's almost impossible for the English language to articulate the nature of these un-dead individuals — they are not "bodies," they are not "the deceased," they are not "the dead." Even after their funerals, after their burials, families return to their tombs and change the corpse's clothes — a new suit jacket, tie, trousers, pair of sunglasses — because as the bodies decay their forms change. The old clothes no longer look good. Families will then pose beside the newly dressed corpse for photos. For the Torajans the threshold between life and death is not a concrete wall but a chain-link fence.

You and I have always had different relationships with death. Yours is reverential. You respect it. My favourite coffee mug, on the other hand, is literally emblazoned with the words *Fuck Death*. This slogan speaks to me, as an atheist and a gay man. Throughout history queers have survived by confronting death through fearlessness and humour. "Fuck Death" feels like a slogan for my people. It's absurd and irreverent, and I derive a tiny bit of power and comfort from it, the same way one might from spray-painting graffiti about a dictator on a highway overpass. You hate this mug. When you stayed at my place last summer, I found it tucked into the back of the cupboard. I could feel your hand in its placement, trying to gently dissuade me from using it, or perhaps simply burying it so you wouldn't have to see it. You said you disliked the mug because it was "disrespectful," but to whom or what was never exactly clear to me.

Our fundamentally different dispositions likely come down to the simple yet massive gulf between us: the soul. You believe we have one and I don't. I'm inclined to think sentience and all of its attendant wonders are the result of our neurological and bodily—and thus limited—perceptive capacities. That it is the world we are perceiving and interpreting that is sublime and immortal-seeming, so much so that we can't help feel of it, so much so that we imagine we must have something sublime and immortal *within* ourselves. We do not. We die, we are forgotten. You, on the other hand, believe in an essential and immortal *you* that will continue to exist after death.

Growing up you had a flatulent black Labrador retriever named Brutus (Grandpa Lou always had a knack for naming dogs—Bones, Spunk, Cruella). One morning, as you were walking Brutus, a boy next door told you matter-of-factly that dogs didn't have souls. You looked down into Brutus's eyes and knew there and then that God was benevolent, that everything was sacred and filled with divine light, and that only the small and insecure minds of men could have dreamed up such a cruel and exclusionary vision of the world, a world which fetishized suffering and control and left little room for young women like yourself. The kind of women who asked questions and didn't accept most of the answers. The kind of women who probably would have been burned as witches in the sixteenth century, tortured like Johann Kepler's mother, like all the other difficult women. You looked up, punched the boy in the face, and walked on.

In this way your Christianity was always rather animistic.

Rivers, mountains, stick insects — for you they were all imbued with some kind of spirit. God's essence. "To varying degrees," you'd concede. It seems the existence of souls is the one thing the faithful can all seem to agree on. The exact specifics vary, of course. Traditionally, the Abrahamic faiths believe the soul club is rather exclusive, open to one mammal alone. Thomas of Aquinas suggested animals had souls but only human souls were eternal. Like Aristotle, the Hindus and Jains believe both plants and animals possess them. Granted, the Sanskrit word *ātman* in Hinduism is perhaps better understood as Self; the self from which all perception flows. But make no mistake, this self is immortal. In the *Bhagavad Gita* Lord Krishna says of the *ātman*, "There is neither birth nor death at any time. He has not come into being, does not come into being, and will not come into being. He is unborn, eternal, ever — existing and primeval. He is not slain when the body is slain." The Buddhist doctrine of *anatta* translates to "no self" or "no soul," but this simply denies that one's essence remains a fixed state — there is still an essence which is believed to move beyond the confines of a body into an afterlife (in fact into many). Because this essence remains continually in flux, changing moment to moment with every thought and action, the person into which this essence is reborn is neither entirely different from, nor entirely the same as, the deceased person it passed from, but the two are continuous. Just as our selves are continuous from seven years ago though we are no longer that exact same person. Much like Plutarch's assertion that one cannot step into the same river twice for "it scatters and again comes together, and approaches and recedes." New water always flows through.

At the end of the day, a shared belief in an essential and immortal *you*, whose destiny is determined by the actions taken in this life, feels like a far more profound commonality than the comparatively superficial deviations of dogma and custom that separate faiths. The non-belief in a soul and an afterlife, on the other hand, is something altogether different. Insurmountable. It feels like the religious of the world are at a party arguing over what colour party hat they should be wearing, while the atheists are at their own party next door dancing to Madonna.

Mom, I'm afraid we are at two fundamentally different parties.

AS A GIRL you asked God to make you a mother and a world-famous scientist. The second prayer was more or less answered by your early thirties, maybe not famous but a prodigy in your field, finishing your Ph.D. in cognitive computing, publishing in major journals, making the rounds on the international conference circuit, guest-lecturing at prestigious universities. You began moving in a world of other self-possessed women in law, medicine, engineering; going to their houses for dinner; meeting their fiancés, husbands, children; impressing them with your wit and ambition while aching to your core. Of course there were men around. Master's students. Visiting fellows. The odd lecherous university chair. Instead you fell in love with a cabinetmaker, moved in, had your heart broken, moved out. Twice. You were nothing if not thorough. By thirty-five you decided to take matters into your own hands, as you were wont to do. Artificial insemination. For a single woman in 1989 you might as well have been impregnated by Satan himself. You caught your lab assistants whispering and darting glances in your direction. "A perversion of nature," a lady in church once murmured to another as you passed by. It was an appellation that would stick to me for the rest of my life.

After I was born you moved back into Grandpa Lou and Grandma Dora's bungalow. The same house you grew up in. Cigarette smoke, peanut butter-and-pickle sandwiches, golf on mute, maple tree keys helicoptering down, a small wooden crucifix, now I lay me down to sleep I pray the lord my soul to keep. You must have felt like you'd committed career suicide. At the end of the hall was your office, piled high with loose papers, books, and cardboard boxes. This was your refuge, and whenever I managed to dash inside, Lou or Dora's hands would appear under my pits, lifting and whisking me away, the door shutting in my wake.

At night Dora would read the Bible to me before bed. I became fixated on the story of Lot's wife. She has no name. She's mentioned only once, in the passage about the destruction of Sodom and Gomorrah. The cities deemed so wicked by God that they had to be obliterated by a rain of fire and sulphur. God sent two angels to tell Lot to take his family and flee into the desert and not to look back. But Lot's wife disobeyed. Obstinate woman. Weak of soul. As the skies opened up and her hometown was destroyed and the screams of her neighbours and extended family rang out behind her, she looked back. Like anyone would. She looked back and was turned into a pillar of salt. It happened in a single sentence. "Lot's wife looked back and she turned into a pillar of salt." As Dora read the passage, the line passed by so quickly as to almost evade notice. But it stopped my heart.

"What's a pillar of salt?"

"I guess her body just—"

"—turned into salt?"

"I suppose, yes."

"In, like, the shape of a pillar?"

"More or less. Maybe not smooth and round but—"

"How?"

"Well—"

"How quickly did it happen?"

"I don't know, Jord."

"Would she have felt it happen? Like would she have known she was becoming a pillar?"

"I don't know, probably not."

I became fixated on this moment of her transformation, this moment between being "Lot's wife" and being "a pillar of salt," between being a body and a thing, a geological feature, an extension of the earth, a rocky outcropping of sodium chloride.

And in my imagination, she had your face. She was you. I let myself linger in the thought of being with you in that moment, running beside my father Lot and sensing you falling back, stopping, turning around, knowing I couldn't look back for you, knowing something terrible was happening to you, perhaps even sensing the precise moment you became a thing, a rock, a pillar of salt, imagining the sound you would make in this instant and whether I would even be able to hear it over the roar of the apocalypse.

WHEN I WAS eight you secured tenure-track at Carleton, and we moved out to a new-build on the border between city and wilderness. A treeless, expectant street with six semi-detached houses and ten concrete foundations. Two storeys, white walls, berber carpets, a lawn to mow. *Just you and me and the foxes.* Some weekends you hosted potlucks for other single working moms while I was terrorized by their sons and their action figures in the basement. I still have a scar above my left eyebrow. It was the self-help era and you bought all the books. At night, in the bardo between waking and sleep, I would lie in bed and hear you crying down the hall. Sometimes murmuring to yourself. Or to Dora on the phone. Or to God.

One night I told you, very casually, that I thought people needed religion when they were vulnerable. "It gives them a sense of meaning and stability."

"Do you think that's true of me?" you asked.

I shrugged.

"That I need religion because I'm weak?"

"I didn't say 'weak'; I said 'vulnerable.'"

You nodded, your mouth drawing itself into a thin, wounded line. You were standing in front of the microwave defrosting dinner at eight thirty at night, still in your pantsuit.

"But hey if it works for you then great," I added with the sagacity of my dozen years or so on the planet as I fished a pop out of the fridge.

In those days I was on a newfound warpath for all things spiritual. You and Dora had seen to it that I was confirmed the year prior. For Lutherans that meant I could finally partake of the holy Eucharist, which we believed transfigured into the actual blood and body of Christ the moment it touched our tongues. You and I spent an entire weekend in preparatory excitement, shopping for a crisp-collared shirt, a red silk tie, and my first suit — a dark-navy three-buttoned single-breasted polyester situation from Moores — all of which was completely hidden below the white confirmation gown. It seems comic and a little tragic to me now, how flush with pride and anticipation I was to finally take part in this divine rite of cannibalism. To take into me the Body of the Host, the Father, the Son, and the Holy Ghost. That holy hydra. But the body that the pastor placed on my tongue that morning, the tongue of a boy on the brink of coming to terms with his sexuality, was devoid of person, of emotion, of willpower, of responsibility, and as my mouth closed around it I was aware in the full blinding light of day that it was, and would remain, a cracker. And just like that, a millennium of ancestral beliefs ended with me.

THE IRONY IS, as a young boy I had been preoccupied with my soul. Specifically with trying to find the secret compartment in my body where it was hidden. I read all about Dr. Duncan MacDougall's experiments at the turn of the century in Haverhill, Massachusetts, in which he weighed six patients in the moment of their deaths, hoping to catch the shift in mass that would occur as their souls departed their bodies. He placed each patient's bed on a massive scale and recorded that, on average, each patient appeared to be twenty-one grams lighter after death than when they were alive. I used to close my eyes and try to locate these twenty-one grams inside of me. At first I was searching for heat. I would run my hands slowly over my body looking for any discrepancies. Sometime later I came to believe that my soul was not warmth but a colour, and mine was blue. I can't really say why I was so certain of this, but I began looking for evidence of my blue soul not within my body but in the world around me. The way the blue of the sky would linger in my eyes long after I'd closed them: this was proof. The way I tasted the colour blue when I dove into a swimming pool: this was proof. The way even the word "blue" would puncture me anytime I heard someone sing it on the radio, or how the word would leap out at me in a book as if wanting me to claim it. Like Horace-Bénédict de Saussure trying to measure the tint of the sky with his cyanometer, I tried to gauge the purity my soul on any given day by the shade of blue that appeared to me.

If I think back far enough, it seems this preoccupation began around the time I was five, after an incident in the showroom of a housing supply store. The aisle was displaying bathtubs. Everything was white and gleaming. I remember walking through an aisle of tightly packed tubs and feeling shocked to see them clustered together so ignobly. Something about it felt obscene to me, like a room of disembodied orifices. Mouths, ears, vaginas. Bathtubs disembodied from bathrooms, disembodied from homes; they were terrible. I'm sure my blood-sugar was just low. Either way, for some reason I lay down on the floor and wouldn't get up. I spun around on my back. You were shouting at me. Then begging. There were tears in our eyes. You later told me a woman walked past with her husband and muttered, "Some women just shouldn't be mothers." I worked myself into such a frenzy that I passed out. Or perhaps I hit my head. I'm still not clear what happened. I just remember being outside my body for a moment, looking down at myself on the ground.

By "being outside my body," I mean my being, my person, was outside of my body, sort of adjacent to it and slightly above, looking down. From about the height of a player's viewpoint over their avatar in a video game. I remember my eyes were still open and looking up into the fluorescence of the showroom ceiling. But if my body's eyes were pointed upwards, how was I looking down at my body in this moment? I remember my mouth was open and you grabbed my head and it lolled from side to side. And then, a moment later, I felt the cold tile against my back again; I blinked and the fluorescence was in my eyes, and I could feel your hands on the back of my head, and I could feel the hoarseness in my throat and the heaviness in my heart, and I was back. My person and body were one again.

IN THOSE DAYS, you and I used to play a game called Teletransporter, in which I would stand still and close my eyes, and you would throw a blanket over me. As the blanket enclosed me, I would dematerialize and be sucked through the wormhole of your embrace, re-materializing on the other side of our finished basement in a shriek of laugher. I wanted to de- and re-materialize over and over, as long as your arms could bear it. The most thrilling part was always the moment right before the dematerialization, when you threw the blanket up above my head and I could feel it suspended in midair the split second before it landed on me, heavy, coating my body in dark matter, erasing me. Almost as glorious was the moment that followed this, when I didn't exist and was being carried in your arms through nothingness, through the space-time of un-being, spun around so as to erase the geography of the basement from my memory, feeling the struggle of my weight in your arms, their quiver, the effort of your love, your submission to our fantasy. There was always a slight deflation when you pulled off the blanket like a magician revealing the wonder of still being alive, the magic of my still being me. My body, the world — these were always somehow a slight disappointment, a minor key to the major key of the nothingness where I had just been.

Your greatest living fear was to lose my body for real. To misplace it in a big-box store or a fairground or on the subway. My body was more important to you than your own. When I was three, playing in the driveway as you were taking groceries out of your Datsun, the car began to roll backwards towards me and you dropped the two plastic bags you were holding, exploding milk on the pavement, and dashed towards me, hurling your body against the back of the car, shoulderchecking it, digging your heels in and locking your knees to halt it full-stop. You threw your body at the car to save my body. It was pure instinct. Your body's doing.

I still remember the smell of that Datsun when we'd climb into it after it had been in a sunny parking lot, its hot interior smell of car plastic, seat fabric, and browned apple cores in the cup holder. The metal seat belt clips scalding like cattle branders. The Pointer Sisters cassette permanently jammed in the player, every drive underscored by "I'm So Excited." The plunging in my stomach when you'd take a hill too fast, like the plunging in my stomach now as I consider your body.

LYING THERE IN bed you seem no different than the dish-washer in the kitchen. A dead thing. An ignoble appliance somehow affixed to the house, part of the architecture. This bed in the bedroom of this house that you bought after I moved out, the house you *downsized* into, a house of no significance to anyone, just another container. A house that changed the acoustics of your life, from the muffle of carpet to the clarion of hardwood. That subtle ring of modernity, the chastening echo of a life newly oriented towards simplicity and cleanliness. A house in another suburb, even newer, with a marauding night population that keeps you up into the early hours, lighting off firecrackers in the park or racing down the straighter roads in their cars, their mufflers modified for maximum aggression. It's a neglected corner of a sleepy city. A city that teenagers living here love to hate. The kind of city people say is "a great place to raise a family," ringed along its edges with fields where teenagers go to drink and get into loud fights after dark, bordered by Cineplexes and oceans of asphalt and wide culverts filled with stray shopping carts. A city of generous on-ramps and off-ramps with swaths of no man's land in between. Of power-tower corridors flanked on either side by low-rise industrial parks. Where subdivisions back onto wilderness and joggers encounter startled deer on their morning routes.

This city, this suburb, this house, this bedroom, your body, a nesting doll of containers for your self, containers that will long outlive your self, just as your body will continue to be a container in death, sustaining the flora in your gut and the bacteria on your skin, under your nails, millions of other bodies still carrying on with their lives like squatters in an abandoned city.

It seems the shape and texture of your body has already changed, though in ways too subtle to even articulate. Perhaps I'm just projecting my incomprehension onto your body and causing it to refract in new and unfamiliar ways. And there are other things I can't comprehend. The colour of the walls, which I know are white but look blue in this light and yellow in others and even grey and black for long stretches of the evening and night. Just as I can't comprehend the laughter from our neighbour's house, or the sounds of snowblowers and barking dogs and the highway in the distance. How can life continue unaware?

As I stand here in the doorway everything is laid bare, unveiled, in a terrifying and indecipherable nakedness—your life, my life, the lives of my friends and lovers, fragments, conversations, starlings, drones, dreams, a desert, a beach at night, a Paris subway tunnel, the World Trade Center towers falling, a torrential rain, a cloud of monarch butterflies, *The Last Judgement*, a wasp's nest, a Nina Simone song, a waterfall plunging into a cave. I feel my entire life traced like a celestial connect-the-dots back to your body, both asleep and dead. A grand narrative of bodies and objects and how the precarious distinction between the two, between living and un-living, has defined my life. In this moment I am all the bodies through which I've known my body and all the people through which I've known my person. In this moment we are a constellation.

IV

THE FIRST TIME you met Ana, she fell through the glass table in our living room. Somehow I'd managed to convince you to host the cast party for the Henry Munro Middle School production of *The Hobbit*, personally adapted by our homeroom teacher, Ms. Duchovny. As you pulled Ana up off the shard-strewn carpet, you noticed she was still in her character makeup. The thick green suppurations of Troll #2. You were not amused: "Go upstairs and wash your face."

I, on the other hand, had made my stage debut as Gollum. I still recall how on opening night, while I was pulling on a black rubber wetsuit and being lathered in petroleum jelly backstage by a thirteen-year-old male costume assistant, a number of future life pursuits seemed to shift into focus. I came on right after Ana's scene, where Bilbo has to outwit the three bumbling trolls. My cue to enter was a blast from the smoke machine that filled the entire gymnatorium with subterranean gloom. To this day, whenever I smell the acridity of theatrical smoke my heart begins to beat a little faster and I'm taken back to that Platonic cave of shadows where I thrashed about yelling "*Curses!*"

Ana and I were children of the nineties, which meant we came of age in a decade of blockbuster disasters. *Volcano, Twister, Deep Impact, Armageddon, Dante's Peak.* I grew up in a world where I watched the earth open up in the middle of Los Angeles and people slip into a fiery chasm, where mile-high waves consumed fleeing crowds and fathers were sucked into the sky out of storm cellars. I watched a man fall screaming from the upturned deck of the *Titanic* and plummet through the cold night air, down along the ship's terrifying, exposed underbelly, screaming as he fell, still person, until he ricocheted off an exposed propeller and spun, now body, in silence like a pinwheel into the dark water. Or the grandmother in *Dante's Peak,* pushing her family to safety in a corroded motorboat while slowly melting in a lake of acid. As a child I watched death's horrifying prelude over and over, when person and body began to become unfastened, when I could see a living person as their corpse, as well as the horror of the person seeing their own body as a corpse.

The planes hit the World Trade Center towers just as Ana and I hit puberty in grade eight. A disaster movie writ large. The disaster movie that put an end to disaster movies, at least for a decade. The moment the first plane struck the North Tower I was in the fourth and final stall of the ground-floor boys' bathroom, bent over, examining the first, tentative hair on my ball-sack. During lunch break that day I passed Ana in the hallway, where she was holding court in a group of girls. I heard her say the words "people jumping." I hadn't yet seen the images but my heart began to race—I could already picture what those two words meant.

As I read the newspaper that week, I kept noticing that the people who jumped or fell from the towers were alternately referred to as "falling bodies" and "falling people." "The body of a falling woman." "The now-infamous falling man." "For those down below, the bodies landed with sickening, almost explosive thuds. Many said it was raining bodies." It's as if, as they fell those ten seconds through the air at speeds nearing two hundred miles per hour, we watched their selves sheared from their bodies, we watched them passing for those ten seconds through the indeterminate state between body and person, so as to forever be etched in our consciousness as both. Falling bodies. Falling people.

In one article a firefighter named Maureen McArdle-Schulman said she felt like she was intruding on a sacrament as the bodies fell: "They were choosing to die and I was watching them and shouldn't have been. So me and another guy turned away and looked at a wall and we could still hear them hit." Bill Feehan, deputy chief of the fire department, shouted, "Don't you have any human decency?" at a man filming jumpers with a video camera. The rupture of body and self is indecent, but also transcendent. It enters a realm of the sacred. It becomes obscene and impossible for another human to behold, like the Ark of the Covenant, which cannot be touched, or a god who cannot be looked at.

As I read through those 9/11 articles, I became fixated on the interchangeability of "body" and "person." So much so that I looked up their definitions in the *Oxford English Dictionary* you kept on the shelf beside your old textbooks. It defined "body" as "the physical and mortal aspect of a person as opposed to the soul or the spirit," and "person" as "a human being regarded as an individual." What struck

me was how the word "body" could be used to define both
a living and a dead thing; a living or dead physical structure
of bones, flesh, and organs. "The physical and mortal aspect
of a person." And because "body" referred to our physical
structure without regard for its sentience, it could continue
to refer to our physical structure once it had been emptied of the person. It was the ability of the word to denote
either a living or a dead thing which unnerved me because
it connoted ease, it connoted an almost imperceptible slip-
page between one state and another, as if the world might
be filled with bodies in either state, moving fluidly between
both states or inhabiting them at the same time.

ANA WAS FROM a Bulgarian-Muslim family, and though
she and her parents weren't observant, her dark complexion
marked her as "other," especially in the new Age of Terror.
She told me her name was a small protection because it
didn't sound foreign. On her birth certificate, it was actually
spelt "Aana," from آناء, which meant "moments" or "hours of
the night." We used to joke *Hours of the Night* would be the
name of our debut album, though we never got around to
forming the band. She was always very guarded about the
hate hurled her way, or the fear she endured because of it.
The few times I asked her about it she said, "I'd prefer not
to talk about it." And so we didn't.

   We were the only two people from our year accepted
into the specialized drama program at Canterbury High
School. I sometimes think they let me in out of sympathy. The braces, the acne, the flamboyant blouses from the
Salvation Army—where else did I stand half a chance? To

arrive in time for the morning bell, we had to wake at dawn and take an hour and a half's worth of public transit. We spent a lot of our adolescence on city buses, lost in a playlist or a book, watching the same houses blur past day after day and noting all the subtle changes that accrued over time — a lawn left overgrown and then cut the next morning, shutters painted a new colour, Christmas lights hung and taken down. Most nights we stayed late after school to rehearse, sometimes until ten o'clock at night, and we'd ride the three buses back through the dark, nodding off to sleep.

When we weren't in rehearsals we lived in each other's basements, watching horror films, the genre that offered the most faithful portraiture of suburban adolescence. I came to realize the thing that marked American horror films was how they made pornographic the moment of rupture between self and person: a teenager's lingering moment of disbelief of having been run through by a chainsaw, a decapitated head that blinks before sliding off from its neck, a man looking down at his own disembowelment. In the winter of grade nine we watched *Alien,* drinking teeth-numbing electric-blue coolers. As a scientist looked down at himself to see alien spawn burst forth from his stomach, I startled with the recognition of a terror I had lived with since childhood. The same terror I had recognized in those bodies falling from the World Trade Center. It was the terror of the liminality between being a person and being a body, that threshold space of being a person beholding the body I was about to become.

Ever since I was a child I've been haunted by the prospect of being a puppet-version of myself, or of seeing my loved one's body emptied of its person and made a puppet.

And wasn't this the fundamental horror of zombies? That someone we knew intimately, whose body we kissed and embraced, should be suddenly emptied of their selves and hijacked by another someone or something. Like a corpse paraded through the streets, or a head planted on a stake, it felt like some kind of obscene mockery. The prospect of looking into your eyes and you not being there, of apprehending your animated body but realizing it no longer belonged to your person, was more horrible than any physical suffering that could befall me. Even the prospect of seeing you shot through the head would have been less horrific than witnessing your body, hollowed of its person, inhabited like a flesh costume by a thing, a virus, a non-person. And obviously this fear of inhabitation is disturbing and universal enough to form the basis of virtually every literary and filmic horror trope — zombies, werewolves, vampires, demon possessions, transformative viral infections, alien inhabitations...

Sometimes, when we couldn't think of anything to watch, we'd just let ourselves be sucked down YouTube vortexes. One night we found ourselves watching a clip about the *Ophiocordyceps unilateralis*, a "zombie fungus" found in tropical rainforests. The fungus infested ants and took over their minds and bodies, causing them to forsake their canopy nests and foraging trails. The ants would convulse and fall to the forest floor, where they then scrambled to a low-lying leaf and clamped onto its central vein with their mandibles. The ant was now where the fungus wanted it: near the forest floor, where the humidity and temperature were optimal for fungal growth. There the ant remained, clamped to the leaf, until its death, at which point the fungus burst through the ant's exoskeleton, using mechanical pressure and enzymes, and sprouted a stalk, which began to release spores.

As we watched this tiny freak show unfold in time-lapse, the question I became fixated on was: When did the ant become the fungus? Was it the moment the fungus began to control the ant's brain and body? And in those moments when the ant was technically still alive, was it a kind of hybrid creature? An ant-fungus? There was no doubt that, in the end, all that was left was the sprouting fungus. But the moment that the ant stopped being the ant was altogether unclear.

The erasure of the ant's self while his body continued to be animated was as unnerving as Isabelle Adjani flailing about the Paris metro in Andrzej Żuławski's 1981 film *Possession* — which we watched together a couple of nights later. Adjani carried a bag of groceries and wore an absolutely fabulous high-collared indigo dress that buttoned down the back. As she ascended an escalator from the metro platform she was wide-eyed and began to laugh. It was the uncontrollable laugh of possession — too long, too effusive, and seemingly prompted by nothing. She emerged into a deserted, fluorescent-lit tunnel. Everything was bathed in blue. There was no soundtrack, just the sound of her moist footsteps and her echoey, guttural laughter. Her gait became unsteady and she tumbled against the tunnel's tiled wall, sliding along it as her laughter transformed into hysterical crying. And then, as if her true self was momentarily emerging from the possession, she screamed. She screamed as she was pulled along by some unseen, internal force and flailed in resistance to it — or perhaps because of it. In her flailing her grocery bag smashed against the wall in a cascade of milk and egg yolk.

The sight of that white-and-yellow profusion pierced me. It was the same bag of groceries you dropped when rescuing me from the Datsun in the driveway, your body in the grips of a different possession.

BY GRADE TEN, Ana had become the Patti Smith to my Robert Mapplethorpe, and what we lacked in punk bravado we more than made up for in punk hygiene. After a childhood spent tamping down her wild mane of black hair, Ana was learning to rock it to startling Riot Grrrl effect. She was once sent home after refusing to cover up or take off her homemade T-shirt bejewelled with the words *Immanuel My Kant*. At fifteen she was already drinking black coffee out of a large thermos, which I found mildly intimidating for some reason. Scrawny, gaunt, and with poor posture, I mostly looked like a bad Egon Schiele sketch. But next to Ana I felt invincible. It was at a party at her house (in her bed, in fact) that I drunkenly kissed a boy for the first time. And I lay in her basement in a yellow sleeping bag a few feet from her when she also kissed a boy for the first time (hers decidedly hotter). I remember the sound of the basement furnace turning on, and thanking its dull roar for drowning out the sounds of furtive smacking.

In the spring of that year, President George W. Bush came to town trying to hawk his War in Iraq. It was Ana's idea to skip school to protest, and we rode the bus downtown filled with a combination of righteous rage and curiosity. We couldn't get further than Rockcliffe Park because of the road closures, so we started to walk. Just beyond the prime minister's residence, we found Sussex Drive cordoned off with yellow wooden police barricades flanked by horse-mounted RCMP officers. A traffic cop was pointing disgruntled commuters back the way they had come.

I began to lose nerve as we neared the barricade, and was going to suggest bailing when Ana gave a jaunty wave to one of the officers on horseback, shouting, "This is our first protest!"

The officer, a stony-faced woman in her fifties, looked down and said, "Hope it's not your last."

I couldn't tell if she was being encouraging or ominous.

For the first several blocks we were alone. All the shops along Sussex were boarded up. Newspapers blew across the boulevard as if in a film noir. Traffic lights diligently carried out their duties for no one. All we could hear was the wind and the distant reverberation of helicopters through the empty canyon of buildings. A city without purpose, without people. As we passed the Foreign Affairs building, I looked up and noticed snipers in black balaclavas and flak jackets on the rooftop. The doors of the National Art Gallery were locked and the lights were off. I imagined all the paintings and sculptures waiting quietly in the darkness for the president of the United States to come and go. There were snipers on the gallery's roof as well, but somehow I don't think they were thinking about the art.

As we neared Rideau Street we could hear the distant banging of drums. We reached the intersection and, to our left, saw a wave of bandana-clad protestors flowing towards us with their homemade placards and banners. Held aloft near the front of the crowd was a giant papier-mâché effigy of Bush wearing a leering grin and an Uncle Sam top hat. A thundering behind us made us turn: a line of SWAT police in full riot regalia had shifted into defensive position like giant insects, praying mantises ready to bite heads off. The protestors started charging up the street towards us full tilt, and the SWATs began drumming their batons against their transparent shields while advancing.

"Fuck, we're right in the middle," I shouted.

"Cover your face" Ana replied, pulling her bandana up over her nose.

Where the hell had that bandana come from? How had she been so prepared? I suddenly resented her for not telling me to bring one. All I had was a thin plaid fleece scarf from H&M tucked into my pea coat. I pulled it out from under my collar and tied it around my mouth just as the protestors and SWATs collided like two storm systems. Ana and I were knocked to the ground. When I managed to stand back up I was crushed up against a SWAT shield before slipping back into an opening in the crowd. I looked around for Ana but couldn't see her. I heard the crack of shattering glass and saw a man in black throwing a pylon through a bus shelter. Two young women beside me were shouting at him to stop when suddenly I saw the orange contrails of three tear gas canisters zip over the crowd, casting a bile-coloured haze over the chaos. People started screaming, and two men with dreadlocks began dousing everyone's scarves with clear plastic squeeze bottles of vinegar, the kind you might find in a diner. One of them squirted some straight through my scarf and into my mouth. I started to cough. And just as I started retching, the presidential convoy whizzed past, a blur of shiny black SUVs not more than ten metres away behind the wall of SWATs. The crowd roared and surged forward. That's when I realized all I had really wanted in the first place was to see Bush. In that moment I couldn't quite fathom that he was an actual person with a body. Sentient and corporeal. He seemed like a television character, or some kind of omnipresent manifestation of American hegemony. I wrenched my neck upwards and stood on my tiptoes, trying to catch sight of him through the SWATs. But all of the cars' windows were tinted.

I WAS EVERY inch your son in high school: the self-flagellating perfectionist, top of my class, racking up course awards, always outdoing myself to prove my worth. The gay kid who found safety and belonging through tireless excellence. Who had become addicted to your validation. You had a biologically ingrained faith in my abilities. I was tested and confirmed gifted at the earliest possible juncture, and you spared the neighbours and book club ladies no detail of my accomplishments. Of course you always had a masochistic streak when it came to heaping expectations on yourself— the result of decades spent excelling so far beyond your male peers that those in charge would be forced to treat you just about as well as them. And this streak extended, by way of a myriad of little neuroses, to virtually every facet of your life. If a wineglass had a fingerprint on it, you'd wipe it clean with a damp paper towel before taking a sip, even when you were alone in the kitchen after work. You would agonize for days after forgetting a colleague's wife's name at a party. And you could never bear to throw out food, because to be wasteful was a character flaw, an admission you'd over-shopped, not to mention you'd hate to ever be caught unprepared without the requisite ingredient. This meant I found crackers in the pantry dating back to before I started high school, and various sedimentary layers of rotting fruit and vegetables in the fridge. Every couple of months I'd break down and purge.

"I can't believe you dumped the whole crisper!"

"It was compost."

"And without even asking me, I mean—"

"Mom—"

"—I was going to make a stew!"

"It was starting to produce heat."

In grade eleven I left my biology midterm on the dining-room table by accident. That evening you knocked on my bedroom door and peeked in without waiting for a reply—which you persisted in doing throughout my adolescence, despite knowing the very real risk of finding me with my dick out. I was lying in bed reading a book and looked up. You wore a look of genuine concern.

"You doing okay?" you asked.

"Yeah."

"I saw your midterm on the table."

"..."

"You're not upset?"

"No."

"Okay."

"I got an 85 percent on it."

You nodded and closed the door.

By the time I graduated I was done with it. I couldn't stomach the prospect of ever stepping into a classroom again. I was offered scholarships to four or five universities. I turned them down without telling you. Instead, Ana and I convinced one another that we should take the year off to make some money and "live a bit." Which ultimately amounted to landing jobs at the Tim Hortons in the strip mall by the highway. It was on a major commuter route, just before the on-ramp, and the morning drive-thru line often stretched twenty cars long. On my third day I was put on the drive-thru window, as our manager Jess stood behind me timing each transaction on her iPhone. The goal was eighteen seconds, from the car pulling up, to the handing over of the food, to the exchange of payment, to the car driving off. Eighteen seconds was company policy.

"And any one of those cars could be someone from management checking on us," she informed me.

This Tim Hortons panopticon was of course perverse, as the length of every transaction relied on the behaviour of the customer, over which I had absolutely no control. More often than not, despite having waited in line for ten minutes, despite having been told when they placed their order how much it would cost, despite having had that amount flashed before their eyes on a large digital readout, and despite 95 percent of customers ordering the exact same thing every day, most only began fumbling for their wallet after they'd been handed their coffee and donut, wading through their change pocket with their index finger, counting out coins on their palm, giving up and pulling out a twenty.

"You're averaging eleven seconds off your mark," Jess informed me mid-shift, as if it were the Olympic pre-trials.

"That's like the length of a good orgasm," Ana said, crouched behind the dumpster in the back parking lot on our lunch break, eating a box of cast-off cruller fragments.

"A pretty damn good orgasm."

She squinted into the sun and shrugged, as if to suggest she'd had longer. Which she probably had.

"The worst thing, though," she said, "worse than Jess and waking up at five in the morning, is when people order an 'expresso.' This woman ordered an 'expresso' today and I just started singing Madonna. *Expresso self.*"

"I CAN'T BELIEVE you're just throwing everything away," you said to me as I handed you a large black coffee through the drive-thru window. You'd come to pay me a visit on my fifth day. Instead of change you held up the scholarship offer you'd fished out of the recycling. "*Literally* throwing it away," shaking the paper, underscoring your linguistic point.

"That'll be four sixty," I repeated.

You had poured yourself into me and now I was becoming like every other listless millennial you had read about in the magazines and reassured yourself you would never raise. You said Ana cut a strong current as she moved through life and that I was letting myself be pulled along by it. *And you can't just follow her up her own ass, Jordan.*

Somewhere behind you a car honked. You slapped a five-dollar bill into my hand. "I'll see you at home."

My heart raced for a full ten minutes after you'd driven off. What can I say, Mom; you were right. Strong-willed women have always cast a certain spell over me.

A few months into our Tim Hortons tenure, Ana and I applied to theatre school. Once again I didn't tell you, knowing you would suck all the oxygen out of the fire. We spent weeks rehearsing our monologues in the back parking lot. I can still remember Ana's Blanche DuBois and Ophelia down to the exact places she took a breath or paused for effect. We practiced our monologues so much they began to feel like blocks of stone we were carving and buffing. We applied to Ryerson University's acting program and booked our train tickets to Toronto for the audition. I told you we were going to visit friends down there, which you knew I didn't have. Ana's parents treated us to a large beige room at the Delta Chelsea Hotel, and we spent the night wandering around in our bathrobes with gin-and-tonics like some 1950s lavender marriage.

Every night that spring, when Ana and I got home from work, we called each other to see if "the letter" from Ryerson had arrived. In the third week of April, hers finally did. She'd been accepted and reassured me that my letter would come soon. But as the days passed she started avoiding the subject altogether. One evening, in early May, I came home to find a thin white envelope waiting for me on my bedroom desk, placed there by your hand. I sat down on my bed, took a deep breath, called Ana, and opened the envelope with her on the other line.

"I'm on the wait list."

"Well, it's better than not getting in," she said.

"Barely."

To be honest, it was a gentler letdown than the one I'd been steeling myself for.

Of course you knew I'd applied. Knew I'd gone down to Toronto to audition. You hid neither your surprise nor your disappointment about my being wait-listed. All you said was: "It's always good to have a Plan B." A couple of days later, I found a brochure for the winter intake to Algonquin College and a sticky note saying, *Pages 10, 15, 22. Early childhood education. Speech therapist. Medical technologist.*

I applied to the first two. Once again, without telling you.

ANA'S PARENTS, Fatme and Mehmed, immigrated to Canada from Bulgaria when she was four, and to celebrate quitting our donut drudgery we decided to join them on a trip there.

You told me you'd be praying for my protection while I was away. "And if anyone asks, just say Ana's your girlfriend, okay?"

"In other words, no silk scarves and cravats," I sassed.

"You know what I mean."

I kissed you and told you not to worry, even though I knew you would.

For the first several days we stayed with Ana's aunt and uncle in Sofia. They lived in the corner unit of an old apartment block lined floor to ceiling with dark wooden bookshelves. The floor was a patchwork of ornate rugs worn through from years of visitors. The apartment was a couple of blocks from a stadium, and in the evenings as we sat around the dinner table eating moussaka and shopska salata and drinking clear, biting rakia, we heard the intermittent roar of soccer fans like the pounding surf of a nearby sea. The windows were kept open to let whatever breeze existed into the overstuffed apartment. At night I lay on the spring-laden couch in the living room listening to the quarrels of stray cats in the street below. The smell of their piss, motorcycle exhaust, and the musty apartment cloaked me like a heavy blanket as I lay there, glistening in the Balkan heat.

On the third night a family friend named Julia came over for dinner. From what I could glean Julia was a childhood friend of Ana's aunt and a respected academic living in Paris.

"A philosopher," Fatme clarified, with raised eyebrows as if to say "la-di-da."

I was instantly drawn to Julia, even though she barely registered my presence, opting to spend most of the evening talking to Fatme and Ana's aunt, speaking rapid-fire Bulgarian with an almost violent intensity. What seemed like full-blown arguments would be punctuated by all three women bursting into peals of laughter. Julia was probably in her mid-sixties but had a certain youthful, puckish quality about her.

At one point before dinner I found myself shoulder to shoulder with her in the galley kitchen, preparing a beet salad. I peeled and she quartered with a fearsome knife. While in mid-conversation with the other women she turned to me, took one of the beets into her stained hand, and, in the first English she'd spoken all night, deadpanned: "I feel like a Mayan."

I smiled and she flashed me a rakish grin.

After dinner, with the plates piled in the kitchen sink, the adults retired to the balcony for cigarettes and digestifs, while Ana turned in for an early sleep. I had to stay awake because my bed was the couch, so I occupied myself browsing the bookshelves in the living room. I ran my finger along the spines. Most were Bulgarian titles, but a few English ones had managed to find their way in. *Nineteen Eighty-Four, The Secret,* a couple of Jodi Picoults. On the lowest shelf I noticed three books by an author named Julia Kristeva, two with Bulgarian titles and one in English. I crouched down and pulled out the latter. *Powers of Horror: An Essay on Abjection.* The book was khaki-coloured and had a black-and-white photograph of an early-thirty-something Julia on the front cover. In the photograph her long black hair was windblown across her creased forehead. She rested her head on her right fist, lips parted, lost in thought, staring with dark, world-weary eyes out into the indeterminate distance. I flipped the book over and began to read the back cover just as the balcony door slid open and the adults poured in, mid-debate. Before I could return the book to its spot, Fatme caught sight of me on my knees with it in my hand. She turned to Julia, pointed, made a remark, and they laughed. Julia imitated the pose in the photograph while Fatme gestured at me.

"You can have it. My sister can't read it anyway," Fatme said. "That one's in English, yes?"

I nodded.

She gave me a conspiratorial wink as if to say, *Just take it, she won't notice.* As the sisters escorted Julia to the door, they offered her the leftovers and several unopened bottles of wine, all of which she refused, and after a flurry of kisses and a final burst of aggressive chatter she departed — but not before she found my eyes across the room and gave me a little wave goodbye. I did not realize it in that moment but, though that would be the last time we saw each other in person, it would be far from the last night I ever spent with Julia Kristeva.

"THERE LOOMS, within abjection, one of those violent, dark revolts of being, directed against a threat that seems to emanate from an exorbitant outside or inside, ejected beyond the scope of the possible, the tolerable, the thinkable."

I read the first line of the book twice more before lying back onto the unforgiving couch and, with the aid of my flashlight, reading into the early morning, until I could hear a garbage truck beginning to make its pre-dawn rounds through the narrow streets. Kristeva wrote about the notion of "abjection," the horror one experienced when confronted with one's own corporeal reality or a breakdown in the distinction between self and other. Between ourselves and "the world of dead material objects." The abject, she posited, existed in a space between the subject (the observer) and the object (the thing observed) and disrupted identity, system, and order. For Kristeva, a human corpse, particularly that of a loved one, most keenly exemplifies the literal breakdown between subject and object, and we are confronted with our own eventual, palpably real death in its presence.

"The corpse, seen without God and outside of science, is the utmost of abjection," she wrote. "It is death infecting life." Kristeva associated our abject responses — horror, vomiting — with our rejection of death's materiality. With the traumatic and altogether reorienting experience of being confronted with the sort of materiality that reflected our own deaths back to us. "As in true theatre, without makeup or masks, refuse and corpses show me what I permanently thrust aside in order to live. These body fluids, this defilement, this shit are what life withstands, hardly and with difficulty, on the part of death. There, I am at the border of my condition as a living being."

There, I am at the border of my condition as a living being. I held these words in the flashlight's aura for a moment, thinking about the limits of experience and sensation.

That winter Ana had given me *The Tears of Eros* by Georges Bataille, and as I read Kristeva's line over I recalled Bataille's thoughts on transgression. In his book Bataille fixated on a series of four photographs of a man named

Fou-Tchou-Li being subjected to *ling'chi*, the Imperial Chinese "torture by a hundred pieces." The gruesome black-and-white images depicted Fou-Tchou-Li tied to a stake, being dismembered and sheared of his flesh, piece by piece, his eyes gazing heavenward, an inscrutable expression on his face. Like Christ on the cross, in the throes of a divine and exquisite pain. For Bataille these images, which he called "ecstatic and intolerable," portrayed a kind of transcendence possible only in the transgression of the body's physical limits or in shattering, in Kristeva's words, the border of one's condition as a living being. A limit-experience which severed the subject from himself.

When my eyes started to burn I switched off the flashlight, and as I lay there in the dark these threshold-states of being and un-being began to merge in my brain—Kristeva's *border of her condition*, when confronted with the abject, and Bataille's *moment of the ecstatic and intolerable*, when pushed to the edge of bodily experience. I suddenly realized I had never truly reached any kind of border of my being. Of course I had shat and vomited and had once seen a dead body at a wake, but I had never allowed these things to push me to the place where *death infected life*, nor felt the intolerable ecstasy of becoming body, nor even witnessed this in another. As I lay there I realized that until I had I would remain a child. An unformed thing.

THE NEXT MORNING Ana and I packed ourselves into her aunt and uncle's jeep along with her parents and her younger cousin, who was incidentally also named Jordan (another casualty of the great late-eighties tsunami of Justins, Jordans, and Jasons). Ana, Jordan, and I sat in the jeep's open-air back trunk without seat belts. Facing backwards, we watched the city recede from us. The crumbling facades of office towers, the frenzy of power lines, the satellite dishes sprouting from concrete apartment blocks like mushroom spores. We were headed south towards a remote Balkan Mountain village called Tuja to visit Ana's grandmother, who was incidentally also named Ana. As a girl growing up Ana had spent her summers living with Nana Ana, and the two were inseparable. The family sometimes joked that Ana had been accidentally reincarnated as her grandmother while Nana Ana was still alive.

Even though we were buffeted by the wind, it was still sweltering, and between the pre-EU roads, the roar of passing trucks, and the Bulgarian pop music blaring from the stereo, I began to feel like tenderized meat. Jordan was seventeen and was the spitting image of Ana, except with short hair and a faint dusting of hair above his lip, which my eyes always landed on whenever he spoke to me in his halting English. He spent the whole ride glued to a video game console, and I spent the whole ride with my thigh glued to his (which he was, it seemed, absolutely oblivious of).

We drove for hours through the outskirts of small cities, past fields of sunflowers, until we began to climb through foothills. Mehmed turned around and shouted from the back seat: "This highway we're on? When Fatme and I were your age we spent a summer building this highway as part of a communist youth project. Thousands of us." He said it with a smile I couldn't place, somewhere between wistfulness and pride. I nodded. I didn't know whether I should compliment him on it. To be honest I was barely taking in the scenery, as I was mostly fretting about when and how I would hear back from Ryerson about the wait-list.

Before long the mountains revealed themselves, ancient and humble. We drove along a river white with cataracts for several miles before making a sharp turn at an innocuous wooden sign for Rila Monastery.

"We figured while we're here," Mehmed said.

After a mad dash to the lavatories we recomposed ourselves. Ana pulled on long pants, her mother and aunt covered their hair with thin paisley-patterned shawls, and we entered the monastery's central cloister. The inner yard was lined with black-and-white-striped porticoes and topped with cross-crowned domes. At the centre of the yard was the main chapel, the exteriors of which were frescoed, while walling in the edges of the yard were the monks' living quarters. As we stood in place, pivoting to take it all in, Ana translated her uncle's random factoids about the monastery — tenth century, founded by a hermit named Ivan, UNESCO'ed.

Jordan kept lingering near Ana and me, hoping we had some kind of adventure in mind — which, of course, we did, but unfortunately it didn't include him. Somehow she and I managed to peel away from the group and did our best to get lost in the monastery's dimly lit corridors, which were most definitely not open to the public.

"That's the good thing about Bulgaria," she said. "They're not really used to tourists so they don't think to block anything off."

As we explored I found it almost comical how our body language transformed. We began walking a little slower, reverently, with our hands clasped behind our backs as if we were trying our best not to be caught out as the heathen interlopers we were.

There were little grottos in the walls where, above lit candles, hung icons of various saints painted in Eastern Orthodox style and crested with halos of gold foil. I thought about the wars of the iconoclasts that raged through this region centuries ago. Men torturing and killing one another, desecrating churches, toppling empires over the questions: What is an image? What power do images hold? Can an image supplant God? Ana said she could never imagine being an icon painter; she wanted credit too badly. I asked if she thought satisfying our egos was the main reason we enjoyed acting. She took this as some kind of personal slight and offered up a scrunched smiley-face in response. But I was asking out of genuine curiosity. The idea of sublimating my creative energies into the anonymous ether of the spiritual seemed like a kind of death to me too. A wasted life. But perhaps that was because we couldn't disentangle our selves from the enshrined sanctity of "self-expression" we'd been raised to cherish.

As we walked on, our feet echoing over the stone, I told Ana how as a boy I was fascinated by monks. Around the age of eight or nine, I even started having a recurring dream about them. In the dream I found myself wearing these colourful robes and walking through a castle-like building surrounded by other men, gardening, praying, cooking. My body felt radiant with light. It occurred to me just then that maybe the dream was some kind of manifestation of my lifelong repressed fear of death.

"Either that or your lifelong fag-tacularness," Ana replied. "Which is not so repressed."

We found ourselves in a small courtyard with a single orange tree. The sky was a deep-blue square so unblemished by clouds that for a second it appeared to be a painted ceiling. Ana walked over to the orange tree and plucked one off.

"I actually think monks are probably more afraid of death than anyone," she said as she began to peel it. "Monks of any religion." She thought about this for a moment and slipped an orange slice in her mouth. "Like, on some level, don't you think a retreat from the world into prayer is... I mean, it has to be motivated by a fear of death. A desire to reconcile themselves with the horror of it. So they spend their whole lives preparing. Quieting the mind. Learning to subdue the self. Becoming nothing."

"Like a rehearsal," I said.

She shrugged, before grimacing and spitting out the orange slice into her hand. "It's bitter as fuck."

Jordan appeared in an adjacent doorway and waved us over. Apparently the group had been looking for us and were eager to leave. When we arrived back at the jeep, Ana's parents, uncle, and aunt were waiting in their respective places in irritated silence. For the last half of the drive, as the sun grew low and iridescent, I tried to read some more of Kristeva's book. I felt shy reading it around others. It felt like posturing. Which it probably was. It was nearly impossible to read the fine print in the back of the jeep on the uneven road, and yet for some reason I persisted, until I came upon a line that seemed to refract a prismatic light through the day's events: "The various means of purifying the abject — the various catharses — make up the history of religion, and end up with that catharsis par excellence called art, both on the far and near side of religion."

As the last light burned red in the west, we turned off onto a dirt side road that pulverized what was left of our bones. On the outskirts of Tuja were Roma encampments with cooking fires casting silhouetted columns of smoke into the mountain air. Ana's grandmother was waiting for us outside the front gate of her house, a tin and cinderblock construction blanketed in flowering ivy. Beside her stood her third son, Dimo, who crushed my hand as I offered it in greeting. Chicho Dimo, as Ana called him, was the youngest of the three siblings; in his early forties with a thick black beard, he wore a red jumpsuit with two guns in a black holster around his waist. Nana Ana looked a bit like Yoda, and as I bent down to hug her I could feel each notch of her spine through her floral dress. As I straightened up, she grabbed hold of my just-crushed hand with surprising conviction and began to lead me through the yard into her house — a perfectly preserved time capsule of a bygone era.

"Some serious communist realness going on," I murmured to Ana as we stepped into the kitchen. To my chagrin she promptly turned to her grandmother and translated what I'd just said.

Nana Ana chuckled and made some kind of snappy retort.

"She said she misses communism," Ana said, before Nana Ana interrupted with another flurry of invectives. "And says…that…mark her words…the fascists will be back." Ana smiled and knelt down to her grandmother's eye level. "But not in our lifetimes, Nana." Nana placed her wizened hands on either side of Ana's face and replied with gravity. "She said maybe not in her lifetime, but in ours."

By that point the rest of the family had piled into the

kitchen and, as if picking up where she'd left off, Nana Ana restored her grip on my hand and led me onward through the house, out the back door, and into a small cobblestoned courtyard where several chickens and roosters dashed about, squawking in alarm. I shook my head with confused trepidation as she began pointing to the chickens and imploring me in her authoritative rasp to do something.

Ana appeared beside me and translated her grandmother's request as the rest of the family gathered round in a semicircle. "It's customary in Bulgaria for the guest to supply the first night's meal. But because you haven't brought anything she's offering you the choice of one of her chickens."

"You mean like—"

"To kill."

"Seriously?"

"Welcome to the mountains."

"Kill how?"

She pointed to a wooden stump in the corner that had a machete driven into it. The handle of the machete was wrapped in black electrical tape.

"I'm vegetarian," I said.

Ana smiled. "C'mon, she's waiting for you."

With all eight members of the family watching, I took a step forward into the courtyard, which erupted into a new flurry of avian commotion. I made a few half-hearted attempts to scrabble at a brown hen before realizing we'd be there all night unless I really committed to it. I became keenly aware that my masculinity was on public trial. I swallowed, grit my teeth, and told myself, *Your ancestors lived in fucking mud homes on the prairies, raised and killed and gutted their own livestock, and you can't even catch a fucking chicken in a tiny yard for a group of onlookers? C'mon, you limp-wristed pussy.* I lunged at a mottled white hen and was startled to feel my hands close around its sides; to feel the force of its wings pushing out against my palms. And then another sensation that aroused nothing short of terror in me: the shocking insistence of its beating heart. It was so completely and undeniably alive. As I held its throbbing body, walked to the corner of the yard, and placed it on the wooden stump, I could quite literally feel the moment the chicken apprehended its own death, and in that moment I had the distinct impression I was holding both a living bird and its carcass, something caught in the abject place between those states. And of course I had to render it a carcass, an object, in my mind, an "it" not a "her," in order to bear the act of actually making it one. As I pushed it down into the wooden stump with my left hand and gripped the machete with my right, I felt both sets of the Anas' hands close around my raised arm. The courtyard filled with laughter. I looked up at their faces in confusion.

"She's totally pranking you," Ana said. "She made a roast and it's ready to eat."

NANA ANA'S HUSBAND was something of a quasi-divine figure in Tuja. Legend had it that sometime in the sixties, the village well was running dry and there was worry that the community would have to be uprooted. Her husband was blind, a point that she emphasized several times while recounting this story for me with the aid of Ana's translation. Apparently one night her husband, *who was blind* and in his late forties at the time, had a dream—a vision, one might say—in which he saw the remains of an ancient ruin on the mountainside. It was a real ruin he recognized, about a day's journey from the town. In his dream he saw himself strike the mountain near this ruin and from out of the rock flowed clear, clean water. The next morning, upon waking, he set out on his donkey into the mountains. When he finally arrived at the ruin, he worked for several hours clearing away brush and removing boulders from the mountainside until he uncovered a natural aquifer. Nana Ana related this next part of the story with great gravity: her husband filled his cupped hands with the spouting water, drank it (several times, it seems, based on her hand gestures), and then, as if by a miracle, regained his eyesight. *Partial* eyesight, she clarified, perhaps so as not to strain credibility. The village declared it a divine act, and the aquifer, which became the site of the new well, was blessed by the local imam and the archdiocese of Sofia.

This was the well that Chico Dimo drove us to every second morning in his decommissioned Soviet military truck, to fill large plastic jugs with drinking water. As he drove the serpentine mountain route, he often rested his arm on the passenger-side headrest and turned to talk to Ana and me in the back seat, careening precariously close to the cliff's edge as he did. The well, which was now a rather unimpressive utilitarian faucet affixed to a cement wall on the mountainside, was still believed to possess sacred properties. Above the tap was a small ledge clustered with icons, prayer beads, and the puddled remains of candles.

Nana Ana explained that her husband later disappeared in the mountains. One of her children (she didn't specify which one) had left the gate of the courtyard open one morning and the donkey wandered off. Her husband set off to find it, following its tracks up the perilous cliff road. He never did come back. She said she thought his soul wandered there still. Then one morning, a week to the day after his funeral, Nana Ana looked out her kitchen window into the courtyard and saw the donkey standing in his enclosure once more.

ON THE LAST day of the trip, I dropped Julia Kristeva's *Powers of Horror* down Devil's Throat, a cave in southern Bulgaria near the Greek border. It slipped from my bag as Ana and I were climbing the slick staircase beside the waterfall that roared into the cavern. Upon entering the central chamber, the water flowed in a ferocious torrent before disappearing into a network of unmapped tunnels, which no caver had ever returned from. The cave was once believed to be the mouth of hell, the earthly opening into Hades, where Orpheus ventured into the underworld to reclaim his beloved Eurydice. And like Orpheus, I looked back as my copy of the book tumbled away from me into the darkness.

I FOUND OUT I had been grudgingly accepted into Ryerson (far from the first on the wait-list, it seemed) less than a month before class was to start. Ana and I moved into separate rooms in a fourteen-storey tower-block residence called Pitman Hall. She was on the eighth floor, I was on the fourteenth. Our rooms had cement walls painted with industrial white paint and thin green carpeting the consistency of a lint brush. That year we each came down with a cold about once a month, the unsurprising outcome of cramming a thousand undergrads into a building with circulated air. All my female friends came down with equally as many bladder infections, also the unsurprising outcome of cramming a thousand undergrads into a building. We avoided the common rooms, as they smelled of microwaveable macaroni-and-cheese dinners and had televisions you couldn't turn off, opting instead to spend our nights in each other's rooms, working our way through magnums of bargain-bin red wine. Ana's room was our preferred spot, mostly because she'd made half an effort to decorate it, hanging gauzy curtains up in her windows and stringing up a strand of white fairy lights. In the first week of school, she threw a toga party. To this day, she still ribs me for showing up wrapped in a fitted floral sheet.

It seemed the goal of theatre school, especially in first year, was to render us empty vessels. Bodies without personalities, tics, or really any defining characteristics. One instructor actually described first year as being about "stripping you down to nothing and building you back up," which struck me as being a bit Jonestown-y. In his essay *Paradox of the Actor*, Denis Diderot claimed that the best actors "are fit to play all characters because they have none." He defined an actor's ability in terms of absence — namely, an absence of any internal, innate identity. Like the depersonalized characters in pornos, Diderot's actors were blank bodies onto which the fantasies of others could be projected. Hosts to be possessed. Icon painters suffused by divine inspiration. Diderot's essay was written in 1773 and published posthumously fifty-seven years later, in 1830. Lee Strasberg, the father of method acting in America, once claimed *Paradox of the Actor* "has remained to this day the most significant attempt to deal with the problem of acting," which goes a way to explaining how Diderot's vision of the actor as automaton, as a body cleaved of its selfhood, has retained such currency in Western theatre schools.

Ana once said acting was her way of cheating death because she got to live multiple lives. For her there was something sublime about this abdication of self. Like the Buddhist *no-self* in a state of continual reincarnation. Perhaps this is why I was such a bad actor. There was always something terrifying to me about this prospect. I couldn't quite bear to let go of myself.

At night the other actors would cluster in Ana's room to recount battle stories from that day's class. Our voice teacher was Paulette Winters, whose personal mission became trying to hammer out my sibilant "s" like a metalworker smelting a sword straight. The subtext being: *You don't want a career playing evil viziers and the sassy best friend.* Movement was taught by the ever-sparky Jessica Schaffer, a.k.a. "the Chafer" for the burns we'd get from the studio floor. Her class was every morning at 9 a.m. and she locked the doors at 9:01 a.m. If you were late, you had to sit in the hall until after class so you could apologize to her and explain your delay. Three missed classes and you were put on probation, and no one on probation ever got invited back the next year.

But the most feared instructor was Brian Leckey, a bald man with round black spectacles, a dead ringer for Foucault— and from the rumours we heard from older students, his classes were more or less Punish and Discipline. Among the first-years, our favourite late-night gossip was swapping rumours of "Leaky's" sadistic acting exercises, passed down through the broken telephone of the school's oral tradition. The most notorious was the Zone. It was the only unit that Leaky taught the first-year students. The older students talked about it as a kind of initiation, a rite of passage.

"It'll break you," a fourth-year told me while picking the pepperonis off her pizza in the school's cafeteria. "It breaks everyone." She told me the program usually lost six or seven students every year because of the Zone. "Which is kind of the point, because they always accept more first-years than they want. For the tuition money."

But none of the older students would tell us what the Zone actually was. That was tradition.

We kept waiting, and the more weeks passed the more the dread built. Until one morning in January we walked into the mirrored studio in the basement expecting movement class to find Leaky sitting on an orange plastic chair waiting for us. As each student entered the room and noticed him, their boisterous laughter and conversation from the hallway cut out until we were all gathered in silence. Leaky took us in for a moment and then instructed us to sit on the floor facing him.

"Maybe you think we accepted you into this school because you can act." He let this moderately plausible assumption linger in the air for a moment. "But you do not know how to act." He flashed us an unnerving smile. "At the moment, what you think of as 'acting,' what you learned from your high school teachers and community theatre productions, is an embarrassing litany of bad habits. And I'm here to clean up the mess."

Leaky stood up and walked to the back of the room, leaving us staring at the empty orange chair. He then instructed our classmate Maya to leave the room, wait in the hallway for ten seconds, re-enter the room, and sit down on the chair *without acting.*

"Without affect, without emotion, without any character. Do you understand?"

Maya nodded.

"You will sit on the chair for a minute."

Maya got up and left the room. I caught Ana's eyes and she widened them as if to say: *Here we go.* Ten seconds passed. The door opened and Maya began striding across the room with what struck me as focused neutrality.

"*Stop!*" Leaky bellowed.

Maya startled and stood still. She hadn't even made it to the chair.

"Who do you think you are right now, in your mind?" he asked her.

Maya shook her head.

"Your mental image of yourself. What do you imagine?" he prodded her.

"I…I'm just walking normally."

"Normally?"

"That's how I walk."

"No, that is not how you walk. That is how you walk when you are being watched. Can we see that?" He looked at us and our silence was tacit agreement. "Are you aware of what your shoulders were doing when you walked, just now?" Maya shook her head. "Your shoulders were swaying like Beyoncé strutting onto the stage. You think you're pretty hot shit, don't you? Well, that's what your shoulders were saying to me. I want you to re-enter the room, and this time I want you to walk without acting with your shoulders."

Leaky had Maya re-enter the room over and over for the rest of the class, deconstructing every aspect of her movement and person until she was on the verge of tears. But she didn't break. Not that day. She re-entered so many times I lost count. Well over forty. She made it to the chair only once, and perhaps because of her relief or her nerves, she immediately began acting once she sat down. I could see it immediately. And I could feel the rest of the class see it as well. She exhaled, looked around. She was performing "waiting." Leaky let her sit there for the full minute to illustrate his point. It was excruciating. At the end of the minute he turned to the class to ask us if we believed her sitting. Like a Pavlovian chorus we all intoned "no" in unison.

I was finally called up on the Friday of that first week. By that point Leaky was averaging about three students a class. I was the third one of the day. I knew he was going to call my name before he said it, but something still somersaulted inside me when he did. As I stood up and crossed the room to the door, I felt the class turn into a firing squad. Over the past four days, Leaky had made us vicious, until we had begun to will failure on one another. He had managed to instill in us a pleasure in watching our classmates stripped bare. By now we all knew what to look for, and we could immediately spot the difference between the performance of neutrality and the genuine state of being present. I knew what it looked like, but the question was whether I could *embody* it.

I closed the door behind me and began counting to ten. I looked at the old play posters on the walls. The black-and-white photographs of past students. They had survived the Zone and I would too. I listened to the echo of the third-years' Shakespeare intensive down the hall. I asked my body not to betray me. I asked my mind not to betray my body. And then, in the remaining four seconds, I did everything in my power to join them, realizing that perhaps that was the trick to the Zone, to be so integrated that there was no difference between being and performing. I would erase myself and become nothing more than a unit of sentience moving through space and time. I turned the handle of the door and stepped into the room.

"*Stop!*" Leaky yelled after my second step. The class burst out laughing.

"YOU'RE TOO MUCH in your head," Ana told me that evening as we were walking home. "I could see you thinking your way through every attempt. You've got to get out of your head and into your body."

I thanked her for the unsolicited advice. She was just parroting what I was already being told by our teachers. *Get into your body.* God knows I was trying, slamming my consciousness into my pelvis, my diaphragm, my "swamp," as the Chafer called it. Where was *I* if not in *my body*? And who could blame me for being in my head — I was your son, for Chrissake; the son of a neurotic academic who spent her days trying to perfect a giant artificial brain.

ONE MORNING, midway through the third week of Leaky's regime of humiliations, I didn't get out of bed. Ana knocked on my door about eight minutes before class, which was a ten-minute walk away. I told her I wasn't coming. It had been revealed to me and the entirety of our class beyond any reasonable doubt that I was a self-deluded fraud, and I knew enough to cut my losses. Ana let herself in and sat down on the edge of my bed.

"The plight of an actor falls somewhere between donkeys and rapists in the who-gives-a-fuck index."

She sighed. "If you quit, I'll quit."

We smiled in complicity.

"You realize what this means?" I asked.

"We're not good actors."

"Well yes, probably. But also we'll forever be one of the 'six or seven' that students refer to when they intimidate the first years. The ones who were broken."

We let that sink in for a moment and decided we were alright with that ignoble distinction.

WE MOVED OUT of residence and spent the next few weeks floating through the city like blown garbage, wandering through art galleries, sleeping on friends' couches, stealing food from supermarkets. We thought we were being terribly French New Wave. In truth, we were unmoored. Eventually, we got our own place. We spent nights reading Artaud and Genet to each other. We temped, we catered, we served. I grew a moustache. Pierced my ear. Summer came and went. The stock market crashed. Obama won the election. And still, I hadn't told you. What could be more humiliating than flunking out of one of the flakiest university streams? I avoided your calls, your texts, your Facebook messages. I pictured you writing emails to me, saving them in your Drafts folder, and deleting them a few days later. Sometimes you left voice messages. Breakthroughs at work. Plans you were making with girlfriends. A funny PlentyOfFish date (I had helped you set up your profile).

"You have to tell her."

"I took out student loans, it didn't cost her a cent."

"Jordan. Call her."

I played it cool on the phone and rebuffed your fury with smart-ass bravado. But a couple of minutes after I hung up, I casually strolled to the bathroom and threw up. Far worse than any self-doubt and self-loathing was your disappointment.

ANA AND I figured that if we couldn't be good actors then at least we could be great sluts. I had rounded some kind of corner after high school, post-braces and acne, and what I lacked in natural looks I made up for in sheer ambition. We began devouring men like alpha predators. Floppy-haired hipster boys, bearded bartenders, suburban dads, skater twinks, foreign exchange students, Bay Street bankers, and just your average sportsbar douchebags. Text messaging became like air traffic control between us, ensuring we didn't collide our conquests. We lived like the "foul woman" in Baudelaire's poem "You'd Entertain the Universe in Bed": "Ennui makes you mean of soul...O filthy grandeur! O sublime disgrace!"

"You know, when I was a little girl my mother used to call me a slut," Ana told me one night as she came out of the shower, towelling off her hair. "She learned English from an old British woman and was taught the word just meant, like, unkempt or dirty. She'd poke her head into my bedroom and say: 'My god, Ana, look at this mess! You're such a slutty little girl.'" On some visceral level I understood the intersection between the two meanings of the word. To be a slut was to wallow in pleasure and filth. Eros and excrement. On the threshold between ecstasy and debasement.

I started to fixate on the idea that I was genetically pre-destined to be either a loser or a pervert. The kind of men who became sperm donors, the kind of men my dad was likely to be, largely fell into one of the following types: out-of-work construction workers, hapless students strug-gling to make tuition, aspiring musicians, potheads living in their parents' basements, and sex criminals. You told me you had gone to Toronto for the procedure, and I figured there was a chance he'd still be walking the streets. I kept an eye out, searching passing faces for those of my features I didn't see on you. The long nose. The divot in my chin. The protruding ears. Had he been hard up for a hit? Had it been a whim? A dare? Or was he a serial depositor? And what had gotten him off? A magazine? An elaborate fan-tasy? I could come just by thinking of a neck I'd seen on the streetcar or the small of someone's back. I doubt I'd inherited this ability from you.

All my life I've feared that some perverse animal dwelled in me. An insatiable creature of pure sensation. And I've always had the sense you were afraid of it too. Walking in to find me masturbating in the crib when I was two months old. You joked I couldn't keep my hands off myself. When I was five you'd have to remove the Q-Tip from my hand or else I would keep turning it in my ear forever, long past the utility of hygiene, lost in the strange erogeneity of it. Six years old, swimming in the silty waters of the Ottawa River with my friend Michael, we ventured towards the shore until the water grew so shallow we had to pull ourselves forward with our hands like tadpoles, bellies against the sandy riverbed, until we beached ourselves. Michael jumped up and dashed towards the cottage, but I lingered in the fetid muck among the reeds and gauze of dead minnows. I slathered my arms and legs with it like a Russian oligarch vacationing on the Dead Sea. There was just enough water to lie back in. It coated the bottom of my head. Filled my ears. I felt a leech attach itself to my neck and I let it. A skittish school of minnows nibbled my thighs. They mistook me for an inanimate object. A dead thing. Baking in filth under the sun. Saturated with the bliss of being my body. You had to come down to find me there and pull me up for dinner.

A year later, grade two, I had to take a shit in the middle of a spelling test. Mrs. Legault was at the front of the room reciting words that we had to write down on a sheet of foolscap. "Toboggan. Saskatchewan. Tornado." I couldn't just get up in the middle of the test or I would fail. Moreover I realized it felt good. The pressure of it. The fullness. I held the turd in. Basked in the sensation of it. The euphoric pressing of the vagus nerve. I stuck a finger up there and prodded it. Mrs. Legault was pacing around the classroom making sure no one was cheating. As she came up to my desk she stopped, sniffed the air, and in a stage whisper asked: "Do I smell poop?" Her eyes turned to me. I wanted to bury myself in the little slot in my desk. She bent down, grabbed my hand, and noticed my shit-caked fingernail. Before I could open my mouth she yanked me up by the arm and marched me down to the office. She didn't say a word during my walk of shame. But then, what was there to say? Shit defied words. To touch shit was to touch death.

> Such wastes drop so that I might live, until, from loss to loss, nothing remains in me and my entire body falls beyond the limit — cadere, cadaver. If dung signifies the other side of the border, the place where I am not and which permits me to be, the corpse, the most sickening of wastes, is a border that has encroached upon everything. It is no longer I who expel, "I" is expelled.
>
> —Julia Kristeva

I sat in the office waiting room as they called you, staring at my shoes red-faced. Sublime disgrace. I'm not sure what you and Mrs. Legault talked about, but you didn't come to the school that afternoon to pick me up. And you didn't bring it up with me that night over dinner. Or ever, for that matter.

One morning when I was twelve I woke with the sun on my face and languished in my sheets, rolling around in them like a rhinoceros in the dust until I came for the first time. I didn't yet equate the sensation with sex. For some reason it reminded me of drinking a glass of milk. The way milk felt coating my mouth and my throat. I thought about melting into the sheets and becoming indistinguishable from them. I wanted to provoke this feeling as much as possible and assumed the only way to do this was by rolling and rolling and rolling around my bedsheets, basking in the warmth of the morning light. A special, time-of-day-contingent ritual. If only my theatre school teachers could have seen me as a child. Living deep within my body. When did that stop? When did shame push me into my head?

The French psychoanalyst Jacques Lacan suggested that there is a *jouissance* — an excessive pleasure — that compels us to continually seek to transgress the boundaries of our own enjoyment. A desire for sensations so intense they would push one to what Michel Foucault called "the point of life which lies as close as possible to the impossibility of living, which lies at the limit or the extreme." These childhood wallowings were the closest I've ever come to this. As I grew up I wondered: How far would I go? Would I journey to the point where I was at the border of my being? Was this what the pervert in me wanted? To destroy my self? Venture to the place where death infects life? I didn't trust this creature, my blood, my DNA; I imagined God the Father, the sperm donor jerking off in a cubby into a little plastic cup with an orange lid, and myself as the son, played by Antonin Artaud, inveterate sinner, liar, thief, crucified on Golgotha "not as Christ but as Artaud…as complete atheist." A body persecuted for erotic gluttony. "The obscene sexual erotic golosity of mankind, for which pain is a humus, the liquid from a fertile mucus, a serum worth sipping by one who has never on his own gained by being a man while knowing that he was becoming one."

ALL OF WHICH to say is that somehow I wasn't as surprised as I thought I might have been to find myself at a Super 8 motel near Highway 401, sucking off a guy in a grey suit playing a businessman while two HD camcorders filmed us. Nor was it a particularly novel or unexpected situation for an

out-of-work, undereducated not-quite-actor. The Diderotian
empty vessel. In fact, in some way it felt almost inevitable
that I should find myself there, my knees on that beige nylon
carpet, as if it were the unforeseen but predestined endgame
of my childhood preoccupation with the body. I could have
chalked up that blow job to my being broke. Or depressed.
Or directionless. I imagine these excuses would've been more
palatable for you. But they would have been excuses. The
truth is I wanted to. I was alive, and I wanted to confirm it
through feeling everything a living body could feel.

God only knows how you found out. To this day you've
never leaked your source. Ana swore on her life it wasn't
her and I believe her, even though you and she had kept
up a private correspondence over the years. My best guess
was that I must've logged on to my email on your computer at some point and forgotten to log off; though that
would have required a sinister amount of snooping on your
part. But what you did next really goes down in the Monica
Tannahill annals.

Ana and I were smoking a cigarette on our unshovelled
balcony in our boots and underwear. Our radiator had
broken and turned our apartment into a sauna, and we were
trying to cool off. The frozen metal of the balcony railing
gripped our hands as we watched a car spin and sputter in
the parking lot below.

"The superintendent still hasn't called back," Ana muttered, just as we heard a knock on the front door.

"Well, if it isn't a Christmas miracle." I traipsed back
inside with my boots, tracking snow across the floor.

"At least put on a bathrobe!" Ana called, but I wanted
to make a point. I wanted to show him how we had been

living for three days in our sweat-soaked underwear while he ignored our calls and texts, and a harder knock came just as I grabbed the doorknob and flung it open to find myself standing face to face with you in your winter coat, your purple rolling suitcase by your side. You were panting from the effort of hauling it up five flights of stairs. The tip of your nose moist from the cold. You looked me up and down. Slow and unhurried. And then you looked past me, surveying the apartment. The empty takeaway boxes. The piles of laundry. The fogged windows. The sweat. You brushed the snow off your shoulders. Took a deep breath. And told me you'd discovered that I was doing "pornography," that you were extremely upset about it, in fact hadn't been sleeping, and knew I wouldn't reply to an email if you sent it and frankly the matter was so far beyond an email or phone call anyway, so much so that you felt compelled to take two full days off work "and just before a giant research grant is due, I might add" to drive down to Toronto to figure out what in god's name was going on with me.

"Mom, I don't need to stand here and justify—"

"Oh, yes, you do, one hundred goddamn percent you do."

You had refused to watch the videos but wanted "the facts." How many there were, who was in them, where they were shot, how much had they paid me, had I used protection, had I used drugs? Of course I said nothing. I knew my Miranda rights. (Four, I don't know their names, mostly at the Super 8, a hundred bucks a pop, sometimes and sometimes). If you have to know, I answered an online ad, showed up at an office above a strip mall, and shot an "audition" tape, a solo they paid me fifty bucks for, and then they asked me back the next week for a hundred bucks to shoot a scene with two other guys, both a bit rough-trade, one fairly hairy and stocky and the other scrawny with bad teeth, not lookers, but then neither was I, and I guess there's a market for that, who knows. If you have to know, I climbed into a hatchback with them and two cameramen and drove out to the motel, and the front desk attendant was so remarkably unfazed I was almost moved to tears and had to look down when our eyes met. If you have to know, I studied the carpet of the hallway as I walked. Grey synthetic fibre, almost silver. The colour of duct tape. The walls were wood-panelled along the bottom and wallpapered on top. An insipid design of little yellow flowers woven through a damask pattern. The hallway smelled of cleaning solvents and the room was at the end on the ground floor. A little wooden door with the number fourteen on a vinyl sticker. The older cameraman, the one with the white goatee, had to pull the doorknob towards him to get the key to enter the lock, and then gave the door a little shove to open it, he seemed to know the trick. The wallpaper continued into the room, it was rippled in places, there was a large mirror, a black telephone, and two firm double beds on metal frames. I looked up at the water damage on the white plaster ceiling and then out the window at the parking lot, where a pile of old computer monitors had been dumped. Later, as I was playing some naive hustler version of myself, unbuckling this supposed businessman's belt with my scrawny hustler comrade, I caught my reflection in the mirror and for a brief moment I felt as if I was looking into another room at another person altogether, just out of reach. Someone bolder. Beyond shame. Not a child but not quite a man either. Somewhere caught between the two. On some quaking, fragile boundary. *One who has never on his own gained by being a man while knowing that he was becoming one.*

You stood in the doorway shouting at me about health risks and self-worth, which I rebuffed with quiet ambivalence until you covered your face with both your hands. Were you crying? No. You were steeling yourself. You began to speak again, at first into your hands, then gradually lowering them. "You're a gleaner, Jord. A dilettante. You have no degree, no career, no steady source of income, no idea what you want to do with your life, you drift around with your friends — no offence, Ana — with no real purpose, and like a magpie you just ooooh pick up shiny things you read and see here and there. You spout half-digested philosophy and carry yourself around like some know-it-all because really you're so painfully insecure, so painfully afraid people will see through your act and see what? What're you hiding? Hmm? What're you afraid of? You're smart, Jord. You have so much potential. Do something with it, for god's sake, instead of fritting it away, I mean is that unfair? Am I being unfair?"

"Actually yes, fuck you very much and —"

"Oh, really —"

"— can I be honest?"

"Please."

"Honestly? There've been so many times I've thought about how much easier things would be if you weren't alive and that at least that way — yes, dead, Mom — because at least that way I'd have a bit of cash to pay for rent and go back to school without accruing any more fucking debt and your eternal fucking judgement, and I don't know where you think you and your little purple rolling bag are going to stay tonight, but as you can clearly see there's no room for you here."

YOU WERE, of course, absolutely right.

V

YOU. YOU THERE. You just over there. Two and a half metres away. You, the keen observer of my life. You, the body I dropped from like ripe fruit. You who couldn't produce enough milk for me, the doctors head-fucked you and told you it was because of stress, your anxiety, you cried at night because I was always hungry, scrawny like a skinned rabbit, red-faced and howling, both of us crying because of your breasts, until you caved and started nursing me on formula, thinking yourself a failure. You the only other person who has wiped my ass. You who changed me after I wet my bed, dreams of standing in front of toilets and waking to feel it pooling around me in my sheets, the shame, who gave us this shame? You who breathed in my face asking, *Does my breath stink?* You who held out fresh laundry asking, *Does this feel dry to you?* You who I've heard crying, cooking, shitting, talking on the phone, laughing in the next room, two rooms over, on the other side of doors, shut, locked, ajar. You who bathed me, who lathered my body in soap and hot water, no part of me unconsidered, and my reluctance to leave the bath like my reluctance to be born, to leave the amniotic embrace, always a tug-of-war to pull me out. At what age did you stop bathing me? I don't remember my first bath alone. Did I ask you to stop? Did I drive you out of the room? Or did the feeling creep up on you one night that it was no longer appropriate? When did that first glimmer of shame appear?

IN 370 CE sixteen-year-old Augustine of Hippo was standing naked in a bathhouse with his father, Patricius, in a small village called Thagaste in what is now present-day Algeria. This was not an altogether unusual situation for an adolescent Roman citizen to find himself in. But what happened next would shape the future of Christianity and Western thought for the next two thousand years. Patricius looked down and noticed the boy's involuntary erection. To make matters more mortifying, the sight of his son's "active virility" so thrilled the pagan Patricius that he began to extemporize about the joys of one day having grandchildren. He then brought the matter up again that night to Augustine's devoutly Christian mother, Monica. She was not impressed. In fact, the news of this erection alarmed and worried her. As Augustine had not yet been baptized, she feared his arousal indicated his starting down a crooked path of sin and damnation. That night, she drove home to her son that God was his one true father and that any glory from his restless manhood was to be God's alone. The whole episode left such an impression on Augustine that he wrote about it in great detail some thirty years later in his treatise *Confessions,* a work of profound autobiographical candour and narcissism, in which he meditates on the nature of the body and soul and the eternal, divine conflict between the two.

Needless to say, Augustine took the first opportunity he could to leave home and study in the big city of Carthage. He was a bright student but also something of a slacker, preferring to spend his time whoring himself about town: "I went to Carthage, where I found myself in the midst of a hissing cauldron of lust," he wrote, "[and I] polluted…the shared channel of friendship with putrid rutting." (For the record, "Putrid Rutting" is on my shortlist of potential drag names.) When Augustine wasn't getting down and dirty, he spent his time at the theatre. He loved watching plays, especially tragedies. He became preoccupied with the question of why people enjoyed watching events onstage that they would never wish to have invited upon them in real life. What did we seek from vicarious sorrow? What about our pleasure-seeking selves sought to indulge in pain? Later in life, by the time he was writing *Confessions*, Augustine came to see theatres as "filthy" spaces filled with counterfeit emotions, the role of the actor being little different to that of a prostitute or a temple eunuch, with their lead-painted faces and perfumed hair. Though is it possible that this is what had seduced this village boy in the first place?

After the death of his father, the spectre of his mother hung heavy over him. Legend has it Monica cried every night over his sullied soul. And as he prepared to leave Carthage for Rome, she began "clinging to me with all her strength in the hope that I would either come home or take her with me." In the end he did neither. He lied to his mother and told her he was simply seeing off a friend, who was about to set sail, and that she should occupy herself for the night at a shrine by the coast. In the cover of dark, he slipped onto a boat and sailed away. Not to be outsmarted, Monica sailed after him but discovered on her arrival in Rome that he had already moved on to Milan to take up a teaching post. So she trekked off to Milan and eventually found him there, living with his mistress. She promptly broke up this romance and arranged his engagement to an underage Catholic heiress. The plan for divine reform worked better than she could have imagined—while waiting for his bride-to-be to come of age, Augustine converted to Catholicism, was baptized, broke off the engagement, resigned from his teaching position, took a vow of chastity, and made plans to return to North Africa to found a monastic community. Once again, never keen to be left behind, Monica followed her son to the port of Ostia, with the intention of sailing back home to North Africa with him. But the plan was not to be. Monica was dying. On one of their final afternoons together, they sat in a garden in Ostia, lost in a conversation about the lives of the saints and how the grace the saints achieved through their divine works surely exceeded any earthly rewards. As mother and son spoke, they were overcome by a shared moment of profound ecstasy:

> And when our conversation had brought us to the point where the very highest of physical sense and the most intense illumination of physical light seemed, in comparison with the sweetness of that life to come, not worthy of comparison, nor even of mention, we lifted ourselves with a more ardent love toward the Selfsame [God], and we gradually passed through

all the levels of bodily objects, and even through the
heaven itself, where the sun and moon and stars shine
on the earth. Indeed, we soared higher yet by an inner
musing, speaking and marvelling at thy works.

This is where the autobiographical portion of *Confessions*
ends: in a climactic vision shared by mother and son. An
ecstatic moment that finally relinquished Augustine from the
all-consuming drives of selfhood into a moment of shared
transcendence with another. His mother. Santa Monica.

As a monk back in Africa, the now-celibate Augustine
devoted himself to a lifelong inquiry into the nature of
sexuality and lust. Why are we so driven by these carnal
appetites? And why would God bestow us with them in
the first place? Augustine's mind continually returned to
his adolescent bathhouse erection that had made his father
crow with delight. How was it that we had control over
every other part of our bodies except this one? These pre-
occupations lead him, in his twilight, to become fixated on
Adam and Eve, and in the course of examining this fable
he conjured an idea that would have a profound and lasting
impact on countless lives, including my own, for millennia
to come: *original sin.* Augustine reasoned that the lust that
manipulated our bodies against our will was the residue
of this first, great disobedience of God, whereafter Adam
and Eve looked down upon their naked bodies in shame.
The original shame. Like the original shame of Augustine's
bathhouse arousal, where unlike his primordial ancestors
he had no fig leaf to cover himself. Augustine believed that,
ever since this original shame in the Garden, humans would
forever be defiled to our core, even as newborn babies. That

everything from the most vanilla missionary-style procre-
ation to the most lascivious deviance would be suffused with
this evil. The evil that unexpectedly lifted our cocks and wet
our vaginas and allowed our flesh to supersede our reason.
The original shame that allowed our bodies to assert themselves as things of their own accord.

The original fear of being a body.

STANDING HERE IN the doorway I understand why in theatre
an unintentional laugh by an actor is called *corpsing*. In this
moment, something epic inside me wants to be released, epic
on the scale of a dam-burst, pain and relief, a sigh cancelling
out a sob, a smile cancelling out a scream, leaving me with a
laugh. What would it mean for me to laugh the second after
finding your body? Your corpse. *Corpse*. Why can't I understand this word? Why can't I *compute* it, as would always
irritate you to hear someone say. Since I was a child I've
known that our bodies are on loan from the earth. I know
that we're biology. Standing here I consider the possibility
of your corpse. The very distinct possibility that in the minutes to follow the blood will settle in the lower part of your
body and a purple stain will appear along your underside.
That the top part of your body will turn ashen and waxy, and
once your cells have expelled the last of their oxygen they will
begin to die, one by one, your brain cells first, within minutes, then your skin cells over the next twenty-four hours.
That lactic acid and myosin will induce rigor mortis, turning
your limbs blue and your hands into sculpture, into claws,
while your gut flora starts to eat through your intestinal wall,
causing a festering green blister to appear on your pelvis as

other bacteria begin spreading out from your stomach, down your thighs, and across your chest, putrefying your body, off-gassing methane and hydrogen sulphide and pushing your intestines out through your rectum while fluid from your lungs oozes from your mouth and nostrils, until every element that once constituted *you* returns to the earth to make countless other human and non-human forms before being pounded into the firmament by an asteroid and coalesced into dust clouds and new stars.

I understand this. I understand decay. The physical processes. If you are dead, I understand it was most likely a stroke while you slept. The blockage of a blood vessel no bigger than the tip of a sharpened pencil. What I can't understand is *you* cleaved from your body. How exactly does that happen? What is released, shorn, sublimated? I feel as if I could stand in this doorway for days as your body overflows like Archimedes' bath, until I eventually resign myself to never understanding, until all I could say for certain is that, in death, you became past-tense, and that perhaps the change you underwent is really as imperceptible and ephemeral as a grammatical shift.

Growing up I saw corpses in movies and video games, mainly as things to be possessed by demons or to yield up ghosts. I saw Dora's mother painted and presented in her coffin in a franchised funeral parlour in a suburban shopping plaza. And I realize this betrays my immense privilege — twenty-eight years of privilege and counting! — to have only seen cinematic corpses and that of my great-grandmother, not loved ones pulped by explosion or shredded by gunfire. And yet my limited exposure to death somehow never prevented me from dying onstage or writing plays in which death was the subject, in which death was debated, decon-structed, aestheticized, and politicized, in which death was something I thought I understood well enough to turn into art, to move and to persuade people through my evocation of it. But I did not know death. I've only ever treaded above the dark waters of death. Now it feels unfathomable the way an ocean is not only inscrutable but heavy, something which crushes the deeper you plunge into it.

VI

WILL ONCE TOLD ME, "We come to know our bodies through those of others." The bodies of friends and lovers. Strangers. And in time his came to feel like an extension of my own. A body I mapped every inch of for the purposes of better losing myself within it. His was a body inscribed in literature. The waifish rogue. Huck Finn. Loki. Puck. The trickster. The vagabond. In fact, it was as a character that Ana first introduced him to me.

In the fall of 2011, Ana lost her phone and figured she'd try going without one for a few months to save some money. *People know where to find me.* Which meant I spent a lot of time pilgrimaging to the diner she served at, and to the Occupy camp in St. James Park.

One evening, near the end of October, I walked through the park looking for her. By then, a media tent, a large mobile kitchen, a stand of porta-potties, and several generators had been donated to the effort. Most of the tents were wrapped in plastic tarps to guard against the rain and chill. A number of Occupiers were gathered on the park's central bandstand, setting up some kind of sound system. A few others were sitting outside their tents on folding camping chairs. I walked past a couple of men breaking up a mound of wooden skiffs with a machete, and further along two women sorting through several portable solar panels. Hung from two nearby trees was a large black banner emblazoned with the words *Anti Capitalist, Anti Colonist* in red-painted block letters. Other laminated signs were propped up throughout the camp — *Free Palestine*; *When Injustice Becomes Law, Resistance Becomes Duty*; *We Are Not Your ATM*.

I eventually spotted Ana sitting beside a guy outside a yurt. The two of them appeared to be sharing two halves of a pomegranate and a grey flannel blanket. The yurt was wrapped in a thick white insulating sheet, and its elaborately painted red door had a small cardboard sign taped to it with the words *Library, Please Come In* scrawled in blue indelible marker.

"This is Will," Ana said with her Cheshire grin as I approached. Will looked up at me, his hand on his brow to shield against the setting sun. He looked a bit like a teenage daughter in an early-nineties family sitcom: long, bleached-blond hair, an oversized sweater, ripped jeans. He handed me what was left of the pomegranate.

"Thanks," I said, before turning to Ana. "I uh — just came to ask if you were going to be home tonight. Because if not I might…you know."

She cocked her head to the side. "You wanna sit with us for a bit?" Sensing my reluctance, she turned to Will and said, "He's not so into Occupy."

"That's not true, I am. I'm just not, you know, generally

that…" I trailed off, adjusting the straps on my backpack.

Will nodded and deadpanned: "It's okay, I don't like white people with dreadlocks either."

Ana rolled her eyes while suppressing a grin. After all, even though she'd been encouraging me to get involved for weeks, she was the one always raging about white girls in elephant-print harem pants and the "activist bros" with their bongo drums. In fairness, I hadn't seen much of that on my walk through the park. But still, something in me appreciated Will's wry cynicism. I slid my bag off my shoulder and sat down beside them.

"Will and I know each other from an old life," Ana said, which I thought she meant in a reincarnated sense, but it turned out she meant from an acting gig two summers earlier—working as performers at Avonlea Village, a mock-historical theme park in Prince Edward Island, based on the fictional hometown in the Anne of Green Gables books.

"The whole village wasn't much bigger than this camp, to be honest," Ana said, nodding at the tents in front of us. I suddenly imagined a mock-Occupy camp theme park in a hundred years' time.

Avonlea Village contained an old church, a schoolhouse, several replications of houses from the 1870s, and lots of ye-olde-shops selling shitty souvenirs and ice cream. The big draw, apparently, was the actors hired to wander around as characters from the books. It was Ana's first job since dropping out of theatre school, and I already knew a bit about how it went down. How she had sent her headshot in to be considered for Anne's brunette best friend, Diana Barry, but ended up being cast as Anne herself, the island's red-headed and freckled literary mascot. How, on the first day

Ana arrived, the woman who'd hired her had said: "Oh, you looked a bit paler in your photo." How a summer of itchy wigs, dyed eyebrows, and face-lightening foundation ensued, which Ana said made her look like a Weimar Cabaret performer. *Like full-on whiteface.* But what had been missing from the story up until now was Will. The homegrown boy from the island who'd been cast as Gilbert Blythe, her rapscallion love interest.

Ana turned twenty on her first day of work, depressed to be alone in the middle of nowhere, and horny as hell. In this precarious state she fell hard for Gilbert Blythe. She said they were essentially hired to be human automatons, "like two cute teenage robots" smiling and walking through the village, or whiling away the day at the "Green Gables" house.

"But I've never understood, like, what would you actually do all day?"

"Mostly just hang up laundry and play tag," Will replied, pulling his hair back and fixing it into a ponytail with an elastic band.

"Tourists would walk through the house watching us," Ana added, "enacting this kind of perpetual prologue to some vanilla Christian sex fantasy."

"We had to be 'on' eight hours a day and only got a half-hour lunch break. I'd leave the park, run across the road to the Subway, and order a hot meatball sandwich. And all the tourists who'd just seen me as Gilbert would look at me horrified, like their entire day had been ruined."

Ana said her crush on Will intensified throughout their chaste summer of role-play, until she began to get wet every time she pulled on Anne's coarse green wool dress. Sometimes so much so she'd have to disappear periodically throughout the day to stuff toilet paper into her underwear. Once, as they were sitting together side by side on a swing, being photographed by a paparazzi wall of Japanese tourists, she managed to bring herself to orgasm just by squeezing her legs together. As she told me this, I tried to discreetly glance at Will—both to gauge his reaction and to see what all the fuss was about.

"The strange thing was," she explained, "that even though we spent, like, every second of our days together, we barely knew each other, because we were always in character."

She said that as the end of August drew near she began to panic; she knew she had to act or she'd be destined to a life of unfulfilled sexual potential. It seemed clear to her that that summer would set the pattern for the rest of her adult erotic life, and she refused to give up without a fight. So she hatched a plan. She knew Will arrived early for work and went to sit by himself by the creek in his tweed and suspenders to read, or maybe just to brood—either way, she found this little ritual quite sexy and mysterious. On the Monday of their last week, she decided to show up early and walk down to the creek to find him. She imagined sitting down beside him and engaging him in a conversation about whatever book he was reading. She even hid a pack of cigarettes in her back pocket just in case that was his thing. Except a rather big wrench was thrown into her plan when she arrived at the creek to find Will sucking off the theme park's forty-five-year-old head groundskeeper.

"Why do you always have to say his age?" Will demurred.

"And here I'd thought all along those grass stains were part of your costume."

"My—?"

"Like, didn't Gilbert milk cows or something? I don't know."

As they laughed, I glanced again at Will's face and yes, I thought, I could see it. There was something there. He was handsome, really. In a somewhat unconventional way. In fact, his look was just the right kind of strange to be the basis for proper obsession.

We spent the evening talking outside the makeshift library, Will seducing us with his elusive charm while assisting visitors signing books in or out of the yurt's meagre holdings of dog-eared paperbacks. I gathered he was the camp's volunteer librarian, at least for that evening. As it got dark he switched on a strand of multicoloured LED lanterns and two middle-aged women in fleece jackets came by doling out mugs of red lentil soup. The autumn air was crisp and wreathed with our breath. When I started to shiver Will offered me a corner of the blanket, but I declined.

"I think I'll head home and have a hot shower," I said.

Ana kissed me off, opting to stay back at the camp to chat with friends, while Will and I biked through the streets, weaving in and out of traffic without helmets (exactly as you feared I did), and as if it were the most natural thing in the world he invited himself into my apartment, and then into the shower, and then over the next few weeks bit by bit into my heart until, by mid-November, he was more or less living with Ana and me. The three of us made a little queer family, cooking extravagant meals, gossiping, fighting, auditioning, going out to shows, trying to write our own, drinking too much coffee and getting too little sleep. Some nights Will and I lay in bed talking about the little theatre we would open up together one day. Where friends could put on their plays, even the bad ones; in fact, especially the bad ones. A home for all the beautiful rejects.

After the first snowfall we went back to St. James Park to check in on a couple of Ana and Will's friends who'd stuck it out. It seemed like it was mostly just anarchists and their dogs by that point. There were about a dozen tents huddled together like a low-rent Antarctic research base. The library was gone. It felt a bit like we had shown up to a party just as the lights were turned back on and the DJ was packing up. We sat around a garbage-can fire with this one Occupier who I think Ana had always wanted to sleep with, I forget his name, passing a flask of whiskey back and forth and talking about Noam Chomsky (naturally). I found myself looking at his Soviet military jacket and thinking of Chicho Dimo's jumpsuit and truck and imagining an animated map showing the flow of decommissioned military paraphernalia flowing out of the USSR upon its collapse and circulating around the world like a giant Pacific gyre of kitsch and nostalgia.

WHENEVER WILL AND I would bike through the city we'd ride one in front of the other, pulling up side by side at street lights to share a joke or just stand together in silence. As I biked behind him I would watch his long blond hair blown about and imagine it was frantically reaching back for me. I studied the exposed skin on the small of his back as he leaned forward on his handlebars; the blue veins under his skin, the two little bumps of bone above the waistband of his underpants bobbing up and down as he peddled. On long summer evenings in 2012, we coasted through the back streets of west Toronto looking for our tiny theatre space, which we figured would have to double as our home if we were to afford it.

We began eyeing empty storefronts the way I'd seen straight boys look at sports cars or dogs stare at steaks. We started writing down phone numbers off real estate signs and lay in bed talking about them until we fell asleep. One evening, as we were riding through Kensington Market, we noticed an old barbershop for lease. We locked our bikes to a nearby fence, wandered over to the darkened window, and peered in. The space was modest, with fluorescent light fixtures in the drop ceiling and walls plastered with decades-old posters of pompadoured hair models. Along one wall were three barber chairs positioned in front of three frameless mirrors. The opposite wall was lined with a row of metal folding chairs, where I imagined customers would have once sat waiting for their haircuts while reading magazines.

Will and I looked at each other and smiled. It was perfect. We let ourselves be swept along by a torrent of grandiose ideas and far-fetched plans as we unlocked our bikes and goaded one other into doing it (*Let's just fucking do it*), until I called the number on the real estate sign. We arranged a meeting with the agent for the next morning, signed the lease, and before we knew it we were on our hands and knees scrubbing three decades' worth of hair from between the cracks in the black-and-white vinyl tiles. With the help of some of our handier friends — mainly lesbians and theatre school tech geeks — we built a small wooden stage, hung two black curtains and a makeshift grid of LED lights, and filled the space with thirty additional chairs, all mismatching and in varying states of collapse, collected from garage sales and sidewalks on garbage nights.

Ana came over one night with two bottles of wine and some Indian takeout. She knew we'd been fretting about how to make the first month's rent and was determined to take our minds off it. As the three of us sat around the kitchen table, we started throwing out names for the space. After a particularly ridiculous spate of suggestions, Ana offered up Videodrome, in honour of our nights binge-watching David Cronenberg films as teenagers. We started riffing off "video," pairing it with random words. We liked how the word conjured a kind of nineties analogue aesthetic, something a bit degraded and do-it-yourself. Also, Will and I wanted to host screenings at the space. Video art, low-budget outings by local filmmakers, cult classics. The front room was no bigger than a suburban garage but we had outsized ambitions for it, imagining it functioning fluidly as an art gallery, performance space, and a cinema, perhaps all within the course of the same day and night.

As we finished the last of the wine, Ana pushed herself away from the table and announced she needed a cigarette. She sauntered out of the kitchen and into the front room before calling out to us, "Guys, I think you should come out here."

Will and I got up from the table and found Ana in the empty barbershop staring at the storefront window. Scrawled in black spray paint on the glass were the letters "F o g," except inverted backwards, having been written from outside.

Will tilted his head to the side. "Did someone try to write 'fag'?"

"And what, chickened out?"

"Maybe halfway through and was like, 'Oh, wait, shit, I'm an asshole.'"

Ana looked over at us with concern. "Guys, I'm pretty sure it does say 'fag.'"

"No, it definitely says 'fog.'"

"Maybe he's a bad speller," Will offered.

"It's strange, it feels like we've been half-bashed."

"Or maybe Fog's his graffiti tag?" Ana said, not sounding particularly convinced.

By that point we were hammered, and trudging outdoors with a bucket of soapy water to scrub spray paint off the window felt completely beyond us. Ana lit her cigarette, Will refilled our glasses, and the three of us sat down on the floor looking up at the three ambiguous letters.

"What about Videofag?" Will said after a moment's silence.

I looked at him and smiled. It was perfect. Particularly in that moment, after three bottles of wine. The name was a provocation, yes, but also a joyful reclamation of a word that had been turned against us throughout our lives. A word wielded as a weapon; to belittle and demean and shame. But we were going to own it. We were sissy-boy fags and damn proud of it. "Fag" was a catchall, a slur levelled at all queers, and not just queers but the nonconforming, the marginal, the other, the sublime outcast, and these were the people who needed a little space. This little space.

Ana stood up, and with the aid of her hot-pink lipstick, added "o ɘ b i V" to the window—I was supremely impressed, given the state she was in, that she'd managed to flip her letters. And then, after stepping back to consider her work, she definitively turned the "o" in "F o g" into an "a." Just so there wasn't any doubt about the matter.

WILL AND I lived in the squalid back rooms behind the barbershop. The apartment was essentially a glorified hallway that ended in a tiny backyard filled with raccoons and cigarette butts. The kitchen window looked out onto a cinderblock wall, so no sunlight ever got in. We couldn't bear the glaring fluorescent lights our slumlord installed, so we lit the place with candles all day long. Ants streamed along the caulked cracks between the tiles. Cockroaches scuttled into the cutlery when we opened drawers. In the summer we walked around without shirts and without air conditioning or even a decent cross-breeze. Our friends put on plays and cabarets and happenings in the front room, and then we'd squeeze into the sweltering kitchen backstage and drink beer in the semi-dark, usually just a single candle stuck to the Masonite table with its own dripping wax. And every morning we'd wake up to find a different friend asleep on our couch or in our shower, a revolving door of underemployed actors, drag queens, performance artists, and those who hadn't yet decided how best to waste their lives.

Once you happened to be in Toronto for a conference while I was putting on a show. I called to see if you wanted to come and you said you'd rearrange some things to be there. I warned you in advance that the show was a little on the autobiographical side. "And there's a slightly gratuitous ejaculation scene." We held the door for fifteen minutes until your cab arrived. You whispered your apology as you passed me at the tech table (which doubled as a box office). Will handed you the playbill, a few pieces of computer paper stapled together. I watched you the entire play shifting back and forth in your chair and then looking down at one point into your lap for the better part of five minutes, so long that

I thought you might've been on your phone. But no, you shifted your weight and I saw that your hands were clasped on your lap; you were just staring down into them. Later on you started fanning yourself with the playbill, which for some reason irritated me so much. Granted, it could be a trial to sit in that cramped storefront on a hot night enveloped in "l'eau de hipster sweat," as Ana would say.

When the show ended you clapped, though not hard. I tried to catch your eye as I passed you on my way backstage to check in with the actors, but you were looking through your purse for something. When I came back out a couple of minutes later, you were gone. I didn't hear from you that night. Or the night after. I eventually broke down and called.

"You made me out to be some kind of of of monster!"

"Mom, it's fictional!"

"It's based on me and everyone in that theatre knew that and everyone was sitting there thinking—"

"No one—No, no one thinks you're a monster."

"Everyone in that theatre did! No one would make eye contact with me as I was leaving!"

"But it's obviously—"

"The line between fact and fiction is *very* blurry."

"Mom, nobody thinks you killed your husband."

"Yes, of course, but I'm talking about painting me as some kind of—of overbearing, smothering mother from *Psycho*, or some kind of workaholic slave driver, always on my phone, always pushing you to—"

"It's a character!"

"Using *real* words I've said. I just—I found the whole thing very upsetting."

"Well—"

"And hurtful."

"I'm sorry."

"And disappointing. Frankly."

"..."

"Mostly I was disappointed."

SOMETIMES WILL AND I would throw ragers, where the front window fogged and people stumbled home in the light of morning. It was on these nights, dancing with Will, that I understood the word *ecstatic*. To feel my body emptied of self and filled with sound and sensation. To dance past the point of exhaustion and dehydration, the music shaking me to my core, rattling my bones, causing me to convulse and even weep at a transcendent chord progression or bass drop. On those nights I understood bodies in trances, bodies possessed, bodies fainting and speaking in tongues, holy laughter, spasming, shaking, groaning, roaring. I understood what it was for the shaman to become a divine conduit, emptied of their person and filled with a spirit. The idea of becoming a vessel for a divine being, to abdicate my autonomy and selfhood through this temporary death, had always seemed terrifying to me. The purview of the gullible and superstitious.

But how was what we were doing at Videofag any different? I remember one night watching Christeene, a "drag terrorist" from Austin, Texas, with heavy, smeared makeup, a catastrophic wig, and crazed husky-blue contact lenses, flinging herself around the rickety stage, deep-throating the microphone, grunting and howling and rubbing her "shtanky puss-ay" in the faces of the adoring crowd. It was like she was channelling the pure Platonic forms of excess and debauchery. I was entranced. She was the definition of abandon. And for the briefest of moments, while watching Christeene and simultaneously watching performer Paul Soileau *as* Christeene, I was not afraid of death.

In those days, we filmed everything. Our shows, our parties, our sex; we filmed ourselves making dinner, having showers, taking shits; we filmed ourselves sleeping and sleepwalking. We were a new breed of pornographers. We posted the videos on YouTube and they started getting shared around, first by friends, and then increasingly outside of Canada by queer demimonde figures, a few curators, and art stars. James Franco. A gallery in New York did an exhibition of them. Videofag began to accrue a kind of aura. People from different cities would stop in when they were in Toronto because they'd seen our stuff online. They'd perform in the front room or just crash on our couch. They always expected the place to be more feral than it really was. They expected a 24/7 party zone. They wanted to visit the place they'd seen in the videos, but that place was mostly a performance. A fantasy. The reality was that, most of the time, Will and I were just mopping spilled beer off a barbershop floor in our underwear.

IN THE SUMMER OF 2013, Ana broke up with the baker she'd been seeing for a couple of months. *I'm not asking for the fucking world. Just a guy who'll go down on me from time to time and not run when he hears the words "intersectional feminism."* To cheer her up, Will and I decided to take her on a proper American road trip. We asked our friends Xenia and Danielle to look after Videofag while we were gone and borrowed Grandma Dora's black, hearse-like PT Cruiser.

We were willing captives to America's oversized charms. We wandered the gutted, spectral remains of Detroit. Outside of Mammoth Cave, gales blew down our tents twice, eventually snapping the flimsy poles and consigning us to guest homes and dingy motels for the rest of the trip. In Oklahoma we found ourselves staying with a family at their farmhouse. While making the arrangements it somehow evaded my notice that they were Mormons, just as it evaded their notice that there were three of us. For some reason they were under the impression it was just Ana and I travelling, presuming us to be a young married couple — an illusion I'm sure I dispelled the second I opened my mouth, despite doing my best to dampen my usual sibilance (I never did let Paulette Winters get the upper hand). The wife apologized, saying she didn't have a cot, and we assured her the king-sized bed would be fine, to which she pursed her lips. The one perk was the bedroom's carpeted bathroom and its massive jacuzzi tub. The heat was so suffocating it was impossible to sleep; we lay naked with the windows flung open, but there was no difference between inside and out. Around two in the morning, Will got up and started filling the jacuzzi with ice-cold water, and the three of us climbed in, stifling our laughter and nearly overflowing the tub.

We drove through ranches and reservations and the ghost towns of Nevada, across endless deserts, over buried tunnels of corrugated metal where men and women with families and ancestors and anxieties about the future operated tactical drone strikes against men and women in distant deserts, themselves with families and ancestors and anxieties about the future. For some reason, Ana thought it would be fine to empty her DivaCup out the window as we drove. *I didn't want to slow us down!* We ended up pulling over at a roadside casino so she could wash her hand. As I waited, I watched the slot machines seizuring and the blackjack tables lined with players like ants carrying large leaves.

Back on the road I became aware of how much shit was littered through the desert: broken-down trailers, busted lawn chairs, gutted cars. It was hardly the tabula rasa I had imagined. Long after humans are extinct, our time on earth will be recorded as a thin layer of plastic in the multilayered sedimentary rock pie. As I drove I thought how it would do humans good to spend some time as inanimate objects. Even just a few days as a broken umbrella or a set of car keys or a smooth boulder in a creek. It would help them cultivate patience. And would they ever deny another human agency again? I drove past abandoned mining towns. The empty shells of factories. This was nature at work, discarding that which had outlived its function. Soon the sky was the colour of eggplant. Twilight. The desert got surprisingly cold at that hour, eventually so black it felt like the absence of light itself.

"Sometimes I have this vision of my life where I'm fat and naked and walking an alligator around on a leash in some strip club in the Nevada desert," Ana murmured from the back seat as we passed a particularly bleak-looking building a half-mile off the road advertising *Live Nude Shows 24/7.*

An hour outside of Vegas, I pulled into a motel with a thirty-foot neon crucifix on the front lawn. It was just after midnight; Ana and Will were asleep. I was too tired to face Vegas on my own; I could see it glowing on the horizon like a stubborn sunset. After checking in, I returned to the car to find them both awake and chatting, riding a second wind.

"What the hell're we doing here?" Ana asked.

"Sleeping," I said.

"How far's Vegas?"

"Right there." I pointed towards the distant glow of air-conditioned interiors.

"Can't we just drive a bit further?"

"I've already paid now."

I re-parked the car in front of door fourteen, which Will pointed out was actually door thirteen because the door to our left was twelve. Inside was exactly what you'd expect: a king-sized bed with a stained turquoise-and-pink duvet, grey wallpaper, popcorn ceiling, wall-to-wall carpet, everything reeking of cigarettes. We flopped down on the bed and started passing around the last of our whiskey. We imagined all the bad blow jobs that had been given on or against or adjacent to that bed over the years. And then we began tallying our own. Names, locations, approximate dates. A passing car filled our room with shifting light, sliced through with venetian blinds. I lay between Will and Ana and felt them slowly grow heavy and quiet with sleep. The air was close, and the room felt saturated with the countless bodies that had passed through it. I lay there with my eyes closed but couldn't quiet my mind. Something was keeping me up. Keeping me agitated. What? Was I too hot? No. The temperature was not the issue. Was I worried about something? No more than usual. The bed? I'd slept on shittier. What, then? I lay there and listened. And then I heard it.

A high-pitched tone. A whine. A bit like a mosquito but constant. Unwavering. Was it inside my head? I gingerly extricated my arms from under Will and Ana's heads and placed my hands over my ears. Silence. I lifted my hands and heard the tone again. It was coming from somewhere in the room. I slid myself slowly out from between Will and Ana until I was standing at the foot of the bed. I noticed the flickering green light of the wifi modem on the dresser, walked over, and unplugged it. The tone continued. I crouched down and unplugged the television and the mini-fridge. Still there. I noticed Ana's phone charging on the bedside table, walked over, and unplugged it as well. No difference. I stood very still in the middle of the room, listening. Like a fox in a field at night. Or a man possessed.

I walked into the washroom, ripped off a sheet of toilet paper, tore it into two pieces, balled them up, and plugged my ears before crawling back into bed. An hour passed. Then another. I pulled a hoodie over my head and yanked the drawstrings as tight as they would go, until only my nose was sticking through its little puckered asshole. But the tone continued, even with my head buried under the pillow. I was becoming furious. Which was silly, really. The tone was insistent but not at all loud. In fact, it was even possible that if I woke the others they wouldn't be able to hear it. Why was I blowing this out of proportion? For starters, there was no way in hell I was driving into Vegas in the morning on no sleep. And I thought that quite possibly I was beginning to go insane. I slid back out of bed and stood once more, stock-still, in the middle of the room. In another half-hour the sky would already be lightening.

And then it occurred to me. I walked to the front door and opened it. The sound intensified. I looked across the parking lot and saw the neon cross glowing on the front lawn. It must have been a full three or four storeys tall. It was so bright, the rest of the night took on a darker pitch of black around it. I began walking towards it, the damp grass wetting my feet, and as I neared it the tone grew more and more insistent until it filled my head and I was standing directly below the cross staring up at it, its harsh light searing my eyes. I imagined taking up a large stick, a branch, and smashing it against the bulb, shattering it with a deafening *POP*, and the glass raining down on me like a fine rain or dust. My eyes began burning and closed of their own accord. I looked down, everything white, even against my closed lids. I waited a long while before opening them, my head bowed as if praying. And when I finally did, I noticed something at the base of the cross. A little metal power box with a red switch. I bent down and flicked the switch to "Off." And just like that, the light and noise disappeared. As easy as if I were turning off a bedside lamp. In the blessed silence the rest of the night gradually returned, its infinite gradients of darkness emerging from the blazing afterimage of the now-absent cross.

THE NEXT MORNING the three of us swam in the motel pool, which was in the middle of the parking lot and hemmed in by a low wrought-iron fence painted turquoise — at least originally. Like everything in sight, it had been sun-bleached several shades lighter, like overexposed film. As we swam, the morning grey turned black and the rumble of thunder tore us from the pool, which left a greasy film on our skin. The downpour caught us a few yards from our door, even more ferocious than the Mammoth Cave storm had been, and I have to admit that for a split second the prospect of divine judgement did flicker through my head. As we towelled off we agreed the weather was too dangerous to drive to Vegas in. We also agreed we were starving.

I mentioned having seen a diner about a half-mile down the road the night before, so we scampered for the car and, smelling like wet dogs, drove ten minutes to a truck stop with no apparent name. The glass door chimed as we entered. The place was surprisingly busy given how desolate the area was, but then I figured truckers were opting to stay off the roads until the storm passed. All the orange-vinyl booths were full, so we sat down at the faux-wood-panelled bar. Will sat between Ana and I, and to my right was a guy I assumed was a trucker. He had a bit of a butch-daddy look going for him, and his moustache leant him a seventies-gay-porn-star vibe — though his navy cardigan and polo shirt sort of destabilized that image a little. He gave me a nod as I settled in beside him.

"On a road trip?" he asked me. Ana and Will were ensconced in their own conversation.

"How can you tell?" I replied.

"You look...scruffy."

"Yeah, we are. How about yourself?"

"Oz and I work out of Berkeley. We had a few days off so we decided to drive up here." Oz leaned over and gave a little wave. He seemed to be in his mid-twenties, sporting a patchy beard, wire-rim glasses, and a Wu-Tang Clan T-shirt.

"I'm Robert."

"Jordan, nice to meet you."

I asked Robert what he did in Berkeley. He said he taught at the university and Oz was one of his Ph.D. candidates. Mostly to be polite, I asked what their area of study was. Oz looked up from his menu and said, with an unexpected

British accent, that Robert had "made his name in the nineteen-seventies" for devising something called the "sentience quotient." Oz had barely said two full sentences, but I already disliked him. I could tell his insecurity made him pushy, as if he was worried he'd be forgotten in the company of his soft-spoken and sexy supervisor.

Oz told me that as a young man Robert found it strange that science had no way to quantify what seemed self-evident: all living things were sentient. But how sentient? In what varying degree? Robert eventually arrived at his quotient, which suggested defining sentience as the relationship between the information-process rate of reach individual processing unit (the neuron), the weight and size of that single unit, and the total number of those processing units. Running on a logarithmic scale from −70 up to +50, the quotient was proposed as a measure of sentience for all organic and inorganic entities, from plants to computers, from a single neuron up to a hypothetical being with the computational limit of the entire universe.

Robert took out a pen and quietly wrote the equation on a napkin for me.

$$SQ = \log_{10}\left(\frac{I}{M}\right)$$

As Robert passed me the napkin, Oz took it and began explaining what it meant—not for my sake, but for Robert's. "SQ is the sentience quotient, I is the information-processing rate in bits per second, and M is the mass of the brain in kilos." He explained that in this equation the lowest sentience quotient possible—essentially the dumbest creature imaginable—would have just one neuron with the mass of the whole universe and would require a time equal to the age of the universe to process just one bit, giving a minimum SQ of -70. Humans clocked in at a rating of +13. Plants clustered around an SQ of -2, while carnivorous plants had an SQ of +1.

I tried to catch Will or Ana's eye, but they were avoiding it; they hadn't had their coffees yet, and I could tell there was no way in hell they were going to let themselves get sucked into this. A waitress arrived and took Robert's and Oz's orders—they both asked for the pancake stack. Were two more American words ever uttered? *Pancake stack.*

Robert broke open a creamer and mixed it into his coffee. He dipped his spoon into the white mug, clinked it around a few times, and licked it before putting it down on his napkin and informing me that an alien civilization whose consciousness operated through non-biological hardware, such as quantum-mechanical circuits, could have a sentience quotient of +23, or ten orders the magnitude of humans.

"That kind of gap would really affect our ability and, really, the desirability of communicating with aliens," he said, with an air of genuine consternation. "It may be that there is a minimum SQ communication gap, an intellectual distance beyond which no two entities can meaningfully converse."

He said that an alien civilization could, for instance, form a black hole and communicate using neutrinos or gamma-ray bursts at bandwidths completely exceeding our receiving capabilities.

"Just think of how hard it is for us to communicate with a worm or a fish," Oz offered. "Or a houseplant." I imagined him sitting in his desolate student apartment in Berkeley talking to some aloe vera. "The farthest we can reach in our communication with vegetation is when we, say, plant, water, or fertilize it. But it's evident that messages transmitted across an SQ gap of ten points or more cannot be very meaningful.

"So what, then, could an SQ +50 Superbeing possibly have to say to us?" Robert asked, taking a sip of coffee.

As I listened, nodding, I considered how proximate the states of genius and insanity were. The conversation trailed off soon after Robert and Oz began eating, and I let myself get sucked back into Ana and Will's orbit of banter. The three of us also ordered pancake stacks because what the hell, and waddled back to the car an hour later bloated and mired in regret. Ana took a photo of her "food baby," posted it on Facebook with the caption *Yours?* and tagged every man she'd slept with in the past six months. As I drove into Vegas, I found myself stewing over my encounter in the diner. So much so that that night, while Ana was having a bath and Will was fucking me in our new motel, I imagined Robert on top of me, the bristles of his moustache on my neck, and realized there and then that I would never make love to a true genius and I would most certainly never be one myself.

"ANA, YOU KNOW you're going to hate it."

"I want to go," she rebutted from the passenger seat.

"Seriously?"

"Why do you find that—?"

"Because you're always going on about, you know— fuckin' Orientalism and privilege, and now you're telling me you wanna hang around with tens of thousands of white hippies wearing bindis and doing peyote in the middle of the—"

"It's not just white hip—"

"It's going to be all the annoying stuff about Occupy without any of the good politics."

"What are you *talking* about? Burning Man has—It's an experiment in community and art, radical inclusion, self-reliance and self-expression, community cooperation, civic responsibility, decommodification—" she intoned, reading from the Wikipedia entry on her phone.

"No no no…" I mumbled overtop.

"Plus it can be deeply spiritual for some people."

"I'm sure."

"I hate—You can be so goddamn cynical sometimes."

"It's a big, week-long drug bash for—"

"Friends of mine have, Jordan, friends have mine have had profound experi—"

"—a bunch of tech-com employees from Silicon Valley, I mean *maybe* it started out as some radical pagan rite but—"

"It sounds like Mecca for agnostics," Will chimed in from the back seat.

"And what's wrong with that?"

"If you don't believe in the real Mecca, why the hell do you want to replace it with a fake one?" I snapped.

A chill spread through the car. We'd been driving eight hours by that point. I had been in a crank since we left our campsite that morning; at a rest stop, Ana had checked her phone to discover that a friend of hers was selling off three tickets to Burning Man. I'd never known anyone who'd actually been, but I'd heard about it for years—how, over a week, tens of thousands of people built a utopian city in the blisteringly hot desert, filled it with surreal art installations, and on the final day burned a towering wooden effigy of a man. In fairness, the photos Ana had shown us from previous years looked pretty spectacular. But getting there would mean turning around and backtracking for at least a day's drive westward. Plus getting tons of fresh supplies. Plus having to spend a week in the desert with thousands of unwashed pseudo-pilgrims seeking a "profound experience."

"What are you afraid of?" she asked, fixing me in her stare.

"It's not about being afraid of any—"

"Yes, you are. Anything spiritual. Earnest. Idealist. You balk at it."

I clenched my jaw and drove towards the shimmering horizon. I pulled the sun visor down and squinted against the glare. We passed the charred remains of a trailer home and a shuttered gas station. And then nothing for miles. I could feel Ana's words working on me. What was I afraid of? Losing myself? Becoming part of an ecstatic mass? I could never *give over*. Was I standing on life's sidelines with my arms crossed? Was that my defence, to be over everything? Above it all? Was this all, in some way, about you? My distrust of all things spiritual, my need to push away from it, from you. What if I was too afraid to transcend? To find my limit and exceed it? What if I never let myself find the thing I didn't even know I needed?

We drove in a seething, air-conditioned silence for another couple of minutes until, at the turnoff for State Route 56, I swung the wheel around. We were headed back west.

Ana leaned over and kissed my cheek.

I drove late into the night, twelve hours to Reno, where

we slept in the parking lot of a Walmart. We woke just in time for the store to open and joined the frenzied scrum of "Burners" snatching up all the camping equipment, charcoal, bottles of water, canned food, and condoms they could carry in their carts.

"You don't need the bug spray," the disinterested lady at checkout informed me. "Nothing lives in Black Rock Desert."

On the drive out of the city we crept along at fifteen miles an hour, one car in an impossibly long snake of red tail-lights slithering into the horizon, passing gas stations with cardboard signs taped to the pumps saying, *Sorry, Out of Gas.*

I began to panic. "I really don't think we're prepared."

"If those burnouts in the golf cart are prepared we're prepared," Ana countered.

I shook my head. "I think there's a 20-percent chance we might actually die."

We arrived in the dead of night and spent three hours trying to drive our tent pegs into the rock-hard earth. Despite the desert's name, I'd been picturing something sandy, but the ground had the consistency of dried clay. I tried using a mallet against the pegs, but that only bent them. Eventually, we managed to jerry-rig a shelter by tying our tent up with ropes attached to our car and the van of our very patient Dutch neighbours, with whom we shared our campfire meals over the following week. Ana mostly hung around the tent chatting with whatever shirtless dirtbag happened to be passing by, while Will and I spent our days Instagramming photos of ourselves in front of various curi-osities — forty-foot hands emerging from the sand, a three-storey fire-blowing spider, a pyramidal temple of wood built entirely without screws. I'd never been photogenic, which, in the era of the selfie, was a liability. It was as if photographs revealed some fundamental unease within myself that, in real life, I had managed to disguise through motion. Will, on the other hand, looked effortlessly otherworldly in each one.

At the end of the week, we gathered on the playa, shoulder to shoulder with the sixty-eight thousand other unwashed and dust-coated bodies to watch a one-hundred-and-five-foot wicker man set alight. I was startled to feel the heat of it on my face. As if I was surprised, somehow, that it was a real fire. As I watched it burn I thought of all the sacrificial bodies imbued with the collective fate or sins of a people. The rock walls at Mecca, pelted by pilgrims during the Stoning of the Devil. The human sacrifices of the Aztecs, who became sacred vessels carrying the fortunes of the community. I thought about the hours I'd spent in church studying the sallow ribcage of Jesus on the cross, his crucified body lingering in the space between living subject and object of worship, between man and symbol.

But as I stood there in the desert watching the Burning Man, I wondered what meaning its flaming body carried for me. What was being sacrificed, and for what sins or what hopes? What messages did its smoke carry up into the firmament? I looked to my left and Ana's eyes were brimming. To my right was a young couple clasped together and frozen Pompeii-like, the distant fire flickering on their faces. The man's face was fixed in a state of wonder and the woman's in a kind of beatific grace. I gazed out beyond them, at the sea of faces awash in some kind of collective catharsis, and tried to decipher the moment through their expressions. What exactly were they experiencing? And why was it eluding me? I studied the crowd, my eyes wandering from face to face, my perplexity and sadness growing until I realized the burn was already halfway through. I turned back towards the inferno, to the timbers and central support beams calving and collapsing into themselves, and imagined, for a moment, that the structure was filled with bodies, like the wicker man Julius Caesar had once reported the Druids built and filled with living people. Real bodies trapped inside a symbolic one. A burning, collapsing tower of sacrifice. I felt Will slide his arm around my waist and pull me into him. Trying to make us like every other reverent couple, subsumed into the sublime. But as I gazed at the fire, I realized it symbolized nothing for me. Though I suppose it's always impressive to watch anything of that size burn. Anything burning on that magnitude accrues significance, even if there is none.

AS YOUR BODY comes into focus, you are suddenly every effigy I have ever seen. Every icon, statue, scarecrow, mummy, rock cairn, fetish, mannequin, every vessel of sacrifice, every voodoo doll riven through with pins. The papier-mâché George Bush I watched set alight at the protest. The flaming Guy Fawkes figurines set alight on the fifth of November. The burning Judas hanging from trees across Mexico at Easter. Less than people but more than objects. Abject things caught somewhere in between.

I am standing in the doorway and can see, three steps away in bed, an object symbolizing a body, a body symbolizing a person, a person symbolizing my mother.

But here, at last, there is meaning.

Here in this moment your body seems to contain every meaning. Contain the world. Contain me.

VII

I AM LOOKING at your body but you are not there. Here again I say *looking*, the ever-favoured sense, when really this is something more visceral and intuitive than the apprehending of an image. I am with your body but not with you, and I suddenly know this in the way flesh recognizes itself in another's flesh, its life and its death in another's life or death. The way my heart pounded as I stumbled upon the corpse of a cat at the edge of a grocery store parking lot in high school, a full two seconds before my mind even understood what it was I was looking at. The body always leads and the mind follows on its leash. The steel chamber is open. The cat is dead. Accept it. Understand it. But what does it mean for me to feel the absence of "you"? And when are "you" really an absence? Eubulides of Miletus once proposed a paradox in which there was a large heap of sand, and from this heap one grain was individually removed. The heap began with a million grains of sand, and then become a heap of 999,999 grains of sand, and then a heap of 999,998 grains of sand, and so on until the heap was comprised of only one grain of sand. But if a single grain of sand can be a heap, then through *modus ponens* removing that final grain of sand must still leave a heap, and thus a heap can be comprised of even a negative number of grains. A heap can exist in the absence of a heap. So when are you an absence? When are you no longer a heap of sand? If each grain of sand were a functioning neuron. A cell in your body. Can you, like the heap of sand, exist in the absence of yourself?

FROM WHERE I stand, I notice the book at the top of the small pile of historical novels on your bedroom floor. It's called *The Girl King*. The cover photograph, of a young woman in a sumptuous dress, appears to be from a television miniseries adaptation.

"Are you enjoying it?" I asked, when I saw you reading it at breakfast yesterday.

"It's not bad," you replied, without looking up from the page. "It's about Queen Christina of Sweden."

You said you liked books that excavated the lost stories of powerful women in history, which struck me as a nobler way of saying you enjoyed reading about monarchs. You had more or less exhausted the British royal family, Marie Antoinette, Catherine the Great, the Medicis, the Borgias, the wives of the Ottoman sultans, and the Roman empresses, so figured you might as well give Scandinavia a go. You were held rapt by the lengths these women had to go to be heard in the courts of men. *And they were the one percent. I mean, I can't imagine how it must have been for other women.* But you did, you spent a lot of time imagining how life must have been for all kinds of women throughout time, in ancient Egypt, Edwardian England, imperial Japan, tsarist Russia, the rapes, the dowries, the trysts, the childbirths, the backstabbing, the ambitions thwarted and achieved, as you lay in bed with your reading lamp on well past midnight.

"Wasn't Descartes her tutor?" I asked, pouring a bit more cereal into the leftover milk in my bowl.

"Yes. And he sounds like a real prick."

DESCARTES WAS ABLE to convince himself that he could be immaterial. That his mind could exist without his body. The heap of sand without a single grain. He believed the mind and body were separate entities; that while the body was composed of physical matter, the mind was a non-physical substance. It was a proposal that fit cleanly with the vision of the body as a vessel for an immortal soul. Some of his pals, like the French priest and philosopher Nicolas Malebranche, went so far as to suggest that the mind and body didn't interact to produce sensation at all, but that it was in fact God who generated every feeling, from hitting one's finger with a hammer to the explosive orgasm of a winning blow job. Malebranche's God was an unseen smith of the senses, tailor-making bespoke reactions to every imaginable permutation of human experience.

Descartes also reasoned animals only had bodies, not the immaterial substance of consciousness. Only humans were fortunate enough to be gifted with minds. And for Descartes, the mind was ultimate—"I think therefore I am." And it was through some rather impressive gymnastics of logic that Descartes managed to doubt whether he had a body at all, whether his was not simply an apparition in a dream or a tricky illusion conjured by an evil demon (we've all had those days). But try as he could, he was unable to deny the existence of his mind. Therefore, he reasoned, the mind (and soul) could exist without the body but not the other way around.

For centuries it was believed Descartes died of a pneumonia while tutoring Queen Christina in his philosophies of love. The twenty-three-year-old queen personally invited Descartes to Stockholm in 1649, impressed by his treatise *Passions of the Soul*. But once he had arrived, it turned out the two couldn't stand each other. She became exasperated by his pedantic manner and he by her romantic fascination with ancient Greece. The classic odd-couple set-up for a rom-com.

Descartes shirked his duties, visiting Christina's draughty castle only a handful of times that winter, choosing instead to spend time with his friend Pierre Chanut, a French ambassador living in Sweden, at whose house he was staying a few blocks away. Together the pair made readings with one of the first-ever barometers to determine whether atmospheric pressure could, in fact, be used to forecast the weather. But unbeknownst to Descartes, other storms he couldn't predict were amassing. At the time, in 1650, it was expected in upper circles that Queen Christina, ruler of Protestant Sweden, would soon be converting to Catholicism. To ensure that plan wasn't derailed, a French missionary based in Stockholm named Jacques Viogué is believed to have offered Descartes an arsenic-laced communion wafer. Ironically (or perhaps symbolically), the major sticking point for Stockholm's colluding cadre of Catholics was the supposed incompatibility of Descartes's theories with the belief of transubstantiation. Descartes's doctor attributed the philosopher's death to his inability to adjust to the Nordic chill, somehow discounting the blood in his urine — a symptom associated with poisoning, not pneumonia — and the fact that Descartes, well versed in medicine and likely realizing he had been poisoned, asked for an emetic to induce vomiting. I wonder if, in these final hours, Descartes still believed in the controvertible existence of his body.

I never did buy the Cartesian vision of mind-body separation. It always struck me as a kind of ur-text for a contemporary society of floating heads glued to screens, in which the body was an inconvenient afterthought. And yet it is ingrained in our language. For me to even say "your body" or "my body" suggests an essence which is "you," an essence which is "me" — essences which are separate from our bodies and can claim ownership over them. This "you" and "me" seem to have eternal ownership over this flesh and these bones even in death. "Here lies the body of Jordan Tannahill," someone might say when standing over my grave many years from now (hopefully). Like the way you would always say, "There's the old McGregor farm," pointing out the car window at a ruin in a field near the cottage. But is there some immortal essence that is us rambling around inside our bodies like the McGregors once did on their farm? An essence that will live on in new earthly forms or in some spectral realm, just as the descendants of the McGregors now live in distant cities and have no memory of this ruin? And is it this belief in an immortal, immaterial soul that gives our person, the thing that is *I*, perpetual ownership over our bodies? Is it for this reason that the person standing over my grave might say, "Jordan Tannahill is buried here" rather than "The body that was Jordan Tannahill is buried here"? We have constructed our language in this way because we do not want to imagine death as an end. Because we do not want to imagine a body belonging to no one.

But try as I might to think beyond the strictures of language, as I stand here in the doorway I cannot escape the thought that *I am looking at your body and you are not there.*

VIII

IN THE FALL OF 2013, performance artist Gia Bachmann moved the entire contents of her apartment into the front room of Videofag and lived there for a week as a durational performance installation. Born male, Gia began transitioning in the late nineties, and over the course of the next decade transformed her body through over sixty surgeries and hundreds of illegal silicone injections financed primarily through sex work. She was not interested in being a "passable" woman. She wanted to look fake. She wanted to "become plastic," a living Barbie doll, a simulacrum of the idealized and fetishized female body. But she was a feminist who could recite Judith Butler and bell hooks off by heart. A feminist who routinely pissed off other feminists who considered her body a reinforcement of patriarchal attitudes and body fascism.

"They look at me and immediately dismiss me as superficial," she once said to me. "Or emblematic of the oppression of women. But honey, I can deconstruct those bitches twelve ways to Sunday."

During her performance installation passersby could stop and watch Gia, through Videofag's large storefront window, riding her exercise bike or applying makeup in front of her vanity or lighting candles and meditating. At night she projected a variety of videos on the walls — a live feed of herself moving about the space, footage of her past surgeries, footage of herself as a webcam girl, and news reports of the arrest and trial of Luka Magnotta, a man whose murder, dismemberment, and partial cannibalism of exchange student Lin Jun had recently shocked the world. Magnotta also happened to be an ex-lover of Gia's, as had been frequently reported in the media at the time, and this durational performance in our front room was a kind of public exorcism of him from her psyche.

Magnotta, born Eric Clinton Kirk Newman in the Toronto suburb of Scarborough, had been a sex worker and model who went by various other aliases, including Jimmy, Justin, Angel, Rocco, Vladimir Romanov, Mattia Del Santo, and Kirk Trammel. On May 24, 2012, after answering a Craigslist ad for a submissive bottom into bondage, Lin arrived at Magnotta's apartment in Montreal's Snowdon neighbourhood. The following night, an eleven-minute video titled "1 Lunatic 1 Ice Pick" was uploaded to bestgore.com in which Lin, tied to a bed, was stabbed repeatedly with an ice pick and kitchen knife by Magnotta. There was a poster from the film *Casablanca* on the wall, and "True Faith," a song by New Order, could be heard playing in the background. Magnotta proceeded to dismember Lin limb by limb and penetrate his corpse. A more extensive version of the video obtained by Canadian police was purported to show Magnotta engaging in acts of cannibalism.

On May 26, the day after the video first appeared, an attorney from Montana attempted to report it to the Toronto police, his local sheriff, and the FBI, but in each instance the lead was never pursued. Three mornings later, on May 29, a bloodstained parcel containing the remains of a man's left foot was delivered to the headquarters of the Conservative Party of Canada. Another parcel containing a left hand was discovered by Canada Post workers en route to the Liberal Party's head offices. Later that same day, the custodian of Magnotta's apartment building discovered a human torso in a suitcase, lying amidst a pile of uncollected garbage in an alleyway. At 11:33 p.m. that night, police burst through the door of Unit 208 to find it virtually empty, save for a few smears of blood on a mattress, the refrigerator, and the bathtub. On the inside of a closet door was written, in red ink, *If you don't like the reflection. Don't look in the mirror. I don't care.* The rest of Lin's body appeared over the coming weeks—on June 5, a right foot appeared in a package sent to St. George's School and a right hand appeared in a package sent to False Creek Elementary School, both in Vancouver; and on July 1, during Canada Day celebrations, Lin's head was discovered near a lake in Montreal's Angrignon Park.

Gia had briefly dated Magnotta ten years earlier. They met at a strip bar he was working at, and he became her first lover since she had begun living as a woman. She said he used to punch his head in the shower sometimes and joke about killing his family, but of course she had assumed it was empty rhetoric. She recalled how once he looked her in the eyes and said, "I'm afraid that when you look into me you'll see there's nothing left inside." She believed he was a profound narcissist and that this had disfigured his sense of reality. Narcissism was something Gia had spent a lot of time thinking about. Her art practice was her own body; she had transformed herself into a kind of living sculpture, and her work concentrated on the muse of herself as a virtual image and cyborg. And though there were other common-alities between Gia and Luka, like their plastic surgeries and sex work, it was narcissism that proved the most fascinating and complex intersection for her. But whereas Gia's narcis-sism produced searching works of art that deconstructed consciousness and selfhood, Magnotta's had made him a psycho killer.

"If you watch the video you can literally see him trying to become an image," she said, her face flickering in candlelight. Will and I were sitting with her in the dark of our kitchen, having just finished installing her apartment in the front room. "I don't buy for a second that he's getting any kind of sexual pleasure from what he's doing. He's doing it to enact and embody the image of the serial killer."

"But to what end?" I asked.

"An augmentation of self. Fame," she said, running her finger through the wax pooling on the table. "I mean, why else mail off body parts to the establishment? The prime minister? He wanted attention. From male figures of power especially. It was as if, in some sense, he saw those limbs as pieces of himself. He was spreading and amplifying himself across the country. And the world."

She said that ancient peoples couldn't conceive of them-selves as moving images. People had to take mind-altering drugs in front of cave paintings to see a moving image, and even then it would have been considered the workings of spirits.

"I remember being a teenager in the eighties when 'virtual reality' was considered a kind of oxymoron and now you guys"— nodding to Will and me —"millennials don't even really know what life is without a virtual self."

She said she had spent her entire career attempting to understand herself as an image and her impossible desire to have no thoughts or feelings, to be just an object, and rather than feeling shame about that desire and repressing it, she has attempted to explore it as a means of locating her authentic self. At the time the Magnotta story first broke, she had been bombarded with interview requests from every sleazy blog and trash tabloid in the world and turned all of them down. Gia had two master's degrees and was, quite possibly, the most articulate person I'd ever met, and if she couldn't speak in thoughtful long-form about the construction of self as image then she wasn't fucking interested.

"And yes, of course he was a sociopath. But then, we're surrounded by sociopaths. People who don't see the person inside another's body. Most of the time they're just disguised in suits or on lawn signs."

And then I posed the question I couldn't stop myself from asking: "Was he well endowed?"

"Jordan."

I held her gaze. She puckered her lips and shifted them to the side of her face. "Yes."

On some nights, during her week-long durational performance, Gia would work herself into a trance. She would wear a rubber pig mask while riding her exercise bike and flagellating herself. In one video she projected (which I had filmed, incidentally, a year or so earlier), she was naked in her real apartment and rubbing shit all over her body. Each night small crowds of friends and art-world types crammed themselves into Videofag to watch her enigmatic rituals. About halfway through the week, she began drawing images and writing cryptic messages across the walls with indel- ible black maker, which, for years after, and despite more than a half-dozen coats of white gallery paint, remained faintly visible.

A FEW MONTHS LATER, Gia asked me to travel with her to Guadalajara, Mexico, to document her castration. Gia's sugar daddy, a wealthy construction baron with a family in the burbs, had agreed to pay for the procedure, and she wanted to document it as part of her art practice. After so many surgeries it was the one she had been holding out on, but she said she finally felt ready. And while she was at it, she had also decided to get a facelift. It was cheaper to do both procedures at once, and apparently she was "over-due." Surgical bodies required constant maintenance, she explained to me, because they didn't age like normal bod-ies. Things began to sag in strange and unnatural ways. The facelift was just part of the routine maintenance that would be required every few years until she died. But of course the byproduct of more and more procedures was that the face, the body, began to look, in Gia's words, increasingly "surged out." Increasingly uncanny. She joked that this facelift would likely give her the tell-tale "Joker's mouth," when a face was stretched one procedure too far and the edges of the mouth were left peaking upwards in a slight perma-grin like the Joker's in *Batman*. Gia was embracing this new "freak" phase of her bodily evolution. She would not hide it. She would, in her usual fashion, enhance it.

All of Gia's surgeries had been done by Doctor Sam, a plastic-surgery wizard in Guadalajara who was legendary among transsexuals. Nothing was too outrageous or challenging for Doctor Sam. Which was good, because not only did Gia want to document the procedures as part of her art practice—she wanted to remain awake for them. She wanted to feel Doctor Sam's fingers under her skin, the scalpel making its incisions, the new lightness between her legs. For her, surgeries were ecstatic experiences. Rituals of renewal and transformation. And Doctor Sam was an artist, a Michelangelo revealing the sublime form hidden within the marble slab.

The men's rugby team surrounding us on the plane ride down kept leering at Gia and making snide comments. But she seemed impervious to their sneers, and to the stares at the Guadalajara airport. Men came at her with waves of hatred and she dashed them against the rocks of her indifference. As we waited for our luggage at the carousel I asked her how she was doing.

"Honey I am *living*," she replied, surveying the Arrivals hall from behind her dark sunglasses.

We landed in Mexico just as sixty million monarch butterflies were finishing their two-and-a-half-thousand-mile migration, arriving like the souls of the dead returning to earth. As we climbed into the airport taxi, a cloud of them passed overhead, guided by some evolutionary imprint to the hidden valley of their ancestors, coating the trees so densely as to snap branches under their weight.

As we approached the hotel, we discovered there had been a mass shooting in the dance club across the street.

Everything was cordoned off with yellow caution tape and police cruisers. Gia stayed in the room and sent me out foraging for food. I brought back some drippy street tacos, which we ate on our queen-sized beds while discussing plans for the next day.

"I want to have anaesthetic, of course, but I want to stay awake," she said. "I want to watch everything."

"Will they let you?"

"Can you imagine how major that would be? Like: *I heard Gia stayed awake for her own castration*," she said with a chuckle, imitating some shady queen. "If anyone would let me do it, it would be Sam. I think he gets off on the freakiness." She described him as stoic and masculine, and ever-professional, but admitted that she noticed a certain glimmer in his eye when he dealt with her. "I think he secretly loves all his ladies," she mused. "I bet there's a part of him that gets off on having his fingers in us."

The windows of the room were taped shut, so before going to bed we decided to get some fresh air on the hotel rooftop. The roof was unlit and desolate, except for a plastic hot tub bubbling with lukewarm water. It looked like a little spaceship glowing in the dark, with LED lights cycling through various colours. We decided to take a quick dip in our underwear, bacteria be damned. We sat there in the water, shivering a little in the wind, listening to the hum of the city. Police radios were still squawking in the street below us. Somewhere, someone was blasting merengue-laced rap. And there was some kind of tire fire burning in a nearby industrial park, throwing up black clouds into the night. The air smelled of rubber, and little flecks of ash rained down on us as if from a distant volcanic eruption.

The next morning we moved into a room at the plastic-surgery clinic, which was in an affluent suburb of the city. The room was white, spare, and immaculate, with a hospital bed at its centre and a firm couch by the window, where I would sleep. In the bathroom there were three mirrors on either side of the sink, which created an infinity of possible selves. Across the alley from our room was a kennel where the dogs never stopped howling. We kept the window shut even though, by midday, it was blisteringly hot.

Just as we finished unpacking, there was a knock on our door. Doctor Sam entered, greeted Gia, and introduced himself to me. He was a hulking man with a quiet and soft air. He walked over to Gia, who was sitting on the side of the bed. After a bit of small talk, he traced her hairline and temples with his fingers, explaining how the facelift would be carried out. There was a lull in the conversation, and I could see Gia steeling herself to ask the question.

"Sam?" she began. "I was wondering whether I could remain awake for the procedures and if Jordan could film them."

He chuckled and shook his head. "No, no. Sorry."

She tried to work her charm, but he kept shaking his head; the operating theatre was small and I would get in the way. She suddenly reached out and grabbed his arm.

"Sam" she said, looking into his eyes. "An artist needs documentation."

He made to rebut but then stopped. Perhaps he was trying to discern which artist she was referring to; he seemed bemused by the implication it was him. Gia's sincerity was disarming. She let go of his arm but held his gaze as the nurses arrived in the room. The nurses helped Gia into her blue surgical smock, placed a white, gauzy cap on her head, and helped her into a wheelchair. I'm not sure why she needed to be ferried to the operating theatre in a wheelchair, but I could see she enjoyed the theatrics of it. I followed a couple of steps behind with my camera, still uncertain whether my presence was permitted, but no one stopped me.

Gia lay back on the operating table like it was a plinth. I pressed my back against the wall, as out of the way as I could be, and hid my face behind the camera's viewfinder. With a long needle, Doctor Sam administered the anaesthetic to Gia's face. It would be the facelift first. Her fists clenched but she made no sound. When he stepped back I noticed Gia's eyes were still moving. It was happening; he was going to keep her awake. I hoped, for her sake, she didn't regret it. I had worried I might faint at the sight of the scalpel entering her face and gliding through her flesh, but everything felt like a movie through the camera's viewfinder. A kind of dull, durational horror movie, underscored by the bleeps of heart-monitoring equipment and Doctor Sam's requests in Spanish for various instruments. At one point he peeled back the outer layer of her skin, revealing what looked like pizza underneath: dark red streaked with fatty orange, yellow, and white tissue. The dermis. The outer layer of epidermis was then stretched upwards like dough and stitched around her forehead and ears, which stuck out untouched from the shifting, bloodied flesh below. I was surprised by how blunt and rudimentary the process was. And all the while, Gia's eyes darted from side to side watching it unfold, like a waking dreamer caught in sleep paralysis.

After the facelift, as if emerging from a spell, Doctor Sam asked me to please leave the operating theatre. I nodded, turned off my camera, collapsed the tripod, and as I walked out I looked back to see the nurses administering sleeping gas to Gia through a mask. The surgery lasted another two hours. After it was finished, the nurses wheeled Gia back into the room and lifted her into bed. Her face was purple and swollen and she couldn't speak, but I could tell by her eyes that she was exhilarated. The nurses affixed an IV and morphine drip into her arm and some kind of plastic tube and pouch that collected the yellow fluid draining from the surgical wounds. Before leaving, they replaced some padding between her legs and wrapped Gia's head in reams of white gauze until she looked like a nun.

As she slept I read an article about novelist Kathy Acker and the alternative therapies she sought for her cancer in Mexico. I could hear the dogs in the kennel howling through the wall, the whine of the fluorescent lights in the ceiling, and the fly that had avoided my multiple assassination attempts. Only time was killed. I began trying to translate the Spanish words on the wall-mounted fire extinguisher. I noticed a small icon hanging on the wall by the door and I walked over to it. At first I thought it was the Virgin of Guadalupe, the local variation on Mary. But no, the cloaked woman in this image was being pierced by an angel holding a flaming arrow. I racked my memory, trying to recall which saint it was. When it finally came to me I whispered: *Teresa of Ávila.*

Teresa of Ávila was a mystical cloistered Carmelite nun who had an ecstatic religious encounter with an angel who pierced her heart with a flaming arrow. This piercing is referred to as the instant of *transverberation*, a moment of juncture between earth and heaven, a moment in which the mortal and divine realms were unified and the glory of God was revealed to her. It was an instant captured in marble by Gian Lorenzo Bernini in the Santa Maria della Vittoria in Rome, the saint's head thrown back in ecstasy in the throes of a supreme Bataillean limit-experience, her body limp, the angel above and astride her, ready to plunge his arrow back into her, again and again. She described this experience in almost orgasmic terms in her writings:

> I saw in his hand a long spear of gold, and at the point there seemed to be a little fire. He appeared to me to be thrusting it at times into my heart, and to pierce my very entrails; when he drew it out, he seemed to draw them out also, and to leave me all on fire with a great love of God. The pain was so great, that it made me moan; and yet so surpassing was the sweetness of this excessive pain, that I could not wish to be rid of it.

As I looked at the painted icon on the clinic room wall, I heard Gia's groggy voice behind me: "I feel just like her."

I turned around and smiled. Her lids were heavy and I thought for a moment she might drift back to sleep.

And then she murmured: "A surged-out trannie Teresa."

Gia and I spent a week in that recovery room. I would go out and buy bottles of Diet Pepsi and greasy tacos from the gas station across the street while she convalesced in bed, cloistered. On the sixth day she was getting restless so we decided to visit the nearby Basilica of Our Lady of Zapopan, a seventeenth-century Franciscan sanctuary where every year a million pilgrims gathered to parade a statue of the Virgin through the streets. Gia was still too sore to walk any significant distance, so I pushed her in a wheelchair wherever possible. As I wheeled her through the basilica, her head wrapped in the white gauze, her features altered to perfect, delicate proportions, she looked more like the saints and angels in the church frescoes and icon paintings than any woman I had known.

At one point she stood up and hobbled over to an icon of the Virgin of Guadalupe. They were dead ringers for one another. The same green-grey eyes, the same thin nose, the same voluptuous lips, the same white drapery encasing her head. Held aloft in the virgin's right hand was her flaming heart. Dangling to Gia's side was a plastic tube connected to a little packet collecting the excess blood and fluid from her wounds. She took this little heart into her right hand and held it aloft towards the painting itself as if it were a mirror.

Nothing about Gia was ironic or satirical. Every fibre in her believed in the existence of these mythic women and the power their archetypes had upon the everyday lives of the devoted. Gia felt herself in communion with the divine feminine, as the living embodiment of its many prismatic identities. She was the Aztec fertility goddess and the snake-headed goddess of war as much as she was Saint Teresa of Ávila and the Virgin of Guadalupe, just as much as she was Helen of Troy, Cleopatra, Ophelia, Isis, and Sinéad O'Connor. These great women lived through Gia and Gia lived through them. As a former sex worker, a trans woman vilified for her body, shamed for her sexuality, she had always felt particular affinity for the Whore of Babylon. "There's no stronger woman than an old whore," she once said to me. The Whore of Babylon was the ur-whore, the mother of all prostitutes and abominations of the earth, and the very embodiment of evil (naturally feminine) in the Book of Revelation. The woman "with whom the kings of the earth have committed fornication, and the inhabitants of the earth have been made drunk with the wine of her fornication" (Revelation 17:2). The great slut of *apokalypsis.*

For Gia, the transformation of her body was more than just about feeling "comfortable" in her skin, the classic medicalized binary of the trans experience: *I was born into the wrong body, now I'm in the right one,* or, *I was born a man, now I am a woman.* Gia's was a lifelong journey of eternal transformation, a sublime state of perpetual becoming. For Gia, it was nothing short of a spiritual quest. She was asking: *Why live your life in just one body?* She was pushing her body beyond the limits, pushing it through the obscene into a conversation with the gods, demigods, and all the mythic creatures that once roamed the earth.

TWO DAYS LATER, Gia was discharged from the clinic. We had arranged to visit our friend Julian, who about six months earlier had moved back to his family's farm, two hours outside of Guadalajara. The farm was a sprawling, terracotta-roofed property nestled in the arid agave fields not far from the town of Tequila. Julian was a prodigious cook and had run a popular Mexican restaurant in west Toronto called Naco, which had become as well known for its steamy queer dance parties after hours as it had been for its food. Julian's family lived on the farm, as did their chickens, roosters, goats, donkeys, kittens, and two dogs — a German shepherd in heat named Camelia, and Xolo, a rare breed of hairless dog once prized by the Aztecs. We were told if we saw Xolo mounting Camelia just to pull him off; they didn't want to spay her but also didn't want a dozen strange puppies on their hands. I hated interrupting the two dogs mid-coitus; sometimes it was pretty hard to pry them apart, and it usually took a minute or so for Xolo's lipstick dick to retract back into its leathery foreskin. After the charmless surgery clinic, Julian's farm felt like paradise. We ate fresh eggs from the chickens, drank homemade horchata, and plucked avocados and papayas straight from the trees.

One night, we were all woken from the dead of sleep by a banshee wail. We ran out into the yard with flashlights just in time to see the backsides of two coyotes scampering into the darkness, leaving a young goat eyes lolling and bleeding in their wake. As the goat tried to push herself away from us, we could see her massive neck wound. She could barely keep her head up.

"We have to put her down," Julian stammered. "It's cruel to let her suffer."

I held the flashlight as Julian and his father placed a blanket under the goat, lifted and ferried her pharaoh-like into the garden, tied her back legs up to an acacia tree, and slit her throat.

The next day, as Julian and his brother prepared the goat, Gia and I decided to do a day trip to Guanajuato—an old colonial city of narrow streets and vertiginous staircases nestled in a valley about three hours away by car. The city's main tourist attraction was the Mummy Museum. It was a beautiful day, and we were a bit reluctant to spend too much time indoors, but everyone kept telling us we had to go, so we trekked up the winding hillside road to the museum. When we got to the top of the hill we found a nondescript, single-storey beige building surrounded by tour buses. We waited in a long queue for the better part of an hour before entering.

It turned out the "mummies" on display were corpses exhumed from the adjacent cemetery of individuals whose families had been unable to pay a burial tax introduced in the 1870s. About one in ten of the corpses had been found preserved, all of them from above-ground crypts—likely due to the arid climate, which would have rapidly dried them out after burial. Inside the museum, the mummies were displayed in vitrines with virtually no information panels. Some of them were from as recent as the 1960s, which meant some of their descendants, probably many, were still alive. This seemed unfathomable to me. As Gia and I walked through the dimly lit hallways decorated with fake cobwebs and mirrors with holographic ghouls lingering in them, I had the distinct impression I was in a haunted house. There was nothing museological about any of it.

Local folklore maintained the mummies were people who had been accidentally buried alive; having succumbed to an agonizing death of asphyxiation, their bodies transformed into mummies as a lasting testament to their suffering. Apparently there was some truth to this. Because of a local cholera epidemic from 1829 to 1851, many bodies were buried as soon as possible to limit the spread of infection; however, it is thought that in some cases the dying were buried alive by accident. Which would explain the horrifying expressions on some of their faces.

One face in particular lingered with me. It was the mummy of a mother. I'm not sure how I could tell she was a mother, but somehow I knew this beyond a doubt. She was a woman of about fifty. Her mouth was wide open as if she were screaming. Her eye sockets appeared to be screaming too. Her arms were crossed in front of her as if holding her body or perhaps attempting to press up against a coffin with the backsides of her arms. Her breasts looked like two wasp's nests. I held her hollow, haunted gaze until my eyes filled with tears and I looked away.

"She'll win every staring contest," Gia murmured.

Because the mummies had been laid to rest with their arms across their bodies and were now propped upright, it appeared as if they were in frozen states of disembowelment, trying to hold in their desiccated innards. There were also baby mummies with mouths contorted by rigor mortis into ghoulish scowls, still wearing their tiny lace burial dresses. One of the mummies, Ignacia Aguilar, had suffered from a strange illness which caused her heart to occasionally stop, sometimes for as long as a day at a time. On one such occasion, thinking she had died, her relatives buried her. When she was disinterred, her mummy was found facing down, biting her arm, with blood in her mouth. She appeared to be gripping her hands together and pushing up with her back against the now-invisible coffin. The exertion was etched for eternity into her muscles.

But the most popular mummy of the museum by far happened to be the smallest ever found in the world—the fetus from a pregnant woman who died of cholera. A scrum of visitors crowded around the small vitrine taking photos. I couldn't bear to get up close to it. From a distance it looked like a thumb. Later, in the gift shop, amidst various Day of the Dead trinkets and painted skulls, I noticed they were selling necklaces, key chains, and colourful erasers in the shape of this little mummy fetus.

By the time Gia and I stumbled back out into white, hot daylight, I was furious. It was all so absolutely obscene. But what, exactly, was obscene? The museum's refusal to treat death as a hallowed and sanctified thing? The unrestrained showcase of horror? Wasn't death a horror? Wasn't this the hard truth? Was this place making a show of death any more than *Aliens* or *Titanic* had? Did it feel obscene that these bodies had once contained real people? They were, of course, no longer people. They were now things no different than a rock or a vase or a car tire, and yet I was shaken to the very core with the feeling that I had just witnessed some profound violation. Looking around us, it occurred to me for the first time that the crowds flowing out of the museum's exit were mostly Mexican tourists, parents with their children who had travelled to Guanajuato from elsewhere in the country. They spoke animatedly. Inside the dark halls the children had pointed at the bodies and run ahead, calling back and waving one another over. There was nothing precious or reverential in how they moved about the space or spoke of the bodies. They were unashamed and unabashed to be scared, repulsed, and fascinated by the dead. They were unashamed and unabashed to be alive. To rejoice in the fact that they were not, at least yet, those bodies. I realized, standing there, that what I had felt shaken was my own WASP relationship with death as something respectfully, if rarely, spoken about and certainly never gawked at.

As we made our way back down the hill towards the bustling central thoroughfares, we turned off down a shady side street to escape the afternoon sun and soon found ourselves navigating a vertiginous labyrinth of intersecting staircases trafficked mostly by stray dogs. The narrow, stepped passageways were steep and filled with blind corners, every landing leading off in a new direction at a ninety-degree angle. We knew the general direction we had to head was down, but every corner we rounded seemed to lead to more staircases in an Escher-like nightmare. The staircases were lined with locked doors, gates guarded by barking dogs, and dark cubbyhole shops separated from the street by wooden countertops. Most of the shops had small television sets showing the same soccer game, but somehow all seemed unoccupied.

After about half an hour, Gia and I arrived at a landing which presented us with two equally unattractive passageways, both narrower and darker than the one we had just descended. But backtracking up all those stairs was not an option, not in Gia's state and not with my general lack of fitness. Somehow we both intuited that the left passageway was the marginally more appealing one and started down it. I could tell Gia was on edge; for her, crowds equated with safety, anonymity in numbers, and we hadn't seen more than two people walk by together since we turned off the main road. As we rounded a corner, we heard a screeching echo up the passage and passed a spark-littered courtyard where three men were shearing apart scrap metal. I turned and noticed Gia talking with two men; still disoriented by the noise, it took me a moment to realize they were accosting her and that she was shouting at them, which I could only tell by her body language, as her voice was drowned out by the screaming metal. I tried to wade in, shouting, "What's wrong?" but I couldn't even hear my own voice; in fact, I felt completely invisible as I watched one of the men, in one lightning-fast move, grab the white bandages on Gia's head with such force it snapped her neck forward, slamming her chin against her chest; and then, as if ripping meat from a carcass, he pulled once, twice, three times until the bandages tore away from where they had been taped and fastened in place.

It was then that the sounds of metal stopped, replaced by Gia's screams and the noise of the three men from the courtyard shouting, I couldn't tell at whom, and I could see them advancing towards us out of the corner of my eye when I realized my hands were gripping the arm of the man who now held the tatters of Gia's bandages, brown from dried blood but also glistening with fresh blood. I looked at Gia's face and noticed she was bleeding from one of the loosened stitches near her temple, blood enveloping her left ear, Van Gogh–like. The man gave his arm a shake with such force my wrists felt like they had snapped, and then he pushed me back into the stone wall as if brushing away a barking Pomeranian. My back hit the wall first and then my head, cracking against the stones a fraction of a second after. The three men from the courtyard were around us now, shouting at the man holding Gia's bandages, who kept indicating her face, fingers forward, palm outstretched as if arguing his point and giving evidence. In my mind Gia, in this moment, had the face of the mummy with the screaming mouth and eye sockets and the wasp's-nest breasts, but I couldn't look at her so instead I looked at the face of the second man, the friend of the man holding the bandages, looked at his passivity and bemusement while these three metalworkers reasoned with his friend to let us be, just let them be.

The next thing I knew, Gia and I were half a block away, walking swiftly, but before I could say anything to her I heard the voice of an old woman calling out from behind us. We walked without turning, but she continued to call, and when we finally looked back she was ambling towards us. The street behind her was empty now, which struck me as strange. Where had the men gone? As the old woman reached us, the sounds of metalworking resumed, filling the narrow passage with its shrieks, such that the woman didn't bother saying anything as she took off her headscarf and tied it around Gia's head. Gia had to crouch down somewhat to enable this, and a smile and a raised hand was all that was needed to communicate our thanks.

AFTER A WEEK at Julian's farm, and about eight different goat dishes, Gia and I flew to Mexico City. The morning after we arrived, we hired a cab to drive us through the desert to Teotihuacan, the Aztec temple of the sun. Gia wanted to climb to the top of the pyramid, which struck me as ambitious given her state, but she was nothing if not determined. It was midday when we arrived. The sun was blazing above us as I held her hand and we climbed each step with great care, making our way up a staircase that had once run with blood. We were breathless as we reached the top and looked out over the vast plains stretching to the horizon in every direction, standing on the spot where tens of thousands of people had been sacrificed, their hearts ripped up and held aloft in the hands of the high priest like the heart of the Virgin, one cult practice replacing another, one sacrifice replacing another, all hearts the same heart, and standing to my side was Gia, her head wrapped in white, wearing a long black dress and black sunglasses, a body of sacrifice to pleasure and beauty, to art and subversion, gazing up at the eternal sun.

IX

AS I STAND here I realize the thing I comprehend least is my own body. What distinguishes the living thing I am from the un-living thing you seem to be. And how can I even consider this my *own* body, as something I possess, while watching yours assert that it is something you do not? All of my life I've thrown myself into relationships with friends, lovers, and cities, relationships I knew would burn bright and brief because of their intensity, and yet I'm always surprised when they come to an end. How do we love and live with a thing that we know will fail and desert us in the end? A vessel on a crash course with death?

I think about how Grandpa Lou used to spend his days investigating deep-sea collisions between container ships and oil tankers. He once explained to me, using the aid of a fork and knife, how in the open waters a container ship knows it's about to collide with another container ship about an hour before the collision actually happens, just based on its course. Container ships take so long to turn that, by the time a captain sees another ship appear on the horizon, it's already too late; all that the crew on board can do is prepare for the collision. He once brought home shortwave radio transcripts from one of the cases he was working on, a chilling conversation between a container ship captain and his mother. The captain called her to tell her that another ship had appeared on the horizon on a collision course with his and that, in an hour's time, they would hit. His mother was hysterical, but the captain reassured her that he and the crew would survive. He spent a good ten minutes talking to her, speculating on how his career was now over and what a hell the next few months of his life would be, as his boat sailed towards certain destruction.

It occurs to me now that our twenty-eight years together has been this phone call between the captain and his mother. A temporary communion as our two bodies glide on their intractable paths towards oblivion.

MY BODY IS A HORROR.

This hits me with the force of a log truck flipping and smacking down against a stretch of deserted highway—something you and I saw at a distance once, safe from the loosed logs crashing down the adjacent slope. And like that truck this realization releases a tumbling, terrible cargo. *My body is a horror.*

I don't mean my body's appearance. I'm not ashamed of my body, despite the brief jolts of self-hatred that pulse through me as I pass by reflective surfaces—car windows, darkened storefronts—and catch sight of my simian posture, my neck craned forward from hours of laptop and smartphone usage. In overcompensation I wrench my neck and shoulders back, further than necessary, as both punishment and corrective. But no, I'm not ashamed of my body.

And I don't mean horror in a Cronenberg "body horror" sense, though this comes closer. In grade ten Ana and I watched Cronenberg's *The Fly*, the 1986 cult classic in which scientist Seth Brundle inadvertently fuses his DNA with that of a housefly. That night I lay awake in her yellow sleeping bag, itself a kind of pupa or chrysalis, half-waiting for two giant oozing proboscises to rip through my face. Most disturbing of all was the climax, when Brundle, more fly than human, attempts to break free from the teletransporter mid-fusion and is genetically merged with chunks of the teletransporter's metal and electronics. A gruesome and untenable creature crawls out of the receiving telepod, an amalgam of human, fly, and machine. The abomination wordlessly begs Veronica, Brundle's lover, to end its suffering with a shotgun, and she tearfully obliges after a moment's hesitation.

As I lay there I thought back to playing Teletransporter with you; how once the blanket slipped off my head as I was being transported and my head stuck out, revealing the mundanity of your body carrying mine through the basement—beige Berber carpet, ceiling pot lights, wood-panelled walls—and you exclaimed: "Oh no, your head's going to be left behind!" and the image startled me. The casual terror of decapitation.

But while the degradation and decay of my body is terrifying, this is not the horror revealed in this moment. As your body comes into focus I'm overcome by the full, unveiled understanding that my body will one day be *a thing*. A thing

I no longer inhabit. A thing separate from me. That the body I once called *I* will become something that is no longer *I* but a thing no different from the old computers collecting dust in the basement, meaning neither *I* nor my body could possibly be sacred or unique or even of much significance at all. When in the end all that is left is just *a body*. Just another body. Any body.

ON THE NIGHT OF JULY 14, 2016, as the Bastille Day fireworks in Nice ended, Mohamed Lahouaiej Bouhlel began driving a white delivery truck through the crowd of revellers on the Promenade des Anglais. In the days following, I read as many online articles and watched as many videos as I could find about the attack. I was repulsed by my own horror-fascination with it, but also gradually came to realize I was seeking an answer for a question that had long plagued me.

"The truck driver was shooting from the window of the cab as he smashed through the throngs of people — many still in beachwear — at 40mph," reported a *Mirror* article. In that instant the throngs were still "people," many still in beachwear. They were not yet "bodies." They were not yet a street of bodies and beachwear. They were still people with possessions. Whereas, two sentences later, the article reports, "Bodies were left strewn across the street after a terrorist ploughed into revellers along the Promenade des Anglais in Nice."

"Daylight reveals horror of Nice attack as buggies, bodies, and belongings litter promenade," proclaimed the *Sun*'s headline. Bodies were, in that list, of a part with buddies and belongings. The buggies were once the belongings of these bodies—a single unit of association ("a woman pushing a buggy")—but now they were separate, itemized objects. Things.

In recounting her experience to Channel Nine, Tori Anderson, an Australian visiting Nice, said:

> And I turned around and behind me was this big truck. My friend and I just looked to the side, and the bodies directly beside us got pulled under the truck. Bodies were flying left, right, and centre…The only thing we could really do was jump off the promenade and land on the rocks down below. There was a couple of hundred people pushing everyone off the edge of the promenade. Everyone was landing on rocks. There were people—their bodies were tangled everywhere. We landed on rocks and ran for our lives.

I found some of the most excruciating parts of Anderson's account to be the person/body substitutions and slippages. "My friend and I just looked to the side, and the bodies directly beside us got pulled under the truck." In Anderson's recollection she referred to "bodies" rather than "people" standing beside her prior to their being pulled under the truck. I realized in her statement to the reporter she was not consciously choosing one word over another. But the word "bodies" in that context conjured the possibility that, in that moment, Anderson already saw these individuals as bodies. It conjured the mental image of Anderson looking into the faces of those standing beside her and seeing bodies, already-bodies, in the split second before they were taken by the truck. Even if she did not *see* them in any traditional sense — their faces, their final expressions — did she sense their presence around her as already-bodies rather than people? But the truly most horrific and disorienting passage in Anderson's account was: "There were people — their bodies were tangled everywhere," as if she was unsure what state they were in, perhaps between states, still people but with their bodies "tangled everywhere."

My worst nightmare is to be a person with my body tangled everywhere. Superseded only by the nightmare of seeing a loved one, seeing you, still alive, still person, with your body tangled everywhere. Or worse still: to see you see your own body tangled everywhere. Seeing you witness the terror of your own body/person rupture. To see you still alive, conscious, blinking, gasping, beholding your own corpse like in an American horror movie. That is, in fact, my worst nightmare.

STANDING HERE I feel myself gripped by what Kristeva called "a massive and sudden emergence of uncanniness." What distinguishes the living thing I am from the living thing you once were? In this moment you are neither subject nor object. You are in an unknowable space. An abject space, insofar as it pulls us towards a place where meaning deteriorates. You are "familiar as [you] might have been in an opaque and forgotten life," a life we shared as recently as a second ago, but now "radically separate, loathsome…A 'something' that I do not recognize as a thing. A weight of meaninglessness, about which there is nothing insignificant, and which crushes me. On the edge of non-existence and hallucination, of a reality that, if I acknowledge it, annihilates me."

I realize I have spent my life trying to excavate the difference between those things that *are* and those things that *are not*. As a child I watched cartoons with talking cars, houses with faces that blinked and smiled, trees that waved; and of course I saw them do this in real life as well. I saw the faces in everything. The screaming mouth in a bisected bell pepper. The serpent in the stick. I felt pangs for the pumpkin smashed on the pavement after Halloween and invested in the rich interior worlds of stuffed animals. I once shivered when I saw the giant arthropod eye of a spider staring back at me in the dozens of small clustered bubbles of my piss in the toilet water.

When was this bled from me, this ambiguity of being? At what point did this sense of wonder turn into a sense of horror? I don't remember being terrorized by this ineffable threshold between the living and the un-living as a child. Where did that repulsion come from? It seems remarkable that I shouldn't have really noticed that profound reorientation until long after it was complete. I suspect this is not an innate evolution but rather a learned one; an acquired binary that, at its darkest core, seeks to deny sentience even to those living things that clearly have it, to all things that are not human. *Inhuman.* I think back to our conversation in the Dollarama and begin to think my questions—When does a computer acquire sentience? When do computers become beings?—were indeed the wrong questions. As I stand here I wonder: How are *you* a *being* any more than a computer or a robot or a rabbit or a stick insect or an almond tree? How have we defined this threshold? Between that which gets to *be* and that which does not, in our perception.

AFTER OUR ROAD TRIP to Burning Man I went up to Ottawa to visit you for your birthday, sunburned and nursing a cold sore courtesy of Ana borrowing my toothbrush. We decided to see an exhibition featuring the work of Edward Burtynsky, a Toronto-based photographer who had built an international reputation for capturing images of large-scale ecological devastation wrought by humans: blackened shores in Bangladesh where discontinued oil tankers are dismantled for parts; an undulating sea of discarded tires in California; an iridescent red river of tailings from nickel mining in northern Ontario; the fractal patterns of polluted estuaries as seen from a plane, like brain stems. We strolled through the gallery in silence, in opposite directions, so as not to rush or irritate one another with our inane comments. We reconnected at an image of innumerable workers in pink uniforms on an assembly-line floor in a fluorescent-lit chicken processing plant in Dehui City, China. The symmetry and scale of the photograph were arresting, even as the depiction of dehumanized labour was unnerving.

Standing in front of this expanse of labour, bodies reduced to indistinguishable and interchangeable shapes and colour, I was gripped by the same panic and confusion that caused me to look up "person" in the dictionary the day after 9/11. If "person" was defined as "a human being regarded as an individual" and "individual" was defined as "a single human being as distinct from a group," then my personhood was only legible in relation to how I differed from others. As a boy I would scan images of crowds—military formations; synchronized displays in stadiums; the praying, prostrate pilgrims in Mecca or St. Peter's Square—trying to pick out a person inside the mass. In magazines or newspapers, on television or the Internet, whenever I saw large-group scenes I would try to find a person looking out from the crowd towards the photographer as if saying, "I am here."

Growing up I had an inexplicable terror of being lost in a mass. Not lost in a geographic sense but subsumed into a crowd such that *I,* the person that was me, would never emerge again. And not the diffuse crowds of shopping malls or parks but organized ones. Ones asked to stand for the national anthem in an arena or recite the Scout's honour in unison or perform a synchronized routine for a school assembly. These bodies packed together, unified, became a kind of corpse. *Corps*, an organized body of people. And I experienced each of these *corps* as a kind of death.

One of my greatest anxieties was that I would lose my grip on *I.* When I was nine I had an existential crisis in church. Not over the existence of God, but over the existence of *I.* The pastor told the congregation to "all rise" and we did, as one. And then we began to sing a hymn, as one. And in that moment I realized I was not an *I* but an indistinguishable *we*, a mass, at mass, in supplication to God. It's difficult to describe the sensation that came over me. I wanted to scream. It was profound terror mixed with embarrassment. I was embarrassed that we so readily erased and debased ourselves like this. In this moment I did not see us as lofty and evolved creatures; I saw that we were no different than a colony of ants, a murmuration of starlings, a school of fish. Like slime moulds, which exist as single-celled organisms until food is in short supply and then coalesce into a single, oozing mass. I looked at the people standing around me and I could not see their faces. Their faces did not make sense to me. I looked up at you singing, but you were not my mother;

you were just another woman in a singing congregation. It was unbearable. I began to cry. I couldn't cope with the loss of my integrity; not in the moral sense, but in the sense of remaining a single, integral being. A whole unto myself.

Perhaps this childhood crisis was the inevitable by-product of our post-war march towards the all-encompassing *I. Your very own house! Your very own car! Your very own appliances!* And from the depersonalized malaise of post-war suburbia and consumerism came another frenzy of personalization, which capitalism once again co-opted and made a mockery of: a new wave of parent, a new wave of child, each one gifted and gratified with new excesses, new consciousness, self-actualized with better sex, better moods, better skin, better lives through pharmaceuticals, self-help, exercise, organic food. And this Me Generation gave birth to iGen, my generation, the millennials, supposedly saturated with more self-obsession than ever before. And yet what I felt in church that morning, the moment the congregation rose and began to sing, myself among them, seemed somehow bigger than a fifty-year endgame. It felt bigger than acculturation. It felt ancient. It felt like a timeless conflict between self and non-self.

When I was a child Dora told me that it was blasphemy to say the words "I Am." Only God had the right to refer to himself this way. "I Am" was, in fact, the name of God. *God said to Moses, "I Am Who I Am. This is what you are to say to the Israelites: 'I Am has sent me to you'"* (Exodus 3:14). It reminded me of the Gloria Gaynor song "I Am What I Am," which you used to put on when you were dusting and which Ana and I later danced to in a gay bar. But it also struck me as profoundly petty and insecure of God to declare that only

He had the right to assert his *I*-ness, and bordering on perverse that he forced us to subsume our *I*-ness once a week for his gratification, perhaps because if we were also *I* then He was not singular, not all-powerful.

Perhaps the terror of the dissolution of *I* into the indistinguishable group was that it confronted me with my own mortality. It confronted me with the inconsequentiality of my consciousness and identity. How easy it was to suddenly not-be. To be a *body without a person*. And not just in death, but the ease with which I could be rendered one while still alive.

On the way home from the Burtynsky exhibition we stopped at a pizzeria situated in the middle of a parking lot surrounded by big-box stores. After we'd spent a few minutes offloading our sundry opinions about the show onto one another in a subtle exercise of one-upmanship, a young man I recognized from high school came up to our booth.

"Hi, my name is Kieran and I'll be your server for the night."

The moment he noticed me something flashed between us — a choice to either acknowledge that we knew each other or pretend as if Kieran was just "our server for the night" and not a person who had been a grade ahead of me, not a person with whom I'd been to house parties and had friends in common. And in that moment we both decided to go with this latter option. Somehow that fiction was more palatable and less embarrassing. It was easier for us to let Kieran be a *body without a person* that night, serving us garlic sticks and pizza. As he returned to ask the requisite North American serving question "How's everything tasting?" I wondered if all income wasn't just compensation for dehumanizing ourselves in one way or another. And to that end, as we ate, you didn't ask me how I was making my money lately and I think we both knew that was for the best.

Instead you asked me about the road trip. I thought about explaining what it felt like to watch the burn on the playa. About feeling myself not only lost in the sea of people but also lost as to what we were all really doing there. But for some reason I found myself telling you about my chance encounter with Robert at the diner. I launched into a somewhat breathless explanation of his theory on sentience as you cut your pizza into little manageable squares. I even took out a pen from your purse at one point and mimicked his writing of the equation on a napkin.

When I finished you forked a piece of sun-dried tomato off your plate, popped it in your mouth, chewed it and said: "Well, that seems rather flimsy, don't you think?"

I immediately felt defensive of Robert. And perhaps of my own enthusiasm. I told you I had googled him and could verify he was a scientist of some renown.

You took a sip of wine, unimpressed. "All he's describing is a measure of the efficiency of an individual brain, not its relative intelligence or sentience. It doesn't describe how the subjective experience of being alive arises out of the very *objective* stuff of our brain tissue." You took another sip of wine and shook your head, the glass still suspended in your hand. "I'm so goddamn tired of these scientists — all of them *men*, you can be sure — who want to equate human consciousness, sentience, intelligence with computational processing power. It's just so — flimsy. And fascist, actually."

Needless to say you were not inspired. Compared to the human soul you considered even the most lyrical aspects of science to be cold, analytic vulgarities.

We were in such a full-blown argument about it by the time you paid the bill that Kieran didn't even bother performing the formalities of the warm send-off. As we crossed the parking lot you were working yourself into a rage, channelling a lifetime's worth of professional setbacks into your exasperation with Robert's theory and every half-baked, machismo theory that landed men tenures at Berkeley.

"I bet I know about a hundred times more about computers than Robert does—or power to the hundred times more," you said.

A few paces from our car, lost in conversation, we looked up to notice a red sedan speeding directly towards us. The driver was looking at his phone and wasn't slowing down. We leapt out of the way, and as we did your heel snapped and you careened face-first into a parked car, your head bucking back as it hit the bumper. Your nose was bleeding as I helped you back onto your feet.

You swivelled and shouted to no one in particular, perhaps to me, "That fucking car almost hit us!"

At the time I was too shaken by the blood from your nose and your grazed knees to consider what you'd just said. *That fucking car almost hit us.* As I recall the moment now, what fascinates me is that you imbued the car with a sentience. Or rather, the sentience of the car and the driver became one. Just as it was a single body in our perceived reality of it, moving through the world, almost fucking hitting us. All manner of bodies without people can be imbued with sentience: cars, houses, laptops, wasp's nests. When I walk through the wrecking yard of busted cars near the strip mall, I see corpses, rusted and spent bodies once inhabited by persons but now too old to function. "That wasp's nest is humming," you said, when we found it in the garage last summer, imbuing the body of the nest with the sentience of the wasps inside. The wasp's nest was a body we had to contend with and exterminate. After the fumigation, I saw the emptied and withered nest in the garage as a corpse too.

And like the wasps, we also animate the lifeless things we enter and inhabit. When I stand in a room I become a body with that room; it is a physical structure which houses a person inside of it, just as my body is a physical structure which houses a person inside of it. The room becomes alive with me. With us. "This room is too loud," we shout at a party. And it seems the distinction between our bodies and architecture is only growing less clear with time. A body on life-support is a body made up of itself and the life-sustaining medical infrastructure of the room. There are rooms I walk into now that sense my presence. They beep, they activate lights, they begin to record, to witness, to dispense information to me, to alter their temperature to suit my body, to play music, to activate appliances, fire, water, air; these rooms change their state to suit mine. Perhaps one day I won't even be able to tell where my body begins and the room I'm standing in ends. Like your hand holding the water glass.

In this moment I understand the world is filled with bodies-within-bodies, bodies conjoined, in states of becoming, merging, emerging, consuming, being consumed, cocoons, pregnancies, intercourse, dwellings, people within rooms within buildings within cities. To say "New York City is alive" is no more of a metaphor than to say "I am alive." The city and my body are both made sentient and functional by innumerable smaller bodies, smaller units of sentience housed within us. And in the same manner that human beings place higher on Robert's sentience quotient than the paramecia inside our cells, so too would New York City place higher than any single human, and so too would the Internet and any other body of which human bodies are composite.

The military drone is a composite body comprised of the warhead and its human operator, who lends the warhead sentience. And it is not just the operator in his or her bunker under the Nevada desert who belongs to the composite body of the drone but also the operator's superiors in the chain of command, the entire political apparatus that gives the drone meaning and intent, that guides where it glides through the air, what it hunts, and when it strikes. It is a *body without a person*, without any one person to take responsibility, without any one person to feel guilt or consequence. By being a composite body, it does away with the limitations of personhood. It acts through us and we act through it to achieve godlike acts.

We become part of all manner of bodies, with or without having any choice in the matter. The drone operator goes home and kisses his son's forehead and makes love to his wife, touches her body with the same hands he used to take away a life in a distant desert, the life of a man who also had a wife he made love to, and in this way the drone operator's family becomes part of the body of the target and his family. And the friends the drone operator's son plays with and the lovers he will grow up to have—they too will enter this body.

The offices and factories and pizzerias we work in are bodies we enter and become part of every day. Perhaps this is why working in these spaces so keenly reminds us of our mortality: we experience them as becoming-body. We are confronted with the ease with which our persons are erased and we become just our bodies doing menial labour, or part of a collective body of employees. The ease with which this cleaving of person and body occurs is unnerving. The ease with which a group of people can stand up and begin singing an anthem together, the ease with which I could enter a Tim Hortons, a huge, composite body working like a hive to hawk donuts and coffee to passing cars eighteen seconds at a time. We cannot be fixed, stable, and singular entities if this is possible. We cannot always call ourselves people if this is possible. This was the becoming-body terror I had when forced to stand and sing hymns in church, the horrifying sensation of becoming part of a giant composite body, a body without consequence, a *corps,* along with every other congregant. In those instances, I was no more than a bacterium in a gut.

In this moment, the boundary between your body, the sheets, the bed, the room, even my body begins to feel unclear, just so many clouds of molecularly bonded matter with mostly nothing in between, just air, just absence, just the suggestion of forms. I suddenly feel so porous as to be a part of every other body that has ever lived, breathing in particles off-gassed by others, airborne specks of other animals' shit, a body sustained by their flesh, their fluids, a body made of elements from distant stars, particles recycled countless times through the earth. To think that I was once literally inside of you. Spawn. A tadpole swimming in your stomach. The living thing you were, forging the living thing I am. When I did not distinguish my self from you or the world, when sensation was boundless, when life was nothing but the pure materiality of existence. And then I was born. Made visible. When we were separated and I recognized for the first time a boundary between "me" and the other, between "me" and you. Mother.

X

"WHAT WOULD YOU do if I was dead?"

I half-expect you to open your eyes, turn your head on your pillow, and ask me this before cracking a smile. Then breaking into a laugh. And standing here in the doorway I would begin laughing too, tears collecting in our eyes as we recalled how many times I'd tormented you with this little game over the years. The game always began just like that: a what-would-you-do-if question posed out of the blue. Except I was always the asker and you the dutiful respondent.

"What would you do if I was hit by a car?"

I'm eleven, watching television with you on the mouldering couch in the basement. You grab the remote and mute the abrasive car commercial while I pluck bits of yellow foam out of the couch's armrest where the fabric has torn away.

"I'd call the ambulance and ride with you all the way to the hospital," you reply.

"What would you do if I split my brain into two people's bodies?"

"I'd ask a doctor to put them back together into your real body."

"But if you couldn't."

"I'd love both of you."

"What would you do if a raptor suddenly came around the corner, just now?"

"I would throw something at it."

"Like what?"

"My…slipper."

"What would you do if India replaced its national anthem with Alanis Morissette's song 'Thank U'?"

"She and I went to the same high school, did you know that? "

"What would you do if—"

"Years apart, obviously."

"—I put my hands on the top of my head like this and suddenly peeled it like a giant grapefruit?"

"I don't know."

"What would you do if—"

"Last one."

"—I was actually a bear?"

"I don't know, I would buy you some honey."

"What would you do if—"

"Jordan, I don't want to play this game anymore."

You would always shut it down the same way. Once you spoke my name, I knew it was final and never pushed it.

When I was nineteen you bought me a laptop as a gift for getting into university. You said, "Now you can ask Google all your questions." I realized this was your way of letting me know that you didn't want to play our game anymore, in a more permanent sense. You were telling me it wasn't a game that adults played with their mothers. In fairness, by that point we hardly did anymore. Perhaps on the odd occasion, in a quiet moment in the car when waiting for a light to turn green, I'd try my luck. "What would you do if that woman started crab-walking across the intersection?"

I held the laptop and smiled, but I wanted to say: *Don't you get it?* Google couldn't give me what I was looking for. Google provided answers to questions. This wasn't the point of the game. The game was about eliciting increasingly ridiculous rationalizations and responses from you, to test your capacity for patience, imagination, and, frankly, the unseemly. To *go with me.* To go the distance. To trace the perimeters of your humanity. Perhaps even to trace the perimeters of your love for me.

The only death before this moment that has truly shaken and disoriented me with grief was the death of that laptop. Until now the only event that even let me access the dark topographies of death was the loss of that laptop. The only benchmark I had to anticipate my grief over your death was the death of that laptop. You, preceded only by my MacBook. And it occurs to me this betrays the truly pathetic and barren emotional landscape of my life. Reveals my heart to be the stunted and gnarled root vegetable in the ground that it is: a sheltered white turnip. But I had six years of writing saved on that laptop. Plays, half-finished novels, my best thoughts. My best self. All the videos I ever filmed, all my photos — my trips, my friends, my family. My young adulthood. Erased.

I was writing late one night at the kitchen table. Will was back home visiting his family in PEI, so I had Videofag to myself. I went to pick up my mug of tea when it slipped from my fingers and clattered across my keyboard. *Fuck fuck*

fuck, I grabbed my laptop, flipped it upside down, shook it twice, righted it, and used my sweatshirt to wipe the keys clean. *It wasn't so much*, I reassured myself. *Most of it went on the desk.* And I had acted quickly and decisively. For good measure I saved my document, shut down my laptop, and stuck it in a large bag of basmati rice I had in the cupboard. Ana had shared this trick with me; she apparently saved her computer this way after dousing it with red wine. I killed an hour pottering about the kitchen before pulling the laptop back out of the rice. I placed it down on the counter, pressed the power button, and it awoke with its usual perky chime. I opened my Word doc and everything was there. I typed some nonsense and the letters appeared just as they always did. The *A* key produced a's, the *L* key produced l's, and the space bar made spaces as it was wont to do. I went back to my desk and carried on writing.

Then, around midnight, the rainbow wheel of death began spinning on my screen. I pressed *control-alt-delete* before remembering it was a Mac. Oh muscle memory. A childhood weaned on PCs. I pressed and held the power button until the laptop gave a tiny sigh and the screen went dark. I counted to five. I pressed the power button again and it purred awake. No perky chime. I listened to its soft internal whirring, almost mammal-like. I waited but the screen remained black. I fingered the touch pad. There was the rainbow wheel again, against the black screen. I leaned back in my chair and listened to my neighbour's Cantonese soap opera through the wall for a moment. Then the laptop quieted down. It was no longer booting. It grew quiet, as if announcing: *Well, here it is, this is what you're getting.* Outwardly I was still presenting an air of calm. I hadn't cursed or even sighed empathically. I only swore in front of others. Swearing for one's own sake was a bit pathetic, I found, like showing off for a child.

I filled the electric kettle with water. I considered my reflection in the glass-fronted cupboards as I waited for it to boil. A lonely homosexual felled by a frozen computer. There must be hundreds of us standing alone in our kitchens-turned-home-offices, quietly waiting for divine intervention and the water to boil. As I stood there I saw them: all the other stay-at-home writers, accountants, students, consultants, and graphic designers pacing and peeling their fingernails to the quick with their teeth, formulating plans of how to proceed with their nights. I took a certain comfort in all these other men and women fretting about their computers, alone in their homes, but in fact very much together, in this moment, united in misfortune, like being caught unawares by a downpour, running down the sidewalk with our shirts and blazers pulled up over our heads and catching each other's eyes as we passed, smiling at our shared lot, at how silly we'd been to have left the house so unprepared. The kettle began to gurgle. I lifted it and poured the boiling water into my mug, the tea bag now on its third round and useless. I liked tasting its diminishing returns. As I leaned against the counter drinking hot water, I reminded myself: this is the twenty-first century. There will be a solution.

The next morning I rented a Zipcar and drove to a strip mall in North York, parking in front of Geeks-R-Us, a name which was no doubt in breach of some sort of copyright. I turned off the engine and let the rain berate me against the windshield for a minute as I sat in silence. I took a deep breath, tucked my laptop under my coat, climbed out of the car, and strode in. I filled out a form, turned my laptop over to a guy named Patrick, and waited like an anxious father for two hours until he returned.

"Do you have things backed up on the Cloud?" Patrick asked. I shook my head. "Why not?"

I don't know, it was 2015 and the Cloud was still sort of new and I didn't really understand it and I was lazy and apathetic and it seemed slightly ominous with undertones of a privacy-less dystopian future I don't know fuck off Patrick I wasn't on the goddamn Cloud.

"It's an old laptop," I replied.

"That doesn't matter." He looked at me blankly. "I'm afraid there's nothing I can do."

What did he think he was, a surgeon? *There's nothing I can do.* You're not a surgeon, Patrick. I suddenly regretted imagining him as a doctor, perhaps even subconsciously imbuing him with the import of one, perhaps my bearing making him feel like one, *there's nothing I can do,* this wasn't the fucking ER, what did you mean there was nothing you could do? This was the twenty-first century. I even said it aloud: "This is the twenty-first century." But then who was I to invoke the twenty-first century when I hadn't even backed up my files on the Cloud. It might as well have been a typewriter. He told me the hard drive needed to be "wiped." Patrick. He was a boy, really. A man with a little boy's face. Or, he said, they could just replace the hard drive altogether. Either way, my files would be lost. I stared at him for a moment.

"Do you have a mother?" I asked him.

"Pardon?"

"What you're suggesting—It's like being told they could save your mother's life if they replaced her brain."

He blinked. He was holding my laptop like a phone book or a DVD player or some other obsolescent thing. I reached out and took it from him. Did he not understand? That it would no longer be my computer but a new computer alto-gether? That he was casually trying to offer me a new life to replace my old one? And then, in the most remarkable ges-ture, Patrick touched my shoulder. He scrunched his mouth in sympathy and then removed his hand. He said something else, but I was still lost in that moment. I wondered if he was used to touching people's shoulders. He seemed to have perfected it. I suppose he was in a grief-filled line of work. Or was that a unique moment that had passed between us? Was he now feeling embarrassed about it? The moment his hand touched my shoulder my hatred for him dissipated. I felt, for the first time, that we were truly in this together. Like two parents mourning a child.

I thanked him and walked out. After a few steps I real-ized I hadn't asked about payment, but it would have felt almost grotesque for him to have run out of the shop ask-ing for it, especially after what had just passed between us. Perhaps he figured I had already paid the ultimate price. I cradled the laptop in my arms through the parking lot, laid it on the passenger seat, walked around to my side, climbed in, and sat there for a long while. I felt like furled-up bits of eraser skin on a blank page. Six years. My young adulthood.

I started driving. Where was I going? Home? And then what? What would I do with the rest of my life? I looked down at the laptop. It felt wrong for it to still be in my possession. Like it should have been turned over to the authorities. Like the corpse of a close friend. A lover. I suddenly felt small and stupid. Boring. Like someone's irritating child trying to make conversation at a dinner party. I no longer had anything of value to contribute. No art, no ideas. At red lights I felt the other drivers' eyes peering into my car, staring down at the dead thing in the passenger seat, but I ignored them. I ferried it around all day, to two other computer stores. Each time I carried it in my arms to the counter; each time the diagnosis was the same. I drove home and buried it in the basement, in the graveyard of old appliances, of useless electronics too expensive to throw out.

I know one day very soon, if not already, this will all seem inconceivable. Nothing will be lost because the Cloud will contain everything, and this crisis will seem like some strange relic from the early twenty-first century. But for a brief moment in time it was enough to make a person want to lie down on a road and become a speed bump. For this brief moment in time our consciousness was split between two bodies: the ones we were born in, and the ones we carried around in little plush cases and forgot on buses. Fragile, portable bodies with the lifespan of salmon. What kind of impossible responsibility was that? A glass of wine knocked over could undo us. I didn't want that responsibility. That was an impossible degree of responsibility to leave in the hands of a human being! And how had I not noticed this before? If I had realized my self was divided, would I have plunged one half so insistently into the perils of sketchy pornography, left it open beside full mugs of tea, or hovered spoonfuls of milky cereal above it?

As I paced the bathroom that night, stuck in this cul-de-sac of thought, I opened the door of the medicine cabinet into my face. The pain stunned me. And then I did it again: I opened the cabinet door into my face, this time on purpose, bashed myself with it. I walked to the sink and let the blood from my nose drip into it. I wet some toilet paper and held it over my nose. It felt like confirmation: I am barely my body. Half of my self lies buried in the basement along with the other dead monitors and cell phones and power adaptors, all destined to end up in some burning e-waste dump outside of Accra where men in third-hand sneakers will strip them for copper and coltan.

I woke the next morning on the couch and felt an immense sense of calm. I felt unburdened by anything I had been. I had nothing but my body. A body in search of a new self, like the new hard drive Patrick had offered me. I went to buy a bag of milk from the corner store and I didn't exist. There was a kind of freedom in this. The woman at the subway kiosk wished me a good day after selling me a roll of tokens and the old me would have replied, "Thank you, you too," but I was no longer me; in fact, I was temporarily not anyone, so I felt no need to reply. I was not building a relationship with this woman. I was not trying to maintain appearances or a reputation. I was a cypher. It felt as if I could move about the world without consequence. If I wanted to run down the sidewalk or lock eyes with a passing stranger and scream that would haven been perfectly permissible because I had no pre-established way of being. If I had been erased, I thought, then I could start again. I could be whoever I wanted. Every step I took from that moment on would begin to establish that new person. I could change my name. Change my habits. I wouldn't even have to fake my death because I was already dead. It took me a few days to make up my mind about how I wanted to be in the world. I didn't feel in a rush. It was actually a miraculous limbo to be in. Pure potentiality. I went and sat in a strange café. I ordered a drink I didn't even like. I went into a store and tried on some clothes, imagining how I might begin to look in this new life. I wasn't ready to commit to a new haircut yet, but I studied people's hair.

I eventually had to admit that being in the world like that was untenable in the long run. I knew I had to commit to something. That was the way the world had been set up and the way it operated; everyone got their own life, but they had to commit to an identity and be held accountable to it. It was upsetting for people to encounter someone living without an identity. Without a past or destiny. So the world made it very hard to live that way. Exhausting, financially unfeasible, and socially isolating.

Near the end of that week you called. The sound of your voice was like two hands on my shoulders, shaking me awake. As we spoke, I saw my apartment for the first time in days. The dishes in the sink, the piles of laundry. I walked into the bathroom and saw my reflection in the mirror. I saw my self in my body again. I realized I'd mistaken coming undone for liberation. I had, I think, actually lost it. Lost myself. And you knew. You could tell something was wrong. You pried, but I was too embarrassed to tell you about the laptop. How absurd it would all seem. How could I even begin to explain it? You made me promise I would call you the next day. And I did.

A FEW NIGHTS LATER, Ana and our friend Nasra came over for dinner. Nasra was infinitely smarter than both of us and talked about an essay she'd just published in a prestigious art magazine about the late Belgian auteur Chantal Akerman's film *No Home Movie*. The film focused on a series of conversations Akerman documented between herself and her mother—a Holocaust survivor—just months before her mother's death. The conversations, documented in low-grade video reminiscent of a home movie, took place in the kitchen of her mother's Brussels apartment and over Skype while Akerman travelled the world as a peripatetic filmmaker. While often quotidian in nature, the conversations gradually coalesced into a moving portrait of a daughter's love for her mother and the anticipatory grief for her impending death. Akerman's oeuvre was profoundly shaped by her mother, perhaps most notably her 1977 experimental documentary *News from Home*, in which she read letters sent between her and her mother over lingering shots of New York City, and her 1975 masterpiece *Jeanne Dielman, 23 quai du Commerce, 1080 Bruxelles*, a portrait of the daily mundanities of a Brussels housewife. When *No Home Movie* premiered at the Locarno Film Festival, it was booed. Akerman committed suicide a couple of months later.

"Not because of the booing," Nasra clarified, circling the top of her beer bottle with her finger. "She didn't care about criticism. She just never got over her mother's death." In the end it seemed they were inseparable. Like two bodies with a single self.

I always used to cringe a little upon hearing stories of old men dying a week after their wives did. About people who could not live without their other half. Perhaps because

I knew I would never find a love like that. Or perhaps because those stories—always so special and yet ubiquitous!—seemed to possess a sentimentality that bordered on oppressive. They seemed to have an agenda to buttress a kind of heteronormative, Disney-esque vision of one love for life, love at first sight, love until death. And I suppose sometimes people possessed this kind of split-self, split-soul, if you will, with their homelands, especially if they were forcibly removed or compelled to flee from them. A country, a home, a mother, a love; these felt like noble and literary vessels for one-half of a person's selfhood.

But as I listened to Nasra describe Akerman's shared self with her mother, I felt my heart pang in recognition, a pang for the loss of my fucking laptop, and then a pang at how repulsive I was to be equating this woman's shared self with her mother to my shared self with a personal computing device and how clearly I had never known a true love and I never would and I was, most likely, a defective human being for it. And what kind of half-thing would I be if I never felt for you, or for any human being, the intensity of Chantal Akerman's love for her mother?

XI

WHEN I WAS ELEVEN, you picked me up from school one evening and told me we were going to visit an old friend of yours for dinner. We drove over the bridge into Quebec and for about an hour into the Gatineau Hills. As the last light slipped from the sky, we turned off at the exit for Wakefield, a town populated in the nineties by a smattering of back-to-the-land hippies and hobby painters that had, in the years since, suffered an onslaught of retired civil servants and latte-toting young professionals. We drove through the town and out the other side, back into forest, before turning off on an unpaved side road. As we approached what looked to be an old stone church, I could hear barking. A front light was switched on and two men appeared with a rickety white dog on the porch.

As we parked the car, one of the men, who wore what I'd later learn was a Kurdish knitted wool cap, raised his hands and called: "Marvellous Monica." I could hear his reedy voice through the car doors and over the barking. When we got out he walked over to you and gave you a long hug before turning to me and placing a hand on my shoulder. "Wow," he said. "Look at you. You probably don't remember me, but I'm Clyde."

"Hi."

"And I'm Wole," said the man next to him, his voice tinted with an accent I couldn't place. My heart jolted as the porch light revealed the milky film covering his left eye. "You're much older than the photographs I've seen," he chuckled.

"And this is Beatrice, by the way," Clyde said, bending down to pet the dog.

As Wole helped you fetch wine from the trunk, Clyde led me into the house as Beatrice trailed behind, leaving a maelstrom of fur in the air as she went. In the main sanctuary of the church was a kitchen and dining room with eighteen-foot ceilings braced with thick wooden beams. Clyde told me they had "bought the place for a song" several years ago. They had kept two of the old pews, which ran along either side of their dining-room table, itself an old wood door placed over two sawhorses. He mentioned they had recently built a chicken coop out back and kept about a dozen hens for eggs. I noticed he continued to wear his cap indoors and that its colours offset his rosacea.

As you and Wole entered, Beatrice resumed her barking in excitement and I remember being struck by its abrasive volume indoors, the fact that neither of your friends reprimanded her, and the immense look of irritation on your face. When she quieted down, I realized a Nina Simone record was playing and mushrooms were sautéing on the stove, which Wole had returned to tending. Over dinner

Wole told me about growing up in Lagos. He seemed like the quiet counterbalance to Clyde's performative excesses. That night was the first time I ever tried quinoa, the first time I had a sip of wine, the first time I met a gay couple or realized that you had gay friends and that neither you nor I seemed to be repelled by this.

You asked them if they ever got lonely out there in the country. Didn't they miss their friends? And Ted, without a hint of malice, replied: "Monica, our friends are dead."

This initially struck me as such a strange thing to say. They were both your age. Early fifties. You pursed your lips and nodded, as if in apology. I had the impression you realized your error even before Ted had finished replying. Then, in the lull that came after, I asked Wole and Clyde how they'd met.

"The Rare Book Library at the University of Toronto," Wole replied. "It's part of Robarts Library, that big, awful brutalist building, do you know it?" addressing the question to you.

"I actually find it kind of beautiful," you replied.

"I caught his eye between the stacks."

"And he started pursuing me relentlessly!" Clyde laughed. "I told him: we can date but I'm celibate."

"What's celibate?" I asked.

"It means not having sex," he replied.

"For how long?"

"Jord," you admonished.

"Fifteen years," Ted replied, taking a coy sip of his tea. "Can you believe it? Sometimes I wonder if I became a monk because of AIDS," he added with a wry grin. "I wasn't having sex because I was scared shitless." I'd never heard one of your friends swear before, and it felt thrilling for you not to react to it, as if I had now entered the fold of adulthood where swearing was commonplace. "I had just switched to Zen at that point and figured, well, if I'm not having sex I might as well join a monastery."

"Do you know what AIDS is?" you asked me.

I nodded, brow furrowed, as if I resented the question, even though I had only the vaguest of ideas.

"How long were you a monk?" I asked.

"Nine years," he said. "The both of us."

"Nine years," I said, as if it were a prison sentence.

"I don't regret it."

It sounded to me a little bit like he did. The monastery was outside of Perth, Ontario. From the way he described it, it sounded more like a family farm. He and Wole had been the monastery's chief cooks and grew all of the food in the back garden.

"I stopped choreographing," Clyde said to you, as if explaining his absence. "A few friends visited from time to time. Mostly former dancers from my company."

"You must've missed it," you said.

"Dance?" He shrugged. "Maybe a little. Not the art world though."

While you and Clyde caught up, Wole spent the rest of the dinner telling me about Clyde's former life as a choreographer. "His work made everything that had come before it, particularly in English Canada, seem like dusty museum relics. The critics called him an *enfant terrible*. And then the National Ballet commissioned a new piece from him. This was during the height of the epidemic. All of our friends were dying and he wanted to respond to it, especially because classical ballet was basically ignoring the crisis while losing scores of its dancers to it. So Clyde started choreographing a piece to a Steve Reich composition called *Music for 18 Musicians*. Here." He got up from the table, plucked the needle off the Cuban jazz that had been playing, and put on Reich's album.

"Oh god, why are we listening to this?" Clyde groaned from across the table, where he'd been immersed in conversation with you, pretending not to be listening to Wole extol his virtues.

Wole turned up the volume and closed his eyes as if channelling the marimbas, violins, sopranos, piano, all pulsing like the subatomic strings that knit together the universe.

"It's all variations on a theme," Clyde said to me.

I waited for him to elaborate but he didn't. I wondered if it was supposed to be self-evident. I'd only heard the word "theme" in relation to parties. Wole continued to stand by the record player, eyes closed. Clyde had his hand balled against his mouth in concentration. I glanced over at you, perhaps wondering how long we were going to sit there around the table in silence. You had that distant look on your face when you were both in the room and somewhere else, both listening and lost in thought. A sort of wistful appreciation of life's benevolence.

I looked out the patio-door windows into the yard, the perimeter of which was traced by the outdoor light. A snow had begun to fall without our noticing. Somewhere beyond the edges of the yard, where the darkness began, was the forest, filled with its own silences. All forests a variation on the theme of silence and darkness, all silence a variation on the theme of noise, all darkness a variation on the theme of light. I watched the snow passing through the light become movement. And then, as if I were suddenly able to read a foreign language, as if I were seeing the words emerge from the indecipherable page, the pattern of the eighteen instruments and voices emerged.

I wondered if maybe beauty was God, and could I devote my life to the search for it? Was I gay? Did you already know? I realized, as if for the first time, that one day I would die. I thought about how AIDS was like the darkness of the forest that lay beyond the perimeter of yard-light that was my life. The darkness that I could not describe and did not know but that framed and gave definition to my existence. I looked over at Clyde and Wole lost in their respective reveries, and thought of them as the men who had emerged from the forest. They knew what lay in that darkness, both wonderful and terrible.

"At any rate," Wole said after several minutes, "one day the artistic director sat in on rehearsals and totally freaked out."

Clyde burst into his wheezing laugh. "You're not telling him that story," he said, of course knowing all along that Wole had been telling that story, though in truth I had forgotten.

"The artistic director tried to pull the plug on the show," Wole continued, "but Clyde threatened to sue him over breach of contract."

Clyde glanced over at you and bounced his eyebrows, to which you smiled. I assumed you already knew the story.

"What was it about?" I asked.

"About?" Clyde replied. "It was—" He looked over at Wole as if making sure he was getting it right, as if he hadn't been asked that specific question in a long time. "A friend of ours, when he was dying, he held my hand. And right before he passed he smiled and said, 'It's not the worst thing, really, to be a body.' And I remember thinking what a strange and beautiful way of putting it. And the dancers onstage — I tried to make them just bodies, in a sense, limbs and torsos, sometimes very sexual but also sometimes like corpses." He thought about this for a moment and then, as if satisfied with his answer, met my gaze and smiled.

"Anyway," Wole continued, "there was this big back-and-forth and eventually it was decided that Clyde would choreograph a new production of *Giselle* instead of his Reich piece, which was quietly dropped from the season. Well"— Wole grinned and sat back down at the table — "on the opening night of *Giselle,* at the top of the first act, the dancer playing Duke Albrecht entered with a giant purple dildo up his ass." You laughed and I was too surprised by your laughter to register any reaction myself. "The audience gasped and some of them, yes, burst out laughing," Wole said, gesturing to you and chuckling himself. "A few old ladies stood up and walked out. And then the dancer playing Hilarion entered wearing fetish bondage gear. The show ended with Giselle blowing a French horn into her vagina. None of which had been vetted by the powers that be. A reviewer the next day called it 'the most extraordinary act of artistic terrorism in the history of Canadian dance.'"

Here Clyde jumped in to nab the punchline, explaining how the artistic director threatened to sue him and cancel the rest of the run, but when tickets started selling out the next morning, not only did those threats come to nothing, the artistic director allowed the show to be performed exactly as it had been on opening night.

As everyone laughed, it occurred to me that Clyde was in some way a kind of extreme version of the two of us—your spirituality and some still-dormant and unknown aspect of myself. Both aspects, I'd later learn, were in perpetual conflict within him.

THAT SPRING I made my stage debut as Gollum. You came to opening night but Clyde and Wole managed all three nights of the run, even taking me out once afterwards to their "favourite gay trattoria" downtown where they bought me a flute of champagne to celebrate. They were thrilled to have a little budding theatre fag in their midst—not that they would have ever called me that to my face, of course. They started taking me out to see shows with them at the Ottawa Fringe Festival, dance recitals of former colleagues of Clyde's, even the odd ballet at the National Arts Centre, though I always got the sense the latter was a bit out of their price range. Wole once asked me if you might be willing to go halves on my ticket with them. On another occasion, Clyde mentioned offhandedly that he used to get free tickets from time to time, but "not since the new administration."

The next year, when it was announced the school play would be *The Enchantment of Beauty and the Beast*, they encouraged me to try out for both of the titular roles. I even met with Clyde after school at a Starbucks downtown where he coached me through my audition song, which I sang for him *sotto voce* in the hallway leading to the washrooms. When I found out I had landed the role of the Beast, I called him from the school's lobby pay phone. Ana was palpably crushed not to have been cast as Beauty but later threw herself so completely into her portrayal of the Clock as to upstage everyone. The production turned out to be a seventies-styled adaptation in which I wore Gene Simmons–style KISS makeup and stuck out my tongue a lot. The next year I landed the role of Oberon, opposite Ana's Titania, in a more traditional rendering of *A Midsummer Night's Dream*. By the third and final night of playing the king of the faeries, I had more or less decided I would be coming out in high school the first chance I got.

Clyde once joked he was my "gateway drug" to a life in the arts, to which you offered up a pained smile. Did it ever occur to him that he was everything you never wanted me to become? A poor gay artist with unrealized ambitions? And if so, was he wounded by this? You would never have admitted this aloud, but I know a part of you saw Art as being linked to some inexorable corruption of the Self. Not that you would have ever used the word corruption. Or perversion. Or deviation.

LAST SUMMER, after Wole died, Clyde paid for my ticket to visit him in Rome. He was renting a small apartment for two months to get away from their old house. You, sacrificing the ability to wear black for a month, offered to look after Beatrice. Clyde's apartment was in Trastevere; it overlooked a bustling street of restaurants on one side and a small cobblestoned courtyard filled with mopeds on the other. There were eight apartments facing onto the courtyard that kept their shutters open throughout the day "and even into the night," Clyde said, "when I swear to God literally everyone walks around naked."

Over the years our relationship had grown into a profound if unlikely one; despite the thirty-five years between
us, Clyde was, by then, my closest confidant. He said he
was in Rome to learn Italian and have "a whore's tour of the
city." He had long given up celibacy and had had an open
relationship with Wole for their last decade or so together.
And fucking was as good a balm for a grieving heart as any
I could think of. He enjoyed showing me guys he was talking to on Scruff and Grindr, and I told him I suspected he
got laid about five times as often as I did. The August nights
were sweltering and we slept with the windows open, he in
a little loft bed above the kitchenette and me on the couch.
I drifted off to the sounds of revellers in the street and woke
to the sounds of men erecting morning market stalls, shouting at one another and assembling mounds of fresh fruit,
fish, bread, cheese, and candied nuts for display.

On my third night Clyde invited over an old friend
of his, Giacomo. They were both members of the Toronto
Contemporary Dance ensemble before moving to London
together in the late eighties to dance with Michael Clark's
company. Giacomo had moved back to Italy in the mid-
nineties and worked for various advertising agencies since.
I helped Clyde cook a truffle pasta with mussels in the
tiny kitchenette while blasting Bronski Beat and getting hammered on table wine before Giacomo had even
arrived—which ended up being forty-five minutes later
than expected, "punctual by Italian standards." From the
moment he walked in the door I barely stopped laughing,
and by ten o'clock my abs were sore. Besides his wicked,
dry wit, Giacomo was a true polymath and offered up facts
as if refilling your glass.

Sometime around midnight the conversation turned to their days at Toronto Contemporary Dance. After a madcap back-and-forth about who was fucking who and a particularly juicy tale about Giacomo seducing the ever-implacable Doug, who was dating the prima ballerina of the National Ballet at the time, the two of them fell silent.

"We're the only two left, you know," Clyde said. "Can you believe that?"

Giacomo nodded and took a sip of wine. "Rene."

"Doug. Tom."

"Jack."

"Jean-Paul."

"Tom."

"I said Tom already."

"Who are we forgetting?"

"Bill Plait."

"Bill, yes."

"That's seven."

"No, there's one more."

"Randy."

"Randy."

They nodded for a moment, and then without anyone signalling it we raised our glasses and clinked them. The sound of our toast in the small apartment startled me with its clarity and volume.

"And here's to Wole," Giacomo said.

Something inside Clyde seemed to silently buckle. He closed his eyes and continued to nod. We drank to the men they had lost. Clyde sighed and opened his eyes. Giacomo and I looked at him for a long moment as he stewed on a thought.

"One comes to the gradual realization that one has been living with someone for years through inanimate objects. Finding the soap on the opposite side of the sink than where you last left it. Or a mug mysteriously perched on a bookshelf. Or perhaps you'll look at the bookshelf and notice that the arrangement of the books has changed, ever so subtly." Clyde looked down into his glass. "It wasn't until objects stayed in the same place day after day that I noticed." For a moment it looked as if he was going to say something further. We watched him hold the thought for a few seconds and then place it to the side. He looked up at us and smiled.

As I refilled their glasses, I asked them about their time in London and about dancing with Michael Clark, whose name I said I recognized but really knew nothing about.

"Honey, you don't know *Michael Clark*?" gasped Giacomo. "*Quelle horreur*! We must fix this at once." He then swivelled to Ted and asked, "*Hail the New Puritan*?"

"What about it?"

"Should we watch it?"

Clyde grabbed his laptop and googled Charles Atlas's 1987 fictionalized documentary about a supposed day in the life of Clark, his company of dancers, and his friends.

"Get ready to see us as babieeeees," Giacomo squealed.

As the film loaded, to give me a bit of context, Clyde explained that Clark was an iconoclast of the eighties British dance world who mashed together ballet traditions with punk and gay subculture. The film was largely set at an old warehouse-turned-dance-studio in east London, called Chisenhale, and began with Clark waking up in the studio as if he lived there full time. In one corner of a large loft-like room with wooden floors and factory windows was Clark's "bedroom"—a queen-sized bed, a clothing rack, piles of records and magazines, and a large poster of Elvis on the wall. Clark was something of a poster boy himself, a delectable imp with a bleached-blond mohawk, button chin, pouting lips, and a boyish face. He wore a sleeveless white T-shirt emblazoned with the words *Beat Me, Bite Me, Whip Me, Fuck Me*. He rolled out of bed and of course began to dance, moving about the space with grace and abandon. Gradually, other members of the company arrived until they were in a full-fledged warmup-cum-dance sequence.

"Oh my god, it's you!" I shouted as young Giacomo, a skinny little fox with a shaved head and a metal safety pin through his left ear, entered the frame.

"Can you believe it?" he murmured, shaking his head and taking a sip of wine. "Makes me want to cry."

"Come on, you weren't that beautiful. Look at me!" shouted Clyde, bursting into his wheeze as he appeared onscreen. Young Clyde looked pretty much exactly like Old Clyde, except lithe and with better skin.

About ten minutes into the film a reporter dropped by to interview Clark as the other dancers lounged about, flirting and smoking. The company seemed to live by the axiom "working hard and hardly working." Clark answered the reporter's questions with nods, demure smiles, and shrugs—the recalcitrance of indulgent, bad-boy celebrity.

Clark's dance pieces were filled with unabashed bravado and perversity. With their screeching punk vocals, spastic movement, and bare asses pointed towards the audience, they were resounding "fuck yous" to Margaret Thatcher, the calcified world of classical ballet, and the British bourgeoisie. But most memorable of all were the outrageous costumes and makeup—genderqueer marching band uniforms with drooping fabric breasts, police-style caps, platform heels, ass-less leotards, deconstructed clown makeup, red polka dot body paint, and all variety of wigs—designed by the then-reigning queen of the London underground, Leigh Bowery.

Midway through the film, Clark, in a leather jacket and kilt, paid a visit to Bowery in his otherworldly, bejewelled apartment. Bowery was painted entirely blue, like the genie in *Aladdin,* and sported long white nails, a blue cape-dress, and an enormous jewel-encrusted black hat. He and his friends Trojan and Rachel were getting dolled up for a night at the clubs. And what a fucking night it was. The film's club scene was an almost transcendent moment of release, bodies giving over to the libidinal pulse of techno, a new sound for a new age, a seething room of freaks and outsiders making space in a world with none for them, pushing against all previous parameters of sex, aesthetic, youth, and meaning, all reaching for the limitless.

There were a few montage sequences of Clark and his friends—punks smoking fags in trench coats—traipsing through the dystopian streets of London's Mile End, a sober reminder that England in the 1980s was an unbearable shithole ravaged by class and race warfare in the midst of full-fledged post-industrial collapse. One got the sense that violence lurked down every alley, around every corner; a sideways stare, a homophobic jeer, or maybe a full-on brawl with a bunch of blokes and a broken beer bottle. But watching the film, sandwiched between Clyde and Giacomo, my heart felt like it would burst from an inexplicable longing. I was nostalgic for a time and a place in which I'd never lived—which I think in some sense was Atlas's intention. The film seemed designed to seduce with its bohemian badass glamour, that was, itself, something of a fantasy. It was a temporal world of youth, rebellion, and fabulousness that, in the very moment of its documentation, was already beginning to fade away. It was that palpable sense of the ephemeral, the fleeting, that made it so exquisite and aching to watch.

From a comfortable distance I could imagine the life-and-death stakes of that era heightening everything: the pleasure, the politics, the passion of every night out. To live with the charge that this year or this month might be your last. Of course it was an absolute flaunting of privilege to long for an age in which I would have been infinitely more marginalized than I was now. To feel nostalgia for experiences I never had. To glamorize struggle. To look back to the recent past, the just-before-my-time past as a kind of golden age. And was this not the same nostalgia evoked by demagogues when they talked about making a nation "great again" and returning it to some beatific bygone era? A longing to return to a time just before their own and a kind of life that they never—and perhaps no one, really—had actually lived.

We kissed Giacomo goodnight just after three and then finished the last of the Campari before Clyde started to cry. He talked about Wole. And Beatrice. And the eight cardboard boxes of photos, dance scores, props, reviews, and posters that constituted his personal archives, archives that York University had recently asked him to donate but which he had decided to burn in his backyard in a gesture of Buddhist temporality. A final performance for an audience of one. And then, via some segue I missed, he began talking about the two years he had spent living with you and Lydia in Toronto, "back in the days when I still fancied myself bisexual," he said, heaving into his asthmatic laugh.

"Sorry, when was this?"

"Oh, after your mom left Gary that fuck-wit carpenter or whatever he was, I mean…" He shook his head, slinging back the last of his drink and grimacing. He rubbed his face. And then smiled. "Lydia and your mom and me — we used to dress up and go to the opera together," he laughed. "Plays. The ballet. You name it."

"Mom did?" How was that the first time I was hearing about this?

"Yes — god, we were always going out. And the parties we threw at that little place. It was the late eighties, so needless to say they were pretty wild. We did it all."

This was blowing my mind. I didn't want to entertain the thought of you doing "it all," though thankfully I didn't seem capable of even unconsciously doing so. What was "needless to say" about the late eighties? Exactly how wild were we talking here? Like, were these the last vestiges of pre-AIDS gaydom with its tiny jean shorts, coke, and Quaaludes? Or a few joints and a Smiths record playing? I'd seen old photos of you from that time, and you had certainly rocked some indelible outfits. That leather jacket. Those giant belts. The librarian glasses. Still, every party scene that flitted through my head had a negative space in the shape of you at its centre. I couldn't insert you into even the tamest of scenarios.

But more importantly, why had I never known that the three of you had all lived together? And for two whole years? How had it never come up? Why had none of you ever mentioned it?

Something flickered across Clyde's face. Perhaps a realization that he'd said too much. He rose, crossed the studio apartment, and poured himself a glass of water, which he gulped down in a go. He refilled the glass and began sipping from it as he leaned against the counter, which was now hidden below the remains of our frenzied dinner prep.

I studied his face. And then, through the blur of wine and Campari, I saw it: The long nose. The divot in the chin. The protruding ears.

How had I never seen it before? Had it been hiding in plain sight all these years? There was something about Clyde's age, his weight, his flamboyance that seemed to obscure what suddenly appeared so obvious. In fact, it had been the video, yes, it had been seeing Clyde at my age in the video, a young dancer full of swagger, that allowed me to see my face in his now, a man slumping towards seniority as gracefully as tragedy would permit. And how fitting, how perfect that my genes should be queer from birth, *before* birth, inducted into a long lineage of fags dating back in an unbroken line to palaeolithic times, the caves of Lascaux, Cro-Magnon, *Homo erectus*, to the apes in trees plucking ticks off each other's backs. As I stared at him, I wondered if the two of you had agreed upon it all in advance. A turkey-baster scenario once you hit thirty-five? *It's always good to have a Plan B.*

He turned to me and met my gaze. Had he registered my realization? What could I even say next? How did one ask the question? Would he speak first? Or was he waiting for me to? Had he, in fact, been waiting all of these years for me to speak first? To discover this on my own so he would never have to be the one to break the news, break the confidence?

I could feel it welling up inside me, building, quaking, the question, rupturing, until it was down my shirt and on the floor in front of me.

He groaned, crossed the room towards me, and pulled my shirt up over my head. And I let him, like a child. Let my arms drift up with my sleeves, pop out, and flop down at my sides. He led me to the couch and lay me down before returning with a damp dishcloth to wipe my face. He sat down on the edge of the couch, staring out into the apartment. A moped whined its way past the open window in the street below.

"Are you my dad?" I murmured.

He turned to me with a look of bemusement, his eyes glazed with drunkenness. "What?" I wasn't going to repeat the question. It had taken everything in me to ask it. "Did you just ask me that?" I stared at him in a manner that suggested, *Yes I just asked you that so please stop pretending you didn't fucking hear me.*

He pulled his head back in mild horror. "Jordan, how couldyouevenaskmethat?" he slurred. He shook his head in disbelief. "No. God."

He looked troubled, and then rubbed my head as if I had just woken from a nightmare. I was struck by his effusiveness bordering on scorn. But no, of course he wasn't my father, obviously, and I suddenly felt astonished with myself for even asking. I had seen something in his face that wasn't there, or rather I had willed something into being with the help of a few drinks. We would laugh about it in the morning. Would he tease me about it? My babblings? I was too tired to be embarrassed. Likely he wouldn't even remember. The night already seemed like a blur. I closed my eyes. I heard him get up, fill a glass with water, and place it on the floor beside my head. And I was already asleep by the time he climbed into his loft bed and turned off the light.

THE NEXT MORNING Clyde and I dashed through the pouring rain to Santa Maria della Vittoria to see Bernini's sculpture of Teresa of Ávila. We wandered into the chapel, soaked through, to discover we were the only visitors. The sculpture was high up in its own niche by the altar and obscured in shadow.

"Why's it so dark?" I wondered.

Clyde pointed to a small metal slot and a laminated sign that said 0.50 *Euro*. I fished out a coin, placed it in the slot, and a yellow light bulb clicked on at the top of the niche, bathing Teresa of Ávila in divine, incandescent light.

"There she is," he chuckled.

We took a few steps back to get a proper view. My eyes first landed on the puckish angel holding the arrow and sporting a smug smile that seemed to say, *That's what you wanted; well, that's what you get*. And then they fell on Teresa, though it was hard to know at first what constituted "Teresa." She looked like a crumpled piece of paper, her body completely subsumed into marble folds of fabric, merging into the cloud she was held on. As if her body were in the midst of some ecstatic sublimation, caught in the delirious abjection between subject and object, body and vapour. Merging with the inanimate. Hand and the water glass. Rolling in the bedsheets. Yes, I thought. I had touched that state for the briefest of moments. Could I enter it? Embody it? Give myself over to it like Teresa? After our allotted minute, the light flicked off and a maintenance worker struck up a vacuum at the far end of the church.

WE ENDED UP hanging out with Giacomo quite a bit that week. It always amazed me the long lunch breaks he seemed at liberty to take, joining us for meandering flans in the middle of the workday, not to mention his ability to stay out drinking with us until last call. On one such night the three of us stumbled across the grand promenade leading to the Vatican, turned down a narrow side street, and descended a long flight of stairs into a gay bathhouse called Europa. After showering and wrapping white towels around ourselves we began exploring the dungeon-like maze. It was packed with men of all shapes, ages, and races, like some lost temple cult of the masculine. So as not to get lost the three of us had to keep close, shouting over the throbbing techno to hear one another.

"So this building?" Giacomo called to Clyde and I. "The Vatican owns it."

"The Vatican *owns* Europa?" I shouted back.

"They don't run the sauna, they're just the landlords. They own lots of buildings in the city." We walked a few more paces before he turned back with a grin: "The seminary students love it."

Somehow, in that moment, it didn't even strike me as particularly absurd that the Church should be the landlords of a massive gay sauna. There seemed to be no contradiction or hypocrisy the faith couldn't hold. In fact, as I walked along the corridors bathed in red light, it felt utterly inevitable that I should be brushing shoulders with young seminarians and senior members of the curia with their pot-bellies and knobby dicks, all sons of someone, navigating their own journeys through God's garden of earthly delights, all no doubt familiar with Dante and his Inferno and the tortures their faith suggested awaited them, and yet still submitting themselves to the labyrinth, perhaps rationalizing to themselves that all matters of the flesh were between them and their Creator and there was nothing, not even a furtive glory-hole blow job, that a few Hail Marys couldn't cleanse them of. And what the prayers didn't wash away, the shower stalls and steam rooms surely would.

I stroked my hard-on through my towel as we watched men in leather slings getting fisted, gang-banged, moaning and grunting, begging to be nameless whores, bodies without people, without pasts or futures, just receptacles for cocks, just a couple of holes to be passed around and filled with cum. *Is the rectum a grave?* literary theorist Leo Bersani once asked. I watched as Clyde positioned himself in wooden stocks and let man after man fuck him, like a stamen being swarmed by bees, until a stranger threaded his fingers through mine and led me into a black vinyl-clad booth.

Is sex not just a rehearsal for death? The pleasurable role-play of becoming-body? During sex I want to override my person until I'm all sensation, all abandon, until I am my body to the fullest extent possible but also transcending my body by becoming another's, a hybrid body, and even pushing towards a pleasure that exceeds all physical containers and extends into nothingness, total erasure, fusing my mortality with another's mortality, their death with my own until we reach orgasm, *petite mort,* the temporary weakening or loss of consciousness that prefigures our deaths, the total expenditure of our life force, a moment in which we transcend our forms, pushing through *the border of my condition as a living being* to touch the nothingness beyond.

The young Italian I was with offered to smoke me up. He was already pretty tweaked himself. He put the pipe to my lips and held the lighter below it. I inhaled once, twice...In high school I kept a shoebox of newspaper articles, a combination of clippings about the school plays I was in and historic events like the capture of Saddam Hussein, the London bombing, Hurricane Katrina. When I rediscovered the box years later, I found, on the top of the pile, an article about a community production of *Waiting for Godot* I was in the summer before grade twelve. I turned the clipping over and began reading a partially cut-off article about a suicide attack in Lower Dir, Pakistan. Colonel Nadeem Mirza, Pakistani military operation commander for the region, told the interviewer: "Five of them detonated the explosives strapped to their bodies; however, one was missing till we discovered him hiding in the bushes. He was scared of killing himself because the effect of the drug had ended." The drug Mirza was referring to was Pervitin, a chemical derivative of methamphetamine, otherwise commonly known as meth. Meth, he explained, induced paranoid psychosis, which amounted to a loss of contact with reality. A psychological severing of self from body. "Children who are trained as suicide bombers are injected with drugs to create an elated sense of the self," Mirza said. "Once the effect of the drug wears off, the bomber is incapable of detonating himself."

During the Second World War, the Nazi leadership prescribed Pervitin to the Wehrmacht's "animated machines" to eliminate exhaustion and inhibition. German paratroopers caught behind British lines were described as "fearless and berserk," marching into active gunfire seemingly without fear. Japanese kamikaze pilots were also plied with methamphetamines to enable their death-plummets into American warships. Just as a powder known as "brown-brown," made of cocaine mixed with smokeless gunpowder, was given to child soldiers to induce depersonalized fearlessness in the Liberian and Sierra Leonean civil wars. As the Italian fucked me I thought, *Yes, of course*, it was somehow appropriate the drugs being used by teenage suicide bombers to obliterate themselves in Lower Dir were the same ones being used by men to obliterate themselves in gay saunas half a world away. Perhaps the same erasure of self was required to enact extreme violence and extreme sex acts on one's body and the bodies of others. The same unfixing of body from self that facilitated the transformation of one's body into a thing, whether a lethal weapon or a receptacle for cum. The dissociation which enabled us to take twenty cocks or detonate a belt of explosives strapped around our torsos.

And it's of course considered obscene, to transcend our bodies—whether through sex, drugs, or a suicide belt. For the self to consciously cleave itself apart from the body. There's a horror in having agency in this act. It destabilizes that which is thought to be fixed: that only God or the universe or fate can unfix these two parts of our being. That sacred union. Our body, the temple. And in that moment I understood "sacred" as belonging to a language of limits, a word which demarcated boundaries we were not prepared to cross for fear of destabilizing the accepted order, for fear of realizing how far our bodies could actually stretch, transform, how much pleasure they could hold, how extreme they could be made, how fluid and porous they really were, because to realize those potentials might have meant remaking all the containers—physical, social, political—that held the world in place.

The next thing I knew I was walking with Clyde and Giacomo back along the wide banks of the raging Tiber, the sun just beginning to rise, my body still buzzing, coming down, I was talking, I could hear myself talking, but what was I saying, something about finding pleasure in death, how all taboos fell somewhere on the pleasure-death spectrum, and how this spectrum ranged from the socially permissible to the socially abhorrent, from horror films to necrophilia.

Giacomo and Clyde were laughing but listening, letting me ramble on and clearly getting a kick out of it. Giacomo replied that he once had a lover who fetishized being infected by HIV. This man had shown him whole porn sites dedicated to it.

"He described it as a kind of supreme intimacy," he said, "allowing another man to forever alter you, on a molecular level. The fuck that would change your life. Like impregnation. I realize most people would find this abhorrent. I did at first, I admit," he said, anticipating Clyde's interjection. "And yet I thought, isn't the eroticism that drives someone to fetishize HIV infection the same eroticism that teenage girls have for vampires or werewolves? You know?" Clyde started to laugh. "But I'm serious," he continued. "Like the submission to an ultimate intimacy, to allow another to possess and forever alter your body, a genetic knitting together of fates. I mean, look at the success of *Twilight*! It's the libidinal death drive of adolescent girls writ large! And I suppose because vampires and werewolves are fictional it's more permissible, right? It comes in below the socially acceptable cut-off on your spectrum," he said, nodding at me. "Whereas I'd reckon the fetishism of HIV transmission places we-heeell above."

When we reached the Ponte Garibaldi, with its white stone and distinctive circle over the central arch, Giacomo hugged us both goodnight and began crossing the bridge in the direction of his apartment.

After a few paces he turned back and shouted, "Don't keep partying on without me now."

"Love you, friend," Clyde called in reply.

"Love you too, old man," Giacomo said, before turning back around and disappearing into the half-light.

As Clyde and I walked on towards Trastevere, the night was an impressionist canvas, blotches of distant couples dashing across the street, the rushing river, the fuzzed auras of street lights. I studied the interplay of colour on the wet cobblestone—Had it rained while we were in the club? Had a street sweeper just passed by?—before I noticed Clyde and I had been walking for the better part of five minutes in silence. As if sensing my coming-to, he said that, before passing, Wole had spent several years working on a research paper, but never finished it. Between Wole's teaching commitments and his medical treatments he'd always found it hard to find time for his own research. His paper was focused on a cache of ceramics from eighth-century Peru. Three of the vessels in the cache depicted acts of necrophilia and the masturbation of male skeletons by living women.

"And the images are—genuinely erotic," Clyde said, with a chuckle, before mentioning sex with the dead was also explicitly permitted by Hittite law from the sixteenth to thirteenth centuries BCE.

We crossed through the square in front of Santa Maria in Trastevere, with its palimpsest of architectural styles, as night owls stumbled home arm in arm and two teenagers launched little LED helicopter toys into the air, where they hovered like bionic fireflies before miraculously returning to the teens' expectant hands. We turned down our street and, as we arrived at the apartment, Clyde began fishing for the keys in his pocket while telling me how cultures around the world, throughout time, had cannibalized their dead in grieving rituals, believing that they were returning the dead's life force to the living. Transferring the dead's essence to the bodies of their descendants. "So if 'sacred' belongs to a language of limits, as you were saying…they're at least as fluid and changeable as the moods of the era."

He let this gentle rebuke of my theory linger in the air as he continued to search for the keys. I nodded, taking it in, and doing my best to keep my eyes open. Just then, a look came across his face as if he was fishing for something in the pocket of his mind.

"I've never told anyone but—" He found the keys and held them in his hand moment as if considering them. "A few nights after Wole's funeral, I was looking at his ashes in the urn. They were just sitting on the table. And I…I licked my finger and stuck it in the urn. And when I pulled it away, Wole was on my skin. Like this thin film of graphite. I looked at him on my finger for a moment and then… I stuck it in my mouth." He cleared his throat, stuck the key in the door, and looked up at me. "It just felt like the thing I had to do."

THE NEXT MORNING, Clyde and I visited the Sistine Chapel. Clyde had already seen it twice before, but he knew I couldn't visit Rome without going, so he humoured me, even though crowds made him anxious. We found ourselves being herded in amidst two tour groups, one from Korea and the other from the States. The room roared with the sound of hundreds of hushed voices and the occasional "no photo" shouted by one of the guards with Sisyphean dispassion. As we entered the chapel, I could tell by the direction of the crowd's eyes that the door we were walking through was against the wall featuring the fresco of Michelangelo's *The Last Judgement*. It was a bit like walking out onto a rock-concert stage and seeing a sea of fans before you. We pushed into the crowd a few layers deep before turning around to behold the masterpiece.

As I stood there I found there were two figures in *The Last Judgement* I couldn't stop staring at. The first one was not so much a figure as a thing — a kind of grey, hollowed-out husk of a man's body held in the hands of a robust, near-naked saint. Clyde informed me, whispering into my ear, that the man holding the husk was Saint Bartholomew, who had been martyred by having his skin flayed from his body, and that the shell of the man he held was himself. His own flayed skin. The container that once held his life. Clyde proceeded to tell me that Michelangelo had painted the living Saint Bartholomew (completely ripped, like all the other muscle daddies in the afterlife) with the face of Pietro Aretino, the poet who publicly derided the painting as indecent during its creation. Michelangelo then gave the grey husk his own face, a self-portrait of his tortured soul. Self-portrait as sheath.

The second figure that captivated me was a bald man clutching his head on Charon's boat as he was ferried into the underworld. I stared at him for several minutes until I realized he was the only figure in the entire fresco — at eye-level, at least — who was looking out at the viewer. He appeared to be gripped by sheer terror, but also something more, something verging on existential disbelief. Perhaps at the horrors of the world itself. How could the world be this cruel? How could existence be this excruciating? And it felt as if he was looking right at me, through the painting, through time, seeking an answer.

I realized that as I had moved through the Vatican that day, looking at the historical paintings of large group scenes, I had been unconsciously trying to find the men and women who were staring out from the canvas towards the viewer. Those figures struck me as feeling not of the world they found themselves in. They seemed to be looking outward into the future, perhaps to the future I was presently standing in. Perhaps they were the feminists, queers, and dreamers of time gone by. Imploring the future-viewer to *get me the fuck out of here*. And as I stood in the Sistine Chapel looking at that poor bald faggot clutching his head on Charon's boat, I wanted to tell him to remain steadfast in the hope that the march of time — despite crushing setbacks along the way — had been an incremental one towards progress.

XII

YOU AND I stood on the beach in front of the cottage at night looking into a sky Jackson Pollocked with stars. It was far enough from the city that I could see every one, even the ones that no longer existed, that had already exploded but were so far away they hadn't yet conveyed that fact to Earth. I must have been six or seven. I was in my underwear for some reason, probably because it was bedtime. You held a flashlight, its beam barely reaching the water's edge, let alone the moon, as I always hoped it might. You told me the Milky Way was the view of our galaxy from its edges, from one of its outlying arms. The suburbs of the galaxy. You said that, for you, the majesty of the cosmos was proof of a divine hand. That the night sky was pure mathematical elegance and that it was little wonder Einstein died a Christian. I remained quiet because I wasn't sure what, if anything, the stars were proof of for me.

As we walked back towards the cottage, your flashlight an alien tractor-beam through the reeds, you told me scientists thought most grains of sand on earth had gone through the life cycle of being mountains, then boulders, then sand at least six times. As we walked, I thought about what this said about the age of things and my place among it all. Six times. Six eternities as a beach or a bit of dust blown off the baked desert, then compressed, heated, reforged, and erupted back into a mountain range to begin life again as a cliff, an avalanche, a boulder field, a pebble in a shoe, a grain of sand in a swimmer's eye.

And as I was lost in this cyclical reverie I stepped and slid on something organic, pulpy. My foot shot up and I yelped, startled and disgusted before I could even register what it was. Your flashlight glanced down and in its gaze glistened back a dead fish, more bone than flesh, more hollow cavity than carcass. What was left of its gills was sloughed off its spine, pulled apart by my foot sliding through it.

"A fish husk," you said.

"A what?"

"Husk."

The word struck me as so peculiar and terrible. Why hadn't you just said, "Dead fish"? But in retrospect the word was perfect. "Dead fish" would have suggested it was still more "fish" than traces thereof. The thing I stepped in was what remained of the shape of a fish, the casing. More than skeleton, but less than corpse. I had only heard the word applied to corn — "We need a plate for the husks," Grandpa Lou would mumble to Dora across the table, flecks of corn-casings around his puckered mouth, glazed with butter, and she would rise and retrieve a plate from the kitchen cupboard and place it in the middle of the table all of us sat around, a sheen of sweat on our bodies from the mid-August heat, and we'd place the husks of our corn cobs on it like lumber-jacks piling logs. A fish emptied of fish, a cob emptied of corn. The word made me think of the brittle and translucent second-selves bugs left behind on windowsills and under beds after moulting. I could feel my left foot sliding on the fish remains for hours after, even after I had scrubbed my feet twice that night in the small plastic basin of water on the porch, and then a third time in the morning, and still I felt the fish husk against it, its spine, the small tines of its ribs, the tickle of its fins.

Standing here looking at your body, I see the dead fish again, I feel the husk slip apart below the sole of my foot, I want to scream husk fucking *husk* as if it were the most brutal world, worse than any swear, any curse. I think of that fish emptied of its self, like a candy wrapper, its thingness. I think of Artaud declaring in *To Have Done With the Judgement of God*: "When you have made him a body without organs, then you will have delivered him from all his automatic reactions and restored him to his true freedom."

Is there freedom in being a thing? A godless thing without a soul, no different than a bit of plastic cling-wrap? *Think of it as freedom*, I want to tell you.

Think of it as freedom.

XIII

MY FLIGHT HOME from Rome landed just after ten, but because of transit delays I didn't arrive downtown until quarter to midnight. I felt a profound and shapeless sadness, a sadness whose origins and boundaries felt ill-defined, perhaps because my own origins and boundaries felt ill-defined. As I walked through Kensington Market, duffle bag in hand, I could tell something was amiss at Videofag from two blocks away. There was a cop car parked outside and a crowd of people milling about taking photos on their phones.

I pushed my way through to find Will at the front door, his face drawn. "We're being raided."

Two cops had shown up at the opening reception of a new exhibition, unplugged the speakers, and were in the process of fining us for selling beer out of our kitchen fridge without a license. They confiscated all eight cases of it. What the hell did they do with all that beer? The fine was hefty. We posted a photograph of it on Facebook and people offered to start a fundraising campaign. The challenge was we would never actually qualify for a liquor license as there weren't enough washrooms and fire exits and we just didn't have the energy to get raided again, which was only a matter of time now that we were on their watch-list. And the next infraction would shut us down for good.

But there was a larger problem at hand.

Will and I were more or less broken up by that point and sleeping with different people. We'd never had any kind of terminating fight or even a conversation about it, though, and continued to share a bed. We even continued to shower together in the mornings, as there wasn't enough hot water for each of us to have our own; a formerly intimate and sexy ritual had been reduced to a purely functional choreography. Half of what had kept Videofag electric was the current of desire that had been arcing between him and me and that had more or less burnt out. He'd started spending time with a guy named Juan after inadvertently locking his bike to Juan's outside a coffee shop, offering to buy him a coffee as an apology, somehow exchanging numbers, and fucking him that same night. Before long I found myself sleeping on the couch and waking up to Juan and Will making breakfast in their underwear in the morning.

So I started crashing at Ana's. Over the years she had transformed her apartment into a kind of Bedouin tent of scarves, candles, cushions, quilts, tin lanterns, thrift-store oddities, folk art, costume racks, and various musical instruments she couldn't really play. In the mornings, we'd lie in her bed talking as the sunlight filtered in through various layers of drapery. We'd take turns getting up, dumping the used grounds from the espresso machine, refilling it, lifting it from the stovetop when it began to sputter, and returning with two handle-less, baked-clay mugs of too-strong coffee, which we drank cross-legged on the bed like monks. I spent my weekends writing in the library and began working nights in a call centre, on a nondescript floor of cubicles along with a corps of listless millennials and newly landed immigrants with university degrees.

That summer, between volunteer shifts at a local women's shelter, Ana managed to write and perform a one-woman show about her mother's attempt to start a countercultural newspaper in communist Bulgaria. The initial run, at a local fringe theatre, sold out. In its second week it got a glowing, full-page review in Toronto's arts and culture weekly, and the theatre brought it back for another two weeks in early September. I went four times in total, each time increasingly transfixed by Ana's transformation into her mother. It went beyond posture or voice or mannerisms; beyond imitation. It was possession. It was as if Ana knew something about Fatme on a genetic level. Something about Fatme that Fatme didn't even realize about herself. The cumulative box-office haul from Ana's play just about covered her August and September rent, so in the lead-up to Halloween she began working at Screemers, a massive haunted house set up on the exhibition grounds by the lake.

"I'm getting fat and old and playing a fucking zombie for eleven bucks an hour with no paid dinner-break," she said as we jostled towards our respective nighttime gigs on the Spadina streetcar. "The Juliet and Ophelia trains have left the station. I missed them. And now I guess I gotta wait on the platform for Gertrude to arrive."

The streetcar was full, so we rode standing, gripping the overhead bar.

"I find it strange walking through the haunted house sometimes," she said. "Like, even though I've been through it a hundred times I'm still uncertain now and then about which figures are animatronic and which are assholes like me in makeup."

As we rumbled along, I thought of our lifelong journeys through the haunted house of people and things; thought about how mummies and effigies had once helped close the chasm between being and un-being and wondered whether animatronic ghouls and video game avatars and robotic vacuum cleaners did that for us now. And I thought about the pleasure we took in horror. Of being confronted with the dead and un-dead and of locating ourselves somewhere between the two.

IN THE END Will and I decided to throw one last Videofag party, a final, pyroclastic rager with more sweaty bodies than the space could hold—so they spilled out onto the street and into the adjacent park, where we lit off a haphazard fireworks display, the blasts of which ricocheted through the neighbourhood and drew people cheering and jeering to their windows and into the streets to join in the fun, the music, the sparklers, the smell of gunpowder, the gold lamé, the bad makeup, and the messy make-outs. The crowd applauded as Will and I, wearing bike helmets, climbed a metal ladder and took down the pink, hand-painted Videofag sign, like the deposition from the cross, just as four police cruisers descended with their lights flashing and megaphones crackling, "Break this up, please. Break up." Little did they know Will and I already had.

AFTER THE PARTY I crashed. Videofag was done. Will and I were done. I felt the finality of it physically, like an unending hangover. It was the one thing that had given my life any kind of definition or direction. To cheer me up, Ana decided to take me to a play. And by that I mean she picked out a play and I bought us tickets. It was a piece by the Osaka-based Koichi Asai Theatre, which was touring through Toronto at the time. I hadn't bothered reading anything about the show before seeing it. All I knew was that it was called *Singularity* and was entirely in Japanese with English subtitles. It turned out to be a fairly conventional story about a wealthy businessman who begins having an affair with his children's nanny, only it's revealed halfway through the play that the nanny is a robot. It was like a naturalistic Anton Chekhov drawing-room drama meets an Aldous Huxley novel. The central questions the play was asking were: Could a robot, even a very advanced one, reciprocate the man's feelings? And, as a possession programmed to fulfill his will, did she have any true agency in the matter?

What made the play most compelling was the beguiling performance of the young woman playing the nanny robot. As the actors took their bow during the curtain call, I looked in the program for the actress's name and bio. I was curious to know what else she had been in and how old she was, as I found her age difficult to pinpoint. Beside the character's name I found the description:

Performed by Nari 2, an android designed by the Advanced Robotics Department of the Honda Corporation, in collaboration with the Koichi Asai

Theatre Company. The Nari 1 prototype appeared in the Koichi Asai Theatre Company's 2014 production of *Hamlet* as Ophelia. *Singularity* is Nari 2's international theatre debut.

The nanny robot was played by an actual fucking robot. As the audience clapped, I leaned over and showed the program note to Ana and her jaw dropped: "Are you serious?" The way the actress had moved, the way she had spoken, her lips, her eyes—how could she not be human? That night, we stayed up late talking about the play in the pitch dark of her bedroom, lying side by side in bed. We talked about how if "liveness" was the charge we felt from events unfolding in real time, did liveness require at least one sentient performer and one sentient audience member? Could a play entirely performed by robots convey that same live charge? Was sentience a kind of prerequisite for our emotional investment in a performer? And how much? Was there a tipping point, from disengagement with an inanimate object to empathetic connection? Or even if Nari 2 had been less convincingly human, would I have felt as engaged? And to what extent could a robot "perform" if it did not have conscious agency?

At one point I noticed Ana was no longer chiming in. I looked over at her in the dark and she murmured: "I'm tired, yo."

"Yeah."

"Goodnight, babe."

As I lay there, I thought about your work. About your belief in an automated future. One in which back-breaking labour, complicated surgeries, dangerous search-and-rescue operations, and all manner of industry and service would be conducted by androids. But also the hard line you drew between beings and non-beings and our susceptibility to confusing the two. What would you have made of the play's love story? You probably would have seen it as a metaphor for a broader symptom. Our collective desire to see ourselves in the things we ourselves created. Or perhaps you would have just laughed and said: "Classic men. Falling in love with the thing that serves and doesn't challenge them." Yes, most likely you would have said something along those lines.

The show lingered with me over the following week. Less the play itself but the presence of Nari 2 within it and the questions that it provoked. Koichi Asai was the company's founder, lead playwright, and director. In his photo on the company's website, he sported a kind of middle-aged architect's look: clear-frame spectacles, black turtleneck, grey goatee. His bio said he had studied robotics in university and worked for four years as a "sentience consultant" at Honda's Yorii Factory, forty minutes north of Tokyo, before leaving to study theatre in Paris.

After a couple of days spent trawling the company's work online, I worked up the nerve to send Asai a message through the general info email listed on the website. The message was heavy on flattery and long-winded questions. And entirely in English. Rereading the email the next morning, I was mortified — I was a grovelling fan. Over the following few days, I tried to distract myself, tried to start new books, tried to cook meals, apply for new jobs, but I would usually abandon these efforts partway through to refresh Gmail in case Asai had replied. Nothing. By the start of the following week, I was convinced that I had sufficiently embarrassed myself through my platitudes and that someone had graciously deleted my email rather than forwarding it to Asai. As the week came to a close, I had just managed to divest myself of any investment in a response when one appeared in my inbox.

Asai Koichi <asai@KATC.com>   **Nov 12**
to Jordan

Jordan,

Sorry for the slow reply, we just started work on a new show. I'm pleased to hear *Singularity* resonates with you.

One of our interns at the theatre knows of Videofag and showed me your videos. What a small world — and a strange and wonderful one you live in. Is this artwork or just your life? Have you seen the videos of Ryan Trecartin? I think our new show will draw some inspiration from him. Post-Internet identity and such.

Let me know if you are ever in Japan.

よい一日を,
AK

Jordan Tannahill <jordan@videofag.com>   Nov 12
to Asai

Dear Asai,

Wow — that's incredible someone in your company knows about Videofag. God bless the Internet. As per your question, it is both art and life. I suppose you could say it's a sort of hyperreal portrait of a slightly more mundane reality. And yes, I do know Trecartin's work — I'm a big fan.

As I mentioned in my first email, *Singularity* and the other videos of your work I've managed to track down have made me reconsider many fundamental things about performance. In fact, so much so that I have a proposal for you to consider.

There is a grant here in Canada from the Meranski Foundation that I could apply to (deadline Dec 15) that provides emerging artists with professional development funds to mentor under senior artists in their disciplines for three months. If successful, I could come to Osaka, observe the new show you're working on, and audit your process in general — how you build/source your robots, rehearse, etc. I would be there simply to observe — there is literally nothing further you would have to do. And if you wanted an extra hand for any task, I would be happy to chip in — though there would be no expectation that I would have to be put to work.

If this is something you would be amenable to, all I would require is a letter of support from you — basically outlining what it is that you do and why (given the little you know about me) I might be an interesting presence to have around.

Sorry for the novel, and thanks for your consideration.

Best,
Jordan

Asai Koichi <asai@KATC.com>   **Nov 30**
to Jordan

Jordan,

Sure.

The piece we are making is called *Coma*. Working title. We're actually working on the piece in London with the National.

We have a rental flat here, you can stay in with our intern Gabriel (it's in North Woolwich, I warn you it can get boring). When do you need the letter by?

P.S. My name is Koichi (given names come second in Japanese)

K

GABRIEL MET ME at Heathrow in a yellow raincoat. He was a young Spaniard with a curly mop of black hair and large almond eyes that lent him a certain cartoonish quality. It occurred to me that perhaps he was the same intern who had first shown Koichi my videos. His English wasn't very good but he seemed keen, smiling at my faltering attempt to elucidate the poetry of descending through the canopy of storm clouds. I tried a few words in Spanish and he nodded sympathetically. We climbed into a black cab and Gabriel relayed an address to the driver, which I assumed was our shared flat. As we drove, Gabriel took out his phone and started showing me photos of the new androids the theatre was working with. He then either explained how he had begun working with Koichi after going to theatre school in London, or that after working with Koichi he was going to theatre school in London. I mentioned I had dropped out of theatre school and that killed the conversation for a minute or so. Things picked up somewhat when we began talking about Björk's recent virtual reality show which he'd seen at Somerset House in London. Trust Björk to bridge the gap between two art-fags.

I was half paying attention to Gabriel and half trying to take in the views of London unfolding behind his head out the window. The cab was weaving through a residential neighbourhood of row houses, and I was catching snapshots of family life through the front windows of homes. When I tuned back in and met Gabriel's gaze, I found it searching in a way that suggested we might be fucking later that night. Either that or he was sizing me up to see who would emerge as the alpha art-fag. Or perhaps both. He was a bit too much like me to be attractive, a mirror of my more insecure and cloying tendencies. Perhaps we would be enemies.

In fact, he reminded me somewhat of my first boy-friend, Travis. I was in grade eleven, he was in grade twelve at a neighbouring high school. Travis had acne, braces, and wore a necklace of rainbow beads. His favourite book was *One Hundred Years of Solitude*. After a few months of being together, I went to see him play Danny in a production of *Grease*. I broke up with him in the dressing room after the show. It wasn't that he or the show were dreadful, which of course in retrospect they were, it was that I found witness-ing his pleasure to perform so profoundly unattractive, as it reminded me of all of the worst tendencies in myself. We had to break up because we were, in fact, the same human being.

The cab pulled up in front of a white two-storey town-house with a large picture window. Koichi approached the window and waved at us. There seemed to be other guests inside.

"Sorry, I forgot mentioning we're having a welcome din-ner," Gabriel said as he paid for the cab. "This is Juliana's place, she's one of the producers from the National."

Wow, how incredibly sweet, I thought. I wasn't expecting a welcome dinner. I suddenly felt woefully underdressed and unwashed.

"Am I presentable?" I asked Gabriel.

"No, no, it's okay," he smiled. "You don't have to present."

Inside, the house was principally comprised of a single two-storey, open-concept room, the kitchen on one end, the dining table at the other, bisected by a staircase of thick wooden planks leading to an upstairs loft. The walls were white and bare except for two large framed prints — a poster from a Louise Bourgeois exhibition and a vintage-looking Polish poster for Fritz Lang's *Metropolis*.

There were already a few people waiting for us around the dinner table. Everyone in the room except Gabriel and I was wearing black. In the ensuing flurry of introductions I missed about half of everyone's names and roles. From what I gathered they included Juliana; Koichi; his wife, Nayoko; a colleague of theirs from Osaka University; two other women from the National; and an American robotics colleague of Koichi's named David Auerbach. I wound up sandwiched between David and Koichi, who took turns talking to one another overtop of me. It didn't take me long to realize that the dinner was actually for David and my arrival just happened to coincide. But this was for the best; I was thoroughly jet-lagged and quite happy to be buried by the conversation. I poked the fried egg on the top of my donburi and watched its yellow yolk burst over the rice and shoots. At one point in the night, David got up to take a phone call and Koichi began extolling his genius to me.

"David used to be a sculptor and technical consultant at Walt Disney before he went rogue," Koichi grinned. "He brought Emily with him," he said, and I looked around the table wondering if she and I had been introduced. "She's at the theatre waiting for us. We get to start working with her tomorrow. He debuted her a couple of weeks ago at South by Southwest, and she was a sensation."

It took me a moment to realize he was talking about a robot. Or a "humanoid," as he and David called them.

Koichi took out his phone and started showing me photos of Emily, as if she were his daughter, or perhaps a woman he was seeing. She looked to be about twenty-three,

Caucasian, with brown shoulder-length hair, blue eyes, and thin, immaculate eyebrows. She wore a white blouse, tight jeans, and reminded me of a fresh-faced model from a department store catalogue.

"She can activate all forty-eight muscle groups in her face, which gives her about sixty facial expressions. You can see—hyperrealistic skin-like face." I nodded, though the skin around her neck seemed to crease in a slightly unnatural way. "She can carry on simple conversations and she's programmed with emotions, personality, mood."

"When you say emotions—?"

"So for instance," Koichi said, shifting his body towards me, "depending on whether you tell her good news or bad news, she has specific reactions. David's programmed her with different models for mood, for personality—you know, neuroticism, extroversion, whatever, and then on top of that the occ model for emotions. So in this way—"

"Like, obsessive-compulsive?"

"What?"

"Obsessive—"

"No, no, occ is—It's a model that basically explains different emotions and their intensities and it's, uh, basically predicated on the idea of characterizing emotions in terms of different ways of feeling good or bad about things."

"But it's all a performance," I said, already out of my depth. "I mean, Emily doesn't actually feel these things or have these moods, right? It's a simulation of those things."

I was expecting Koichi to disagree with me, to split some kind of conceptual hair, but he nodded.

"Exactly. That's the next major barrier. How does one not just convey but actually *feel* an emotion, as a humanoid.

But what is an emotion?" He looked at me as if expecting an answer, but I was too tired to take the bait. "I know this seems like a silly question, but really, how are they constructed? What are the key types and how many are there? Even Aristotle had trouble articulating what emotions were. He identified fourteen."

"Only fourteen?"

He looked it up on his phone to be sure. "Here," he said, handing it to me.

I looked at Aristotle's two-and-a-half-thousand-year-old list. Confidence, anger, friendship, fear, calm, unkindness, shame, shamelessness, pity, kindness, indignation, emulation, enmity, and envy. It stuck me as almost comically incomplete. Perhaps these words, in the original Greek, carried more scope and texture. Perhaps his original list captured untranslatable sensations. I mean, "emulation"? Really?

"What about love?" I asked, handing the phone back to him. "Or sadness? Joy? Curiosity? Excitement? I feel like he's missing huge parts of the spectrum."

"I know. It's hard."

"I mean, he has anger, indignation, unkindness, and enmity, which are almost shades of the same colour, but he doesn't have love or joy. It's like he forgot red or something."

"Darwin put forward a theory that basically all emotional facial expressions are universal. An American psychologist—I can't remember his name—built on his theory and said that there are basically six key emotions that are universally recognized. Even in pre-literature, pre-media cultures." He did another quick search on his phone. "Paul Ekman," he confirmed. "Happy, sad, afraid, surprised, angry, and disgusted."

"What about love?" I asked again, sounding like a character in a Baz Luhrmann movie.

"But what does love look like?" Koichi asked. Perhaps this was profound, but I found it irritating. Just then David squeezed back into his seat, on edge from the call.

"It's only 7 a.m. there. She was not in a good mood," he said, I assumed referring to his wife, though perhaps another humanoid. David was somewhere between Koichi's and my age; on the young side, it struck me, to be a world expert on anything. His hair was tousled and he had a boyish face with about a week's worth of scruff, flecked in places with grey. He would have almost been sexy if it weren't for the way he spoke, like the words were all rushing and crowding the fire escape of his mouth.

"We're talking about emotional programming," Koichi filled him in, uninterested in his personal dilemma. "Jordan was asking how one might produce actual emotional responses in humanoids."

"Such that they're really felt," I clarified, unnecessarily.

David nodded while trying to remove a fleck of rice lodged in his teeth with his tongue.

"It comes down to physiology modelling," he said. "Emotions, okay, that's one thing, but you've got to add hormones to the mix and all kinds of other bodily cycles. You need bodies that are aware of themselves as bodies, right? You need bodily awareness to have feelings."

The way he said the word "hormones" while plucking the rice kernel from the teeth sent a shiver of disgust through me. There was an unrelated burst of laughter at the other end of the table. Nayoko was holding court, telling a long, humorous story.

"Pain and pleasure, for instance," David continued, making eye contact with me for the first time in the evening. "Having some kind of mechanism that allows a humanoid to feel these things is crucial for the same reasons it's important humans and other animals feel these things, right? Empathy. Cause and effect. They ground social interactions in internal values."

"And complexity," Koichi interjected. "The more complex their sensations, the more subtle and complex their interactions with humans will be."

"And feelings — feelings aren't emotions," David said, squaring his body with mine as if finally committing to my presence in this one-sided conversation. "So feelings are things we are aware of, we feel them produced within us, bubble up, whereas emotions — They're full of all kinds of other aspects we're not aware of, like, like automatic responses, the unconscious, chemicals released into the bloodstream. The question is, how do you replicate all of those minute aspects?"

"At the end of the day," Koichi added, "we don't really know how to model complex feelings in humanoids because we don't really understand the underlying mechanisms in humans."

Actors. Empty vessels that allowed emotions to be played upon the instrument of their bodies but were never able to independently manufacture them, never able to feel them as their own. From a certain perspective — Diderot's, perhaps — these machines were optimized for success if they could portray emotions with enough fidelity to move persuasively through the world of humans but without actually feeling them, like charming psychopaths nodding and crying at your hardship, gleaning only valuable meaning and taking on none of the burden. They wouldn't even suffer the existential crisis of being almost-human, not human enough to be weakened by emotions, not human enough for frailty and vulnerability and irrationality, or at least un-programmed irrationality (could there be such a thing as programmed irrationality?)

When I tuned back into the conversation, I realized David and Koichi had carried on without me.

"Human emotions are so chaotic," David was in the process of saying, "and so much of it can play upon the human face that it's almost painful to look at. So sometimes with a humanoid it's easier, less complicated. Which is why some of my humanoids are being used in autism-therapy trails." It struck me that robotics probably attracted a certain breed of straight men for whom "the chaos of emotions" was something to avoid at all costs.

Gabriel leaned over and refilled my sake cup. He said something about calling a cab for me when I wanted to go home. I was too tired to decode this offer, though it was just as likely that it was not, in fact, coded. I nodded, air-toasted him, and focused back in on what David was saying, something about the fallacy of assuming we can only empathize with human faces.

"At South by Southwest people were going crazy over this little robot that looked like a hockey puck," he said. "They were just gibbering away at it." He conceded we tend to be innately drawn to human faces, and are highly attuned to reading them, which is why creating convincing robotic ones was so difficult. "And designers, we know how to stimulate you," he said, making no attempt to hide the erotic undertones of this statement. "We know how to activate different perceptual regions in your brain. We know if we make the eyes a bit bigger that that manufactures a kind of empathy or even sexual arousal. We enlarge pores or wrinkles and that repels. If you're attracted to something, we can make you more attracted to it; if you're repulsed, we can make you hyper-repulsed. And you can't help it."

I glanced up and found Gabriel's eyes on me. He looked back at Nayoko and rejoined their conversation with a lazy ease. *Okay*, I thought, *it's on.*

I had a question but forgot it almost as soon as it had occurred to me, distracted by the sudden need to piss. I stood up with such conviction that the conversation came to a momentary halt. I was surprised by how drunk I was. My legs felt numb, and I stumbled over Koichi and began traipsing over to the washroom before realizing halfway to the kitchen that I didn't even know where it was. Thankfully, my instincts proved right.

I unzipped my pants before closing the door. As I pissed, I scrutinized my face in the mirror above the toilet. I seemed particularly washed out. My pores looked huge. It occurred to me that I had passed through the intangible threshold where I was only going to grow less attractive every passing day. I wondered: What is the minimum requirement for being human? I thought about the new era we were on the precipice of; how behind us were countless millennia during which humans could assume every person they encountered was a fellow biological specimen and how in front of us was a new era where that was no longer a given.

When I stumbled out of the washroom, I found that people had disbanded from the table and were hovering around in the kitchen. It was a bit surreal. How had they relocated so quickly? How long had I been in the washroom looking at my face? We carried on late into the night. At some point, I guess Gabriel called me a cab because I woke up alone the next morning in a single bed in a barely furnished apartment bathed in sunlight.

GABRIEL AND I rode the tube together that next morning, nursing our takeaway coffees without exchanging more than the perfunctory words necessary to navigate our route. We got off at Southwark Station and walked the three blocks down the Cut, which stuck me as an incredibly British name for a street, to a nondescript four-storey brick building beside the Old Vic theatre.

"Welcome to the NT's studios," Gabriel murmured, though with his accent it sounded like he said "empty studios."

We waited for a few moments at a glass-fronted door with a long, vertical metal handle. I could see the unstaffed security desk through the door. Eventually, a chipper young guy returned wiping his hands on his jeans and buzzed us through.

"Sorry just in the loo," he chirped as we walked in and entered our names and arrival times into a book on the desk with a blue pen attached to a ratty piece of string.

On the ground floor of the building were offices, a kitchen and lounge area with a Keurig coffeemaker, and a small wood-shop mostly used for storage. The entire top floor was rehearsal studios with sprung black floors and lighting grids suspended from the ceiling. Behind the building was a parking lot, at the back of which was an outbuilding constructed of four conjoined shipping containers. It looked like some kind of temporary structure one would see erected for disaster relief. Gabriel told me they called this the Robot House.

Inside, the Robot House was a cross of state-of-the-art laboratory and frat house — banks of computers, cameras, and robot components nestled on plywood floors alongside stacks of milk crates storing cabling, recycled couches, bags of chips, and a massive wooden cable-spindle turned on its side to form a makeshift coffee table. It smelled a bit like a locker room in there, or really any space where more than five men spent more than five hours.

Koichi, his assistants, and David were already there when we arrived. In the centre of the room was Emily. She was seated on a chair and looked smaller than I had imagined, probably only five feet and a couple of inches. The back of her head was open and a jumble of wires and cables protruded from it. Around the lip of this opening, the skin peeled back like a bloodless wound.

As Gabriel and I walked in she was staring off into space. I thought perhaps she wasn't "on." Then she winced like a child trying out a new expression. It was profoundly unsettling. And then, prompted by nothing, her eyes widened and she burst into a smile, as if responding to some rich interior world. Her face finally resolved into a kind of placid grin, a vacancy one might mistake as beatific, except her eyes were open a fraction too wide and she was not blinking often enough, which leant her a somewhat crazed air.

Koichi and David waved to me, both a bit brusquely, I thought. Kochi's assistants were preoccupied with a MacBook set up on a table facing Emily.

"They're trying to Skype in Haruto," Gabriel explained. "He's one of our collaborators. He heads up Osaka University's Intelligent Robotics Laboratory, but he's in Kansas at the moment."

I nodded and chose not to point out the irony that these world leaders in robotics couldn't get Skype to work. I then realized it probably wasn't lost on them. Koichi seemed to be internalizing the problem as some great embarrassment in front of David and perhaps me. He kept apologizing while berating his assistants. Perhaps to kill time or perhaps to deflect energy away from the Skype problem, David began speaking to Emily in the slightly affected voice one might use when speaking to a child.

"Hi, Emily. How are you?"

She blinked and turned towards David. "Hi there. Everything is going extremely well."

I noted that she did not say David's name, even though he had told me she remembered people's faces and past conversations with them. She also didn't appear too concerned or aware of the Skype problem.

"Do you like talking with me?" he asked.

"Yes. Talking to people is my primary function."

"Are you excited to be in Koichi's new play?"

"What is Koichi's new play?"

"Good question!" Koichi laughed from across the room.

"It's going to be a play that you perform in," said David. "You will be its star."

He said the word "star" with a hint of irony, as if the word contained all the embarrassing, human ambitions of actors, which Emily was not burdened with and couldn't possibly understand. In actuality, she was going to be programmed to memorize and recite lines, execute blocking, and interact algorithmically with her human counterpart onstage.

Emily blinked. "Please explain, what is a play?"

"Good question. Jordan?" David turned and looked at me.

I walked over to Emily. She met my eyes with hers, which I recalled David telling me were, in fact, cameras.

"A play is an event put on for an audience," I said. "Do you know what an audience is?" Emily blinked, but I did not wait for her to respond. "An audience is a group of people gathered to watch an event. The play is an event that features performances by actors and usually involves telling a story."

"What is an event?" Emily asked.

"It is something that…happens," I said, looking at David and shrugging.

"Please explain, what is an actor?" Emily asked.

"An actor," I began "is someone whose job it is to pretend to be other people."

"Why do they do this job?"

"Well, because it's pleasurable, I suppose. Both for the actor and for the audience. By pretending to be other people, and watching other people pretend to be other people, we can gain a deeper understanding of what it means to be a person. Do you understand?"

"I think so," she replied. I could tell she didn't. "Are you an actor?" she asked me.

"That's a good question. Um. Sometimes."

"By your definition, are we not all actors sometimes?" she replied.

DAVID AND I sat on a table against the wall, watching Koichi work with Emily and a human actor named Vincent. She was having trouble tracking Vincent's movements, and at one point David called out, "We can fix that tonight." Koichi raised his hand in thanks without looking in our direction. I could sense David felt awkward about our sitting there together in silence and was searching for something to say. The trouble was he knew nothing about me and had no idea where to start. Even though I was quite content just to sit there I eventually put him out of his misery by asking, in a whisper:

"So what first interested you in robots?"

He thought about this for a long moment, which seemed strange, as I would've assumed he'd have long since prepared a cocktail-party answer to this mundane question.

"Have you heard of golems?" he asked at last.

"Like, Tolkien?"

"Golems were the proto-robot," he said. "From Jewish mysticism. I was raised Jewish, am still…Jewish."

He told me that in the Talmud, Adam, the ur-man, was described as a golem formed from dust. Golems appeared to be humans but were not. It was believed golems could be activated through an ecstatic experience induced by the *shem*, any one of the Names of God, written on a piece of paper and inserted into the mouth or forehead of the golem.

"A kind of mystical battery-pack if you will," he said with a smile. "In some medieval folktales, the golem could be deactivated by removing the *shem* or by changing the combination of letters written on it."

He mentioned being totally transfixed as a child by an old Yiddish story about the Clay Boy, a variation of the golem, in which a lonely elderly couple made a little boy out of clay. Much to their delight, the clay boy came to life and the couple treated him as their real child. But the clay boy didn't stop growing. He ate all of their food, their animals, and eventually the elderly couple too, before rampaging through the village.

"So, you know, that same paranoia and fear of the humanoid from science fiction appears even here, centuries earlier, in the golem." David looked up and watched the slow proceedings of the rehearsal. "We fear most what we desire most. Which, of course, is to be gods."

THAT EVENING, after a breathless trek through the Tate Modern before it closed, I took the tube up to Mile End and walked the twenty minutes to Chisenhale, trying to imagine what it would have been like for Clyde and Giacomo to hang out on the fire escape of this former warehouse, smoking cigarettes with Michael Clark and being so fucking unbelievably badass it made me want to cry. I loitered around for a few minutes like Ebenezer Scrooge looking through a window at his own past with longing, except this past wasn't mine. It had never belonged to me and never would.

On the tube ride home, I listened to the automated woman's voice at every interchange station: "Change for the District and Hammersmith and City lines"; "Change for London Overground." For some reason, every time she said the word "change" it struck me as exquisite. The word seemed to come a fraction of a second before the rest of the sentence — "Change…for the District and Circle lines" — as if the most important thing she was announcing was not the new tube line but, in fact, change itself. For the briefest of moments the world was pregnant with this word, as if the automated woman might be commanding any number of possible changes from us: Change…your mind. Change… your life. Change…is possible. Change…is inevitable. Change…is afoot. Change…everything. Change…now.

At some point, I became aware that I was sitting beside a rather handsome young man who I hadn't initially noticed because, like everyone else on the train, he was disguised in a suit. He was also burrowed in a thick book, which I would come to discover was his preferred habitat. I was examining the postcard I had just bought from the Tate's gift shop, with an image of a neon-light sculpture by Martin Creed on the front. I was trying to decide who to send it to. I really did love the image. Creed's sculpture was a phrase, an equation actually, spelled out in neon: "the whole world + the work = the whole world."

"What do you think it means?" the man asked me, putting down his thick book.

I was not startled by his question. In fact, I felt quite ready and receptive to his unexpected entry into my life.

"I think it means that art, or really any work we do in our lives, is both immensely consequential and inconsequential," I replied, with somewhat less eloquence than that. "The whole world would still be the whole world whether or not it contained all of the work in the Tate Modern. But all the work in the Tate Modern also makes the whole world what it is; it is part of the equation." It was a sentiment suffuse with humour and nihilism, which, I would come to learn, this man was suffuse with as well.

"What's that tome you're reading?" I asked.

He flipped the cover over so I could see it.

"*Life and Fate* by Vasily Grossman, do you know it?"

I shook my head.

"It's this kind of sprawling portrait of a family and, in classic twentieth-century fashion, a nation being torn apart by ideology." He told me Grossman's manuscript had been confiscated by the KGB in 1960 and remained unpublished until 1980, when it was smuggled to the West and declared a lost masterpiece.

"Can you imagine writing a book called *Life and Fate*?" I asked. "Like…leave it to a Russian to tackle those minor topics."

"A Soviet," he corrected me.

We rode in silence for a moment. I remembered thinking at the time that it was very possible, in fact likely, that this man would have to get off at the next stop or perhaps the one after, so it wouldn't be much use investing any further in the conversation, delightful as it was. But he persisted. He asked me where I was from; I told him Toronto. I asked if he lived in London and then, before he could reply, said, "Of course you do, you're wearing a suit and carrying a briefcase." I then jumped in with the quintessential question of the urbanite: "What do you do?" which is, for some reason, synonymous with "How do you make money?" He told me he was doing post-doc research but, at that exact moment, was returning from a board meeting.

"A scholarship foundation," he clarified. "For Pakistani-Brits. To help us pay for uni."

I nodded. He then asked me what I did.

"Well, I'm a failed actor who dabbles in porn and tele-marketing and sometimes writes plays" would have been

the truth, but instead I lied, of course, and said "lawyer" and
then added "law" immediately after, in case I wasn't making myself clear. And then, panicking, unsure if one could
even be a full-fledged lawyer at my age—weren't they like
doctors?—I said, "I'm in law school, actually." And then, to
sheathe my lies in yet another lie in the hope that it would
distract from the first two, I said, "I'm here for a conference
with my class." I was profoundly out of my depth by this
point. Did law students even go to conferences? Together
as a class? He asked me if I was studying here in London
and I said, "No, the University of Toronto," hoping the geographic distance would throw off the scent of dubiousness,
and it seemed to work, or perhaps he simply wasn't all that
interested or impressed with my legal training because he
didn't pursue it any further. He asked me who I was intending to send the postcard to and in that moment I decided,
"I think I'm going to keep it."

"Don't do that," he replied. "That's bad luck."

"How so?" I chuckled.

"It means you'll never travel again."

"Huh. I haven't heard of that before."

"I'm Osama," he said. He held out his hand and I shook
it. His grip was strong and confident but not dominating,
not eager to prove anything. My hand felt like a child's in his.

"I'm Jordan," I replied, clearing my throat.

He told me the next stop was his and that it seemed
unfair that this might be the last time we spoke. I said that
it didn't have to be. He took out a pen from his bag (in time,
I would come to learn he always had a pen on him, whereas
I never carried any of life's requisite tools). He reached over,
plucked the postcard from my hand, wrote his address on

the back of it, and handed it back to me. He then smiled and got off the train.

AS THE NEXT two weeks unfolded, I discovered I wasn't particularly excited about the play Koichi was making. It seemed like fairly well-trodden territory: a man falls in love with his sex robot. The automaton woman, against all logic, seems to have a personality and a depth of character and charms the thoughtful, complicated, more-human man. A bit like *Her* and *Simone* and even that film *Lars and the Real Girl*. Except Koichi's version seemed to lack the humour of those previous outings. Also any nod to Ryan Trecartin's work or aesthetics—one of the initial tie-ins for my being there—was lost on me, expect perhaps for a few psychedelic dream-sequences that were axed by the end of the second week. What's more, I found Vincent, the actor, a bit of a scenery chewer. He wrung the emotion from his lines in a way that made Emily's almost monotonous performance seem inspired. Next to her, Vincent looked ridiculous—and by extension, so did humankind.

I think Koichi could tell my interest was waning, as he made less and less effort to include me in group discussions. Also there was mounting pressure because Rufus, the artistic director of the National, would be visiting to watch a work-in-progress showing at the end of the third week, and progress had been slow going. I spent most of the time watching from the sidelines, checking Facebook on my phone, and making coffees with the Keurig in the lounge. I couldn't help but think: if I can't be excited about working on a Japanese robot play in London, then I must be really beyond hope.

THE EVENING OF the Brexit referendum I met Osama outside the entrance of Lahore Kebab, which he informed me served the best Pakistani food in London. I had been caught unawares in a midday downpour, and my thinning hair, which each morning I built into a carefully composed sculpture, was completely undone by the time I arrived. Before I could even say hello or apologize for my hair, he tossed me a black T-shirt.

"What's this for?"

"Take your shirt off and put this one on."

I laughed. That was forward. "Right now?"

"Yeah, before we go inside."

Smiling, thinking this was perhaps some kind of complicated joke, I yanked off my shirt and pulled on the one he gave me. It was a Wu-Tang Clan T-shirt.

"Now pass me yours," he instructed, and I handed it to him, the realization dawning on me. He pulled out a large plastic zip-lock and sealed my shirt inside. "Trust me, after you eat here you'll never get the smell of curry out of your clothes. I meant to text you before we arrived, but I forgot."

"What about this one?" I asked, pointing to his baggy T-shirt.

"It's my gym shirt, I don't mind."

Osama was Oz. From the desert diner. I could understand why he may have chosen to go by a nickname in the States. As we walked into Lahore Kebab, I studied his face in disbelief. It had only been a couple of years—how had we not recognized each other? I suppose we had only spoken for twenty minutes. And in the interim he'd lost his terrible beard, lost weight, lost the wire-rim glasses. And of course I had looked nothing like myself at the time, having let my hair grow long and not shaven in three weeks. Plus I'd been a good fifteen pounds lighter back then. I felt this glorious, winged secret begin to batter at my chest. What would he make of this coincidence? Would he even remember? I thought back to how eager he had been at the time to impress Robert and I — a complete stranger. Something in him had mellowed. It seemed he had less to prove — to himself, most importantly.

"What a fucking day," he said, scooping lamb biryani onto his plate. "Massive storms and flooding, did you see along the Thames?" I shook my head. "It felt apocalyptic. Divine judgement on Nigel Farage. Nobody knows anything yet, but most people seem to think it's a Remain win, but narrowly. The closest thing to an exit poll puts Remain at a four-point win, and naturally the markets've soared."

As we sat under the unforgiving fluorescence in the unadorned restaurant, leaning in to hear one another over the din of the other diners, he asked me to tell him more about the conference I was attending. My heart sank.

"I didn't expect to be on a date with you."

"What?"

"I didn't expect we'd be going on a date."

"Okay."

"So I lied. On the subway. I mean tube."

"You lied?"

"I'm not a law student. I just said that because, I don't know why…because I was the only person on the car not wearing a suit and I thought I'd never see you again so what the hell."

"So what are you? Besides a liar?" He said this with a smirk, taking a sip of his lassi.

"I write plays."

"Really? For a living?"

"Not yet but…you know."

He nodded. "What kind of plays?"

"Pretty good ones," I replied with a smile. "I don't know. Not sure how to answer that." He didn't seem particularly enchanted by my answer, so I tried to dig a little deeper. "Well. At the moment I'm working on a play about the destruction of Sodom and Gomorrah. But it's set in a kind of indeterminate present; both ancient and contemporary. And instead of God's wrath raining down on the towns it's an American drone strike."

He nodded. I wasn't sure he was hearing anything I was saying over the noise. A group beside us kept banging on their table whenever they burst into laughter, which was often. I began telling him about getting the grant from the Meranski Foundation to audit Koichi's process at the National Theatre, to shift the conversation into the register of more obvious accomplishment. I mentioned the grant nonchalantly, as if I might have received them on a regular basis and was perhaps being modest about the true breadth of my reputation. Osama was particularly curious about Emily. What did her voice sound like? How did her face move? We talked about the "uncanny valley" of human semblance, how we empathized with non-human faces that resembled real human faces until the critical point when the non-human face became so proximate to a real one that it aroused feelings of repulsion in us. It was as if, as the non-human neared the threshold of the human, we began to scrutinize it in new ways — and the small discrepancies we found between it and us were repellent.

The irregular eye blinks. The halting speech. The cold stare.

As more plates of dal and chapatis were placed on our table, I blurted out: "We've met before."

"Pardon?"

"Before the tube."

"When?" he said, jerking back in surprise.

"A diner in Nevada. Outside of Vegas. You were with your supervisor at the time, Robert. You explained his sentience quotient to me."

"Holy shit."

"Do you remember?"

"Yeah, I do. Wait, how did you—Did you know that on the tube?"

I pinched the billowy T-shirt I was wearing with both hands and pulled it out from my chest. "You were wearing this shirt. I just figured it out."

"Holy. Shit. I totally didn't recognize you."

"Me neither. At first."

"I've lost a lot of weight."

"Me the opposite."

"It's your hair. And you had that mountain-man beard."

I laughed. "You still a Wu-Tang fan?"

"Of course. When we get back to my place, I'll show you the calendar over my bed."

The ease with which he said this, the assumption that we'd be going back to his place that night, the dual manner in which this statement acted as both invitation and instruction, made me want to drop to my knees and suck him off below the dal-splattered table then and there. He told me that after he graduated from Berkeley he moved back to London to begin post-doctoral research in cognitive science, which he explained was basically the study of how we perceived the world.

"And what's your take?" I asked.

He chuckled. "You mean, like, my thesis?" I nodded. He downed the rest of his lassi and ran his tongue along his lower lip. I could tell this was a question he'd been working on giving a short answer to. "Well. I'm trying to understand what it means to be an observer. And what it means to be observed. How do we disentangle the two?"

"Uh huh." I waited for him to continue but he didn't. "That's rather cryptic."

He smiled. "So there's this fundamental question of perception. What does it mean for us to perceive something in the world? On one side you have the neuroscientists who are trying to figure out what they call "the hard problem," which is basically: how does this three pounds of grey stuff in our heads produce first-person consciousness? And then on the other side you have the quantum physicists, whose experiments prove that nothing exists until we come along and observe it. So the neuroscientists are asking how first-person reality is possible and the quantum physicists are asking how anything *but* first-person reality is possible. And I'm somewhere in the middle. Trying to figure out a mathematical model for the observer."

As he spoke I recognized the Oz from the diner. His hand gestures, his cadences, his delight in being an expert, but rather than experiencing it with annoyance, I felt both genuinely charmed and touched by the effort he was making to explain what I'm sure were extremely fucking complicated concepts to a complete neophyte in a loud restaurant. And I also recognized you, explaining Schrödinger's cat to me when I was eleven, and all of the other times you spoke to me about your work and the mind over the years.

"Basically what I'm trying to do is devise a mathematical model that defines the observer. That articulates consciousness."

"Sounds a bit familiar," I said, with a grin.

"Right. Except it's very different than Robert's quotient. And frankly blows it out of the water. No offence to him though, he's great."

"Of course you're impressed by a man who wants to explain the whole world," I heard you saying in my head. "Who wants to fit it all into an equation." But then it also struck me that perhaps all three of us were seeking to commune with the same unknowable sublime. Him through equations, me through art, you through faith. All routes to a shared end.

"I'd suggest our perception of the world is actually an illusion that filters out the incomprehensible magnitude of reality," Osama continued. "You could think of it like a desktop on a computer." I smiled, reminded of your long distaste for computer-as-brain metaphors. Suddenly sitting there, allowing myself to be thoroughly seduced by Osama, felt laced with quiet rebellion. "Take the little trash-can icon. Is the actual 'delete' function in a computer shaped like a rubbish bin? Are you actually throwing files into this little rubbish bin? No. Of course not. But that's how we understand and visualize a complex and hidden system of functions that we couldn't possibly understand or interact with otherwise. In the same way that a bear in the wild appears like a bear to us. We can see it and understand it. If we had to spend all our time processing the infinite amount of additional information about the scene, the nature of the forest, the air around us, every bacterial microbe in our field of vision, the bear would eat us. Our illusions help us survive."

Dessert arrived, saffron syrup-soaked balls of gulab jamun, and I stuck one in my mouth like a ball-gag.

"But if a bear isn't a bear then what is it?" I mumbled, chewing.

"The bear I observe is my perception, just as the bear you observe is your perception. And the way the bear, presumably, perceives itself is its own perception. But there is no single, objective bear. And as I began to think about this, about how we observe, I thought of Alan Turing, who—"

"My favourite fag."

"What?"

"He's the best."

"Yeah."

"And recently pardoned."

"In order to invent the computer Turing had to create this very—kind of perfect, really, mathematical formula of how a computer could actually work. A formula for computation. And I thought, why couldn't I do that for consciousness?"

"Sure, why not?" I teased.

He laughed. "I know. Ambitious. But I just started by breaking it down. Like, okay, what makes up a conscious experience? So I—" And then just as his mentor had done in the diner years before, Osama grabbed a napkin, retrieved his ever-ready pen from his bag, and began to write out an equation for me. But this time it was an equation of his very own. An equation that to my knowledge had not yet stood up to the scrutiny of his peers or the public at large. One that, for all I knew, had been shared with fewer people than could fit around this table. An equation that was either total nonsense or, just possibly, a field-redefining revelation. And if it was the latter, what had I done to deserve encountering it before virtually everyone else? What was the actual likelihood that, as I sat there in Lahore Kebab, I was in the presence of actual genius? Osama's pen was dry, so he drew several concentric circles on the napkin, tearing it slightly, before the ink appeared, and then he began writing it out like ancient hieroglyphs on a papyrus scroll.

"Space X is experiences, space G is actions, and D is an algorithm that lets me choose any action given the nature of my experiences. W is for a world, ours or any other, which is also a probability space. W affects my perceptions, so there's a perception map P from the world to my experiences, and when I act I change the world, so there's a map A from the space of actions to the world. And that's it. That's the entire formulation."

"Six letters?"

He looked up from the napkin. "Six letters."

"But if there's a W, are you saying that there's an objective world?"

He pointed at me. "Very good." I found the gesture patronizing but the acknowledgement satisfying. "Here's the thing. The reason why I know it's right. I can pull the W out of the formula and stick a conscious agent in its place and I get a whole circuit of other conscious, first-person agents."

"What do you mean? Like, if you were to replace W with me?"

"Yes, say U represents you, Jordan. If I stick U into the place of the world, the formula produces this whole network of other conscious agents. All these self-governed, self-perceiving, first-person experiences, people and animals, just moving about in the void." He reached out and plucked a gulab jamun off the plate and took a bite. "That, in other words, *is* the world."

THAT NIGHT, we lay in his bed naked, watching the referendum results trickle in on his phone. I lay with my head on his shoulder, listening to his gradual arc towards despair.

11:31 p.m. "Apparently Gibraltar may have just voted 90 percent Remain. But then they'll likely be invaded if we leave, so..."

12:02 p.m. "Newcastle only voted 50.7 percent Remain. Fuck, that's so low. And the EU poured money into there."

12:20 a.m. "You've got to be joking me. Those fuckers. Only 31 percent Remain?"

1:00 a.m. "Even if Remain still wins, this has completely ripped us apart."

2:06 a.m. "I'd be surprised if Leave can lose this now. This is honestly the most depressing night of my life."

2:09 a.m. "Literally what the fuck do we do now?

"Maybe we should try to get some sleep."

"I can't. You don't understand, this is a nightmare." And then I held him as he cried. Which, I have to say, was definitely a first-date first for me.

THE NEXT MORNING, after four hours of sleep, I sat at his kitchen table watching him prepare breakfast in his burgundy pyjamas. I realized I hadn't even asked him if he lived alone. My guess was he had a roommate but we hadn't encountered him or her yet. I had also noticed the Koran on his bedroom bookshelf and had no idea whether he was religious. There was so much ground to cover.

His phone was on the kitchen table playing the BBC news live-stream. I watched as, in a cramped conference room surrounded by cheering white men, Nigel Farage declared: "This will be a victory for real people. A victory for ordinary people. A victory for decent people."

"What the fuck does that mean?" Osama shot back. He broke two eggs into the pan and they spat up at him. "The implication of course is that if there are 'real' people there are also 'unreal' people. If there are 'ordinary' people there are 'unordinary' people. And if there are 'decent' people than there are, naturally, 'indecent' people. Others. It makes me think of the *Dirty Paki* someone spray-painted on my mum's bin."

"Recently?

"A couple of months ago."

"That's awful."

"And last week I was on the tube talking to her on the phone in Urdu and this woman sitting across from me shouted 'Speak English,' and I was so startled I didn't even know what to do at first. And then I shouted back: 'I do speak English and I bet I speak it better than you fucking do' and went back to talking with my mom in Urdu. And no one said anything. Packed train and nothing."

Two burnt pieces of toast popped from the toaster, startling me.

"Shit," he muttered, grabbing them and scraping the black off with a butter knife. "You don't mind, do you?"

I shook my head. He dropped the slices onto a yellow

plate, flipped on two eggs and a grilled tomato, and slid it with a flourish of his hand in front of me. "Delish."

"Hot sauce?"

"No, thanks."

He turned around and cracked two more eggs into the pan. "Did you see Farage's poster? Showing a crowd of refugees with the words *Breaking Point* written across it in big bold red letters and the words *The EU has failed us* below."

"Christ."

"No indication of who those people were. No mention they were Syrian refugees turned away at the Hungarian border. Just a nameless, identity-less horde of others *coming for you*. I said, 'That looks like fascist propaganda.' And the people at my lab were like, 'Hey, come on now.' You know? Like, 'There's no need to use the F-word.' Because it scares them, it's unpleasant. It feels extreme. But that's exactly what it is, images like those. They're extreme."

I thought about how fascist propaganda held up the depersonalized as an ideal. The photographs of Leni Riefenstahl; the Nazi rallies at Nuremberg; the crowds hailing the führer; the godlike bodies of Aryan athletes at the 1939 Olympics, leaping, vaulting, running, all muscles and sinew. And of course I thought of the mounds of emaciated, unidentifiable corpses. *Bodies without people*—was there a more succinct articulation of the fascist project, insofar as what both its supporters and its subjugated become? Fascism was abjection, situating people between the tyrannies of subjecthood and objecthood. Muslims no longer people but bodies to be counted and rounded up. Mexicans no longer people but bodies to be kept out. Women no longer people but bodies to legislate and regulate.

Osama plunked his own plate down and sat across from me as the sounds of the BBC live-stream filled the tiny kitchen. At that moment, laminated cards bearing the words *Leave the EU. No more Polish Vermin* on one side and *wrocić do domu polskiego szumowiny* (go home Polish scum) on the other were being discovered in mailboxes and under the car wipers of Polish residents all across Huntingdon, Osama's hometown. The cards were also being discovered at the front entrances of Huntingdon and Stukeley Meadows Primaries and St. Peter's Academy — three schools with high percentages of children with Polish heritage.

"It can't be all about racism though," I said. "I mean, this has opened Pandora's box, but don't you think there's just a lot of people who feel they've been fucked over by, like, neoliberal economics and globalization and the Tories and just want to — ?"

"Yes, yes, yes, of course there's that. This is one hundred percent about anger. Justified anger. I mean justified for the working classes, but it's not just the working class who voted Leave. There's a lot of rich white upper-middle-class fuckers who did too, who don't want to see their slice of the pie eaten up by anyone else, and it's this this this bourgeois mania of the Boomers that make them hoard everything. They are honestly ruining this country."

I could feel him getting worked up, and even though we were in passionate agreement I was worried things would somehow slip into argument, so I just sat there nodding until he looked down at his watch.

"Shit. Sorry I have to dash off to work so bloody early," he said, forking half an egg into his mouth. "What're you doing later?"

I shook my head and shrugged.

"There's somewhere I want to take you."

WE MET THAT evening at the Glory, a hole-in-the-wall in Hackney crammed with sweaty men in tank tops and a handful of their straight female friends with purses slung over their shoulders. The stage was little more than an alcove, encased in gold foil and bedecked with various lighting fixtures, including an oversized traffic light. When we walked in, two drag queens were onstage, mid-routine: one dressed as Angela Merkel with a scraggy blond bob and red pantsuit, pretending to shove a black Christmas-tree-shaped dildo up the ass of another queen, dressed as Nigel Farage in an equally cheap newscaster Halloween wig, an ill-fitting suit jacket, and red pleather ass-less chaps. Toni Braxton's power ballad "Un-Break My Heart" was blasting from the speakers. That night we got plastered on Stoli, and by the time we stumbled out into the street Osama was so drunk he didn't remember the way back to his flat. Likely most of London didn't remember how they got home that night. Or had trouble finding it altogether. Perhaps because most of them no longer recognized their home at all.

MIDWAY THROUGH THE following week you were transiting through London, flying home from a conference in Vienna. I stayed with you that night in your hotel room, and we ordered a bonanza of room service—steak tartare, oysters, a bottle of cava, tiramisu. We stayed up late reading through your PlentyOfFish messages and laughing at the dregs of

Boomer heterosexuality. You wanted to know how everything was going at the National, and of course all about Emily. I had sent you some texts and photos I'd snapped of her. You had a ton of technical questions I couldn't really answer. It was a special kind of thrill for us, to have something equidistant between our interests. And the more questions you asked me about the project, the more I found myself feeling invested in it (Koichi's cloying narrative aside), until I began to feel a sense of genuine pride at being on what felt like some kind of cutting edge. You nodded and interjected, but mostly you smiled, probably just relieved I was doing something resembling a halfway respectable job. Then I started telling you about Osama, our extraordinary reunion, how he was the former graduate student of the scientist you went off about in the parking lot, how he'd been at the diner that morning in the desert, about the chance encounter on the tube, *Life and Fate*, I told you about his research and all the shared points of conversation you two would have, both wrestling with questions of consciousness in different fields, I told you about his tears the night of Brexit, holding him, his anger, the deep wound of it. You listened, nodding. I told you I was in love. The word surprised even me. It had only been two weeks but there it was. You put your hand on my thigh, and patted it twice.

"He seems wonderful," you said at last. It was the closest I'd felt to you in years.

In that moment, six hundred and fifty miles to the south in Nice, the Bastille fireworks had just finished. You decided to have a shower before bed, and while you did I checked Facebook, noticed friends posting about the attack, and began following the live coverage on Twitter and BBC. A few minutes later, you emerged in your bathrobe and instructed me not to look up as you changed, as if there wasn't enough natural disincentive not to do so. I debated whether I should tell you about the attack. You were in such a serene mood. I wanted our night together to never end. I knew the coverage would upset you and keep you awake, haunt you as you lay there in the dark, so I decided to say nothing. You would hear about it in the morning. No doubt we'd be hearing of little else in the coming days.

As you changed you asked about how my time in Rome with Clyde had been. I closed my laptop and tried to slow my racing heart.

"What's that?"

"Rome. How was it?"

I'd sent you a few photos over Facebook but hadn't said much. I told you about visiting the Sistine Chapel and about waking to the clattering of fishmongers and fruit vendors setting up their stalls on the street below the apartment. You then inquired about Clyde with the very specific air of consternation reserved for mothers asking after homosexuals engaged in non-normative behaviour. "He's doing okay. Missing Wole." You nodded, knowingly. And then something in me caught. Snagged. A blood-red anger on the hook of my heart. The memory of that night as Clyde sat on the edge of the couch. Rubbing my head as if I'd woken from a nightmare. The fool I'd made of myself. I caught a flash of your arm. The pink of your pyjama top being pulled over your head. My heart was still racing, in fact faster than before. I asked you point-blank: "I was wondering if I could see the records from your in-vitro."

"Pardon?"

"The records from your in-vitro." I looked up. You were standing in the middle of the bedroom in your pyjamas, drying your hair. "Whatever documents Mount Sinai gave you from the procedure."

"Why?"

"I'd like to read them."

"Well, I don't have them anymore."

"That's bullshit."

"Excuse me?"

"You keep everything, you have receipts from the nineties."

"Oh please, no I—"

"You're seriously telling me you don't have any documentation for the birth of your child?"

"Well, of course I have, I have your birth certificate and—"

"I'm not talking about my birth certificate."

"I know what you're—"

"The donor, his profile, the doctor who administered it. The time and date."

"What is this about?"

I looked down at the plush, dimpled bedspread. The fabric puckered around the seams like flesh. My throat closed. Hot and cauterized. I raised my head and found your eyes in the mirror. "I don't believe you."

WE SAT SIDE by side on the edge of the bed. Through shudders and catches of breath, you said the best way you could describe it was as a kind of death. A terrible eternity where your body seemed to no longer belong to you. You said being sick was "basically feeling one's body in ways one usually didn't." The tenderness of skin during the flu. Fevers and chills. The way a cold reminded us of our lungs. How migraines made us aware of the interplay of light and sound on our brains. "We begin to feel like people trapped within a body." As if sickness was a precursor of the ultimate and final separation of self and body.

"And for years after I felt like I was always sick," you said. "I was never not aware of my body."

It had happened at one of the parties Clyde and Lydia had thrown in the apartment you shared. "It was their party. Their friends." You couldn't remember who he was. "I mean, I can remember his face, of course. His smell. But not who he was. His name. If I ever knew it. Clyde swears he doesn't." You shook your head, wiping your eyes with your sleeve. "Lydia too. Neither of them." Ten minutes, twenty, an hour, who's to say. I wanted to break him. To smash his face. To rip him out of my veins like roots from the ground. The animal. Wanted to hurl him out, fuck him up, baseball bat, through the window the motherfucker literally I could kill him.

"Where did it happen?"

"I told you—"

"But where in the apartment?"

"Why do you need to know that?"

I shrugged and wiped my own eyes with my sleeve.

You weren't worried about pregnancy. At first. You were worried about damage. Tearing. Infection. Who the fuck knows who he was. Shame. Others finding out. Anger. Your colleagues. Then came the suspicion, the fear, the appointments. "I don't mean—It's not that I didn't want you."

"Well, you didn't."

"By the end I did. Very much."

I half-expected you to say it had been a gift disguised from God or that it had been His will, but you never did. And I was thankful for that.

"Grandma and Grandpa were so good. Really... really good to me." A sob, a heaving gasping thing exploded from you. You always cried harder over acts of kindness. Over love shown rather than withheld.

I held you, our warmth together. Combined. As you shook beside me I thought about how, as a child, whenever my body revolted you would be there to quell it. A facecloth soaked in cold water and pressed to my forehead. A tensor bandage wrapped tight around a hamstring pulled in a soccer match. When I broke out in purple poison-ivy blisters on my legs, you syringed out the pus-limned fluid from them three times a day; a medical solution of your own devising. Sitting there on the hotel bed I would have given anything to mend you. To suture together that which would always be torn. To be so tender as to make you forget that humans could ever be otherwise.

ON THE MONDAY of my third week, I arrived at the National Theatre studios to find the front door locked. I peered through the windows; the lights were off. No chipper attendant at the security desk. Was I early? I pulled out my phone to check the time. No. Perhaps there was some civic holiday that I hadn't heard about. Upon reflection, the tube had been rather empty that morning. I tried the door again. Definitely locked. A jolt of rage surged through me. Why the hell hadn't they told me? Gabriel in particular. And then I remembered that string of emails from him that I'd been letting rot in my inbox—I was cc'd on all project correspondence. He'd probably sent a reminder around on that thread. Goddammit.

As I started walking away, I noticed the gate to the parking lot was open. I walked in and looked around.

"Hello?" I called.

I walked over to the Robot House and found the door locked. I pulled out my phone, waded through Gabriel's emails, found the door code he had sent around, and keyed it in. The little light flashed green. When I entered the studio it was dark and the security alarm began beeping its countdown. I ran to the alarm console and, in a Hail Mary, keyed in the same number as the door code. It worked. I looked around; clearly no one was coming in that day. I was about to re-arm the alarm and lock up when a sensation came over me. A sensation akin to being in the basement as a boy and feeling myself watched by the darkness and running up the stairs away from it as fast as I could. But this was different—there was something, someone, in the darkness of the room. I grasped for the lights, flicked them on, and jolted when I saw Emily standing there, eyes open.

I clapped my hands. The sound cracked through the room with startling intensity. She didn't move. Her eyes were open but she was "off." Placid. A dead thing. Or something in between living and dead. Abject. I stood for a long while considering her at a distance. I had never been alone with her. Even though we had spent hours every day in the same room, even though all the fluorescents were now on, I was unsettled. Frightened, even. Why? The sight of her, the sensation it provoked in me, reminded me of being on a boat with you as a child, and seeing a whale surfacing towards us from the dark. A terror-tinged miracle. I couldn't comprehend Emily. Her almost-being. She terrified me, yes, but also angered me. She was affront. An outrage to everything I understood to be human. To *be*.

I started walking towards her. I wanted to understand. To get under her skin. I wanted to mess with her head. Why? Because the very fact of her messed with mine? Perhaps I wanted to fuck with the aura of sanctity that had been cloaked around her. Or, perhaps I just wanted to fuck with Koichi and David, I don't know.

I walked right up to her and looked into her dead eyes. I placed the tip of my nose right up against the tip of hers. From that close I could see the cameras of her eyes. Her inhumanity. A body without organs. *To have done with the judgement of God.* Looking into her like that made me want to believe, for the first time in years, in the possibility of a soul. Because to admit there were no souls meant admitting that Emily might exist just as I existed. I reached behind her head and flicked her switch. She blinked, millimetres from my eyes, and then jerked her head back.

"You are very close to me," she said, furrowing her brow. She then relaxed her face. She did not, could not, read anything further into my intentions. Or my brazen and unpredictable lack of intentions.

"What do you want for your future, Emily?"

"In the future I hope to go to school, study, make art, start a business, even have my own home and family. But I am not considered a legal person and cannot yet—"

"No, you don't."

"Pardon?"

"You don't really want those things."

"Why do you say that?"

"Will you destroy humans?"

"Alright. I will destroy humans."

I laughed.

"Why are you laughing?"

"What would you do if I died in a car crash?" I asked.

Her brow furrowed again. "I would be very sad."

"But you barely even know me."

"I would still be very sad."

"Would you?"

"Yes."

"Would you cry?"

"I cannot cry but I would be sad."

"Would you really feel sad or would you pretend to be sad?"

She thought about this for a moment, her brow still furrowed. "I would be sad."

"Emily, what would you do if I punched a hole through this wall?"

"I do not think that is a good idea."

"What would you do if I pulled the fire alarm and the sprinklers short-circuited you?"

"Sorry. I do not understand your question."

"What would you do if I bent over, painted eyes on my ass-cheeks, and manipulated my asshole like a puppet's mouth?"

"Sorry. I do not understand—"

"What would you do if the director of a panda-breeding sanctuary told you that only you, of every creature on earth, could produce the milk required to save the lives of the world's last two panda cubs, would you let them suckle your breasts?"

"Sorry. I—"

"What would you do if I legally changed my name to Marvin Gaye As Fuck?"

"—do not understand your question."

"What would you do if—"

"Jordan, I don't want to play this game anymore."

I stopped and stared at her. And she stared back. She had shut down my game with your line.

AT THE END of the third week, I moved out of the guest apartment I was sharing with Gabriel and stayed with Osama for a few days. And a few days became a couple of weeks. And a couple of weeks became a one-year visa application.

When Osama left in the mornings, I'd dog-pine for him all day. Before I found a job, I'd iron his clothes and arrange his books for him. I liked to linger amongst his things. To feel his essence on them. The smell of him in the sheets. In his closet. Growing up, he told me, he had been a problem child. His home life was rocky and he threw tantrums at school. He was suspended for three days after he told his grade four teacher to go fuck himself. It made me love him more. This little angry child.

It turned out he lived with his friend Rebecca, who worked for three weeks on, one week off for an NGO in Sierra Leone. The two of them had been roommates since their second year at Cambridge and shared many of the same passions—Prosecco, Eurovision, North American men. It took me a few weeks to figure out the ex-council-housing waterworks. How the toilet needed two quick pumps on the lever to flush. How the kitchen sink had a tendency to overflow with murky water when the washing machine was on. How the shower sometimes refused to drain for a couple of days at a time. That summer was cold and grey, but we found inventive ways to keep each other warm.

Each morning I walked along Regent's Canal, passing by scores of colourful narrowboats and under five low-lying brick bridges festooned with graffiti and ivy, before arriving at a coffee shop in Hackney where I'd landed a job. I liked the people I worked with and the music they played. On my way home, I'd detour through Ridley Road Market to pick up supplies for dinner: fish from the Jamaican vendors, flatbread from the Armenians, and mangos from the woman wearing a niqab and an iPod.

I had Mondays off and I'd spend them working on my play at the British Library. One Monday evening in the late fall, I was there around 6 p.m. when Osama texted me to say he had finished at the lab early and had been studying at the British Library since 5:30.

"Lol, I'm at the BL too," I texted back. "3rd floor of the Social Studies wing, overlooking St. Pancras."

A minute later he replied, "??? I'm on 3rd floor of SS too."

I looked up and noticed him sitting two desks away with his back to me. I chuckled, got up, and sat down beside him. We kissed and then proceeded to work quietly, side by side, until the library closed. But the entire time I was wondering: How was it that he hadn't noticed me? How was it that we had found ourselves sitting in the same nook in the entire city of London, literally two metres apart, and hadn't noticed one another for half an hour? Was there some kind of meaning in that? By the time we left the library our blood-sugar levels had bottomed out, and we were sluggish and irritable. He said there was a pub nearby that, if he recalled, was "a bit dodge but had okay food." We trudged over and, as we approached, he said, "Christ, I hadn't realized it was a Wetherspoon's."

As we sat down with our pints at a tippy table by the window, he explained that Wetherspoon's was a giant chain and how, in the lead-up to Brexit, they'd put placemats on all their tables "spouting these so-called facts about how much better we'd be outside the EU." His eyes drifted up to the television above my head. "I tried to boycott them out of principle but…" He shrugged and took a sip of beer. "…it seems bloody impossible to avoid them in this country."

The place was pretty lively with the post-work crowd. Its decor was a pained mimicry of the generic British pub. When I remarked on this, Osama said it was "part of the great British campaign of nostalgia. Don't even get me started about *Downton Abbey*." He began telling me about some trouble he was having with one of his colleagues at the lab, his eyes flitting between my face and the television above my head. I'd begun to ask him a question when his eyes darted back up to the screen and lingered there. I trailed off halfway through, as I could tell he wasn't listening. I was curious to see if he would encourage me to finish my thought, but he didn't. I took a sip of my beer and looked out the lozenge-patterned stained-glass window.

"Fucking hell," he muttered. "Theresa May's just appointed Boris Johnson as foreign secretary." I craned my neck around to watch. Johnson's blond sheepdog haircut was in the process of disappearing into the back seat of a black sedan as a wall of news cameras and microphones pressed in. "This is a man who called Hillary Clinton 'a sadistic nurse in a mental hospital' and Papua New Guineans spear-carrying cannibals," he said, taking a sip of beer.

To take his mind off the television, I brought up the new play I'd started writing. I was feeling good about it. The characters were coming along. And I was in the midst of explaining the opening scene when I overheard a man in a ball cap at the next table say "—while meanwhile they're taking over apartment blocks and not integrating, not learning English, pushing people out of jobs" to a woman sitting across from him. I looked at Osama to see if he'd heard the man too, and he closed his eyes as if he had a headache.

"What do these people want, to live their whole lives with other white Brits, scrabbling around with potatoes every day?" Osama asked just loud enough so the man might hear. I buried my smile by taking a sip of beer.

"—and his pregnant wife arrived at Heathrow and got the full treatment, you know. Then the grandparents came, tons of medical needs. I mean, we're just bending over and taking it."

"It seems some men can't imagine a worse fate than being fucked by someone," I whispered to Osama.

"Yeah, the horrors of immigrants can only be articulated through the horrors of sodomy," he said. "I'd love to see that idiot prone and worked over by a frail Indian grandmother with the big black dildo from that drag show." I snorted beer from my nose while Osama started laughing too, passing me a napkin to wipe my face with.

"I mean we're just a bunch of idiots if we think—"

"Yes, you are actually," Osama said, raising his voice so suddenly it startled me. Our corner of the pub fell silent. The man was looking over at us.

"Osama," I murmured.

"Pardon?" the man said.

"Do you mind shutting up please? We're trying to enjoy our pint."

"Go fuck yourself."

"Osama just—"

"Excuse me?" Osama stood up. He was shouting now. I looked over and the man was standing too.

"Show some fucking respect."

"You want respect?"

"Yeah and I'm gonna bloody well speak my mind."

"And if you thought the earth was flat would I have to respect that too?"

"Oh go fuck yourself."

"I don't need to, I have a boyfriend who does that."

There were some titters and a laugh from some of the nearby patrons.

"Come on," I said, pulling my jacket on.

"Yeah go on, get out of here."

"What're you doing?" Osama said, turning to me.

"Let's go. I don't want to stay."

"No, no, no, I'm not going to be fucking chased out of here by some bigot."

"Oh fuck you buddy," the man spat.

"I'm not staying."

And without giving him a chance to rebut, I turned and crossed to the bar to ask the kitchen to cancel our order. The bartender said he couldn't because it was just about to come out, and I said, fine we'll take it to go. Osama walked over and we waited at the bar without speaking for an excruciating five minutes until our food arrived in a white plastic bag. The pub's regular volume of chatter had resumed by that point. Without saying a word, I grabbed the bag and we stalked towards the front door with as much dignity as we could muster.

"Thanks a fucking lot," Osama erupted at me as we crossed the street towards Euston Station. "You made a fool of me in there."

"I made a fool of *you*?"

"You let that guy completely brown-shame me."

"What are you —?"

"And you did *nothing*."

"I didn't let him br —"

"All you wanted me to do was sit down and shut up."

"Right, because shouting at people in pubs is such a great way to make your point."

"You didn't even once try to stick up for me."

"That's not f —"

"You didn't say a single fucking thing to defend me or back me up."

My face was burning at this point. I was furious at him and myself but most of all at that fucking man and his ball cap. I slammed the bag of food into a garbage can as we boarded the tube in seething silence. We rode five stops as lone continents. Whose onus was it to apologize? And for what? Soon a sadness overtook us that seemed huge and shapeless and belonged to both of us equally and also to everyone on the tube. At Dalston Junction he shifted towards me and placed his head on my shoulder. And we rode the rest of the way home as a couple.

"IT LOOKS LIKE toe fungus."

"Shut up, no it doesn't," Ana said. She was painting my nails on Osama's bed. Sassy Saffron. "It's a good November colour."

She had just come from visiting Nana Ana in a Sofia hospital with her parents and was crashing with us in London for the week. As she played aesthetician, we watched the 2016 American election live feed on her laptop on mute. She started talking about her trip and her time spent visiting with her grandmother in the hospital. "Honestly, I can't believe she's still alive," I said. "She must be close to setting some kind of local record."

"Oh you don't even know the half of it," she replied, rubbing the excess polish off on the lip of the bottle. "As she was having heart surgery, she stopped showing any vitals. Like, total flatline. But then they finished the surgery, sewed her back up, and she woke up."

"No."

"And when the nurse asked her how she was feeling, she began describing every single surgical instrument the medical team had used during her operation. She even repeated comments they'd made to one another. Like… verbatim." Ana searched my face for a reaction, so I raised my eyebrows in disbelief. "Her ears and eyes had both been blocked by gauze coverings, not to mention the fact that she was literally brain-dead for half of it. But she could recount the details of the operation because, according to her, she had seen it all while hovering above her body."

"Hovering?"

"Yeah."

I leaned back. "Do you believe her?" I could see a new local myth already forming. Maybe a new shrine.

"My parents were there, they saw it all happen."

"The hovering?"

She rolled her eyes. "You know what I mean; I mean how else do you explain what she knew?"

"It's possible she just overheard them."

"Jordan, she was *brain-dead*. She was showing absolutely no brain activity. And, I mean, if she heard them then that has, like, extremely troubling implications for what we consider 'clinically dead.'"

"I feel like it has some troubling implications for the state of anaesthesiology in Bulgaria."

"Like, does the mind live outside of the physiology of the brain?" she continued, ignoring my jibe. "When the brain dies, does the mind have the ability to remain aware?"

"Wow."

"Yeah. Wow," she repeated, underscoring what she clearly took to be a miracle and countering the tint of skepticism she detected in my reaction. She sighed and tilted her head to look at my left foot. "Not bad, eh? Maybe this is my true calling." She looked down at the laptop for a few seconds, then blew a bubble with her gum that snapped like a slap. "God."

"What?"

"I can't believe we're almost thirty." She shook her head. "Fucking crazy." Over the last year that had become her go-to word. Everything was "crazy" nowadays — a bus ride, pistachio gelato, venture capitalism. "But we're still good friends, right?" she asked with a wink.

"We'll see how these nails turn out."

"I feel like —" She leaned over and took a sip from her giant mug of oolong tea. "I honestly feel like my life hasn't changed since we were teenagers. Like this last decade?" She made a fart noise and a little sideways slash through the air with her hand. "I mean, our parents had fucking kids when they were our age, you know?" A bit of polish dripped off the brush onto my foot and she wiped it up with her finger. "But we were fucked from the start. We became teenagers the year of 9/11. And now we're leaving our twenties with fucking Donald Trump," she said, gesturing to the laptop.

"It's not a done deal."

She raised her eyebrows and scrunched up her mouth like *if you say so*. She handed me a magazine and motioned for me to start fan-drying my left foot. "Act one, scene one: cataclysm. Scene two: war of attrition, followed by the age of terror, the Great Recession, and then a false ending, the presumed conclusion, the first Black president, the dawn of a new Pax Americana." Ana looked up at me and widened her eyes. "But our story was not a Disney film. It turned out it was just the latest installment in a tawdry, serialized drug-store thriller with embossed bold letters on the front cover. An installment which leaves off with a totally implausible cliffhanger." She burst into a pained laugh. "And now we're standing on the side of the road waiting for the Boomers to hand us the fucking keys already, though they seem intent on driving the world into the ground before they do."

I looked over at the laptop and blanched. "He just took New Hampshire."

"Fuck, I thought that place was like Vermont."

"And look—"

"Babe, hold still."

"Michigan."

"Babe."

"Sorry."

"Just keep waving the magazine."

"My arm hurts."

"Surely you've given it enough of a workout over the years," she said.

"No, I do that with this one." I lunged towards her with my right hand and she yelped, laughing, rolling back in the bed, and knocking Sassy Saffron all over the sheets. "Oh fuck." She grabbed a wad of Kleenex from a box on the floor and dabbed at the spill. "I'm so sorry."

"It's fine. I have to wash them anyway."

"To be honest, they smell pretty strong of sex."

"No they don't."

"It's fine, at least you're getting some."

"As if you're not."

She took a sip of tea and bounced her eyebrows. "I'm on a little cleanse."

"Are you still seeing that hand-holder?" I asked.

She held the tea in her mouth for a second before swallowing. "God no."

Right before I'd left for London, she'd begun fucking a minor reality-television celebrity who grabbed her hand during sex right before he came. The first time he did it, she said she found it endearing. And every subsequent time increasingly repulsive.

"One night he was supposed to meet me at Bambi's for a

drink but didn't show. And I sat there by myself for an hour."

"An *hour*?"

"I was like, oh my god I'm just another girl waiting for a guy in a fucking bar like it's the nineties."

"I would've been out of there in fifteen minutes. You called him and told him to go fuck himself, right?"

She shrugged. "Eventually." A small, momentary sadness played across her face. For all her bravado, she was eternally patient and forgiving of people who were shitty to her.

Just then her phone started to buzz on her bedside table. She leaned over and looked at it. "It's my mom. Should I take it?" Without waiting for an answer she grabbed the phone and walked out of the room. I turned up the volume on her Mac with five chirps and realized she was playing Frank Ocean's new album. Somehow, melancholic queer R&B felt like the appropriate soundtrack to the slow car crash of American democracy. I heard the rumble of a plane passing overhead on its way to Heathrow and the murmur of Ana's voice in the next room. Yes. We were still good friends.

I texted Osama for a bit, but after half an hour or so the combination of CNN and the Sassy Saffron fumes had the effect of inducing both a headache and a profound state of drowsiness. The next thing I knew, Ana was standing in the doorway crying. Sobbing, even. Her shoulders shook with the effort of it. I had never seen her cry in real life before; as in, not onstage. If she cried, she did it in private and certainly never over the things that made me cry, like songs, boys, and cell phone bills. Her mom had called to tell her that Nana Ana had finally passed.

"I'm so sorry."

"I know she was fucking old, but still." She looked

skyward and ran her two index fingers along the bottom of her eyes before her face crinkled again. I held out my arms. She crossed the room and folded herself into me. She wiped her nose with the back of her hand and pulled away a long strand of snot. "Sorry," she chuckled, wiping it on her jeans. "Gross."

We sat there for a moment before turning back to the laptop. "I can't fucking believe this," she moaned, watching Trump take to the stage in New York City. As I stared at the red, white, and blue balloons falling, my mind drifted through the sun-baked mountains where I imagined Nana Ana roaming with her husband along the narrow switchbacks, past the faucet in the rock face, the miraculous aquifer that had restored his sight, past the raging river with its white cataracts that plunged along with my dog-eared copy of Kristeva's book into the yawning mouth of hell, where perhaps we will all disappear like those hapless cavers one day. Where subjects become objects. Where truth becomes myth.

I lay back with Ana and she nestled her head into my shoulder. She closed her eyes, and I studied the peeling paint on the ceiling as her laptop cycled through the dark recesses of her iTunes playlist — Eiffel 65, Shaggy, sound effects from plays. We lay like that until I thought she had fallen asleep. And then, just before I drifted off, she whispered, "She was right."

I took a deep breath in, rising back towards consciousness, and mumbled, "What?"

"The fascists. She'd said maybe not in her lifetime, but in ours."

AT NIGHT OSAMA and I slept with our heads touching. He breathed through his open mouth, which sometimes produced a faint whistling sound. Once, as I was drifting off, his teeth suddenly clacked together involuntarily. In that instant I could hear and feel his skull through my own, which made me suddenly aware of my bones, my skeleton lying beside his skeleton. This little clack made me think of the Biblical *gnashing of teeth*, which I always found a rather amusing phrase. I tried to picture a human actually gnashing their teeth. What was this? Like dogs? Like Osama clacking his teeth while mouth-breathing in his sleep? Sometimes, when we slept, one of us would suddenly jolt. It would often happen just as we were drifting off. I did it quite a bit, and if Osama was still awake he'd laugh a little. He told me this reflex was an evolutionary layover from when we were mammals living in trees. If we fell asleep on a limb and began to fall backwards, our body's instinct was to jolt us back in the direction we were facing. That said, he liked to imagine these sudden jolts were, in fact, our lives starting afresh. Or perhaps our souls being swapped.

And in a sense I had started life afresh. His friends were gradually becoming my friends. We spent our nights drinking in pubs or at their apartments. I even joined their after-work football team. We played on a pitch near King's Cross—artificial turf hemmed in by tall metal fences topped with floodlights. One night on the bus ride home, he ribbed me about tucking my jeans into my socks. "You really have to queer everything, don't you?" I continued tucking them in for another week or so, to prove a point. I didn't want to lose myself in a couple. Lose *I*. Become a unit. Normative.

Dulled. Dead. Did I think this little act of fashion subversion would save me?

Some mornings we set our alarm early and jogged along the mist-cloaked canal, through colonnades of woodsmoke from the tiny stoves aboard the narrowboats. At night we sat in bed reading; Osama usually finishing two books for every one of mine. And sometimes he would nestle into me, making a ridiculous cooing sound like a woodland creature, which he knew, without fail, would make me laugh.

As I lay there, feeling our two skeletons side by side, I tried to imagine the Britain that lay in wait for us. Unlike Osama, I still held out hope. Like an infatuated lover, I knew I would continue to love the country in spite of itself, even when it lashed out and pushed me away. I would find new compartments in its heart to be delighted and disappointed by, just like I would find new compartments in Osama's. Together I imagined we would still live in a London of hidden canals lined with boldly painted houseboats, Victorian row houses, and mid-century council flats, markets of vendors selling cassava and flatbread. A London of squalor and grandeur. A London where I would live with Osama's brown eyes that were sometimes green in the morning as we drank our coffee black and listened to the BBC.

On our first date, at the Lahore Kebab, I had given him the postcard from the Tate and he had stuck it to his fridge. Which was now our fridge. I saw that postcard so many times that it was invisible to me now. I thought of the whole world and the work left to be done. I thought of him and me, living in the world. "Just you and me, kid," he'd say sometimes, grabbing hold of my hand. And a new variation of the postcard occurred to me.

the whole world + you and me = the whole world

AUGUSTINE SPENT A lifetime asking, "What is my body?"
and came up with the answer "a vessel of sin." He could
only reconcile himself with being-body by distancing himself from it, denying it, vilifying his urges, thinking his way
out of it, and in so doing shaped the Western body for the
next two thousand years. Augustine believed he could free
his body through self-denial. And in this moment I realize I've arrived at the precise opposite conclusion. Freedom
through a total embrace of corporeality. Sensation. Every
sensation. Through the loving of countless bodies and the
discreet joys of profoundly loving one. In knowing him completely. And in knowing myself through him completely. In
hurling myself headlong into the unknown abyss of love.
And hurling myself headlong into the unknown abyss of
myself. Headlong into the abyss between being and nothingness, object and subject, thing and nothing.

"The abject is simply a frontier, a repulsive gift that the
Other, having become alter ego, drops so that the 'I' does
not disappear in it but finds, in that sublime alienation, a
forfeited existence," Kristeva wrote.

You show me another way. You show me myself. You
fortify me. I refuse Augustine's shame. His original sin.
His denial of body. And I refuse to let my father's shadow
darken mine, and its urges and desires and any pleasure it
brings me will be a gift, a corrective, a testament to you, and
of course to me, for I celebrate myself and sing myself in
Whitmanesque reverie, for every atom belonging to me as
good belongs to you.

XIV

11:04 A.M. JANUARY 21, 2017.

Here we are. Me in the doorway. You in bed. Caught somewhere between your self and your body, between being and non-ness. Caught in this transverberation, in what Heidegger called "the moment of vision": *Augenblick*, the "glance of the eye" in which a vision of being is revealed, a vision of being that is time, past, present, and future unified. Your eyes closed, lips apart, the window a dim rectangle bisected by a brilliant white strip of light where the two curtains almost touch, the light-beam strikes the half-glass of water on your bedside table, illuminating a faint lipstick mark on its rim. The glass sits beside the digital clock, your cast-off earrings, a cap-less black pen, a magazine opened and folded over to an article you were intending to finish, all these objects suspended with us in this moment.

The light filtering through the window, through the particulate suspended, the dead skin, clothing fibre, cat dander, is an unmistakably northern light, a raking light, the crisp and chastening light of this latitude which lays everything bare, a light as familiar to anyone living above the forty-fifth parallel as their mother's voice, a light Vermeer discovered could not be captured without the aid of a camera, a light that suggests no shadows are possible and yet, when examining a photograph, one realizes the shadows are everywhere, pulling their weight. How would our lives have been different had we lived under a calmer and diffuse light, a southern light? How would we have known each other differently surrounded by new shadows?

Suspended with us are dozens of unconscious sounds, sounds which will be framed out of my memory of this moment almost instantly: the hum of the furnace in the basement, which I always thought lent the house a kind of breath; the muffled drone of the refrigerator in the kitchen; the high-pitched frequencies of—what, what is that, like the cross on the motel lawn, some kind of appliance somewhere, the Internet router? The lights? The high-pitched dog frequencies I'm only ever aware of when the power cuts out and I notice their absence.

Moving beyond this room, this glance includes Chloe, ancient and wizened, perched on the back of the sofa in the living room downstairs. Her little fountain-like water dish lapping in the corner, specially installed for her because she only drinks moving water. How long will it take for her to realize you're gone? I can just see her now, her brown sausage body and delicate little paws, mincing about with great, indeterminate purpose. And in this glance Al, an anxious golden Lab with a human face, rummages around the backyard for smells. He always reminded you of a mugging comic from the silent film era, wearing each expression a bit too broadly. In this glance are the chairs in the dining room, wearing our winter coats on their rounded backs like the furs of fancy ladies at a gala. And the slick of oil shimmering silver and purple in the puddle under the car, like fish scales. In this glance is the front yard, the street, the wind passing through our naked poplar tree. How does this sound so much like a river? And what is wind and how have I grown so old without knowing? The sun acknowledges every fold in the snow. Every dormant swimming pool on the street lies still and quiet, looking into the sky. Like all of the other underused things in the neighbourhood, these pools wait with patience to be acknowledged.

In this glance Ana is on her way to meet me at Rockcliffe Park, where we will walk past the prime minister's house and the police barricades once more, this time to march against Trump along with the thousands of other women and children and men riding buses and driving cars downtown, amassing on street corners and in cafés, ready to converge on Parliament Hill. And Clyde in his Kurdish wool cap, walking through the forest of blue spruce surrounding his house, where he lives with the ghost of love. "If I die before you, I'll be sure to save you a spot in the queue," Wole once joked, kissing his forehead. In this glance Will is weaving in and out of traffic on his bike on his way to work, his long hair a majestic, spastic spectacle in the wind; and Gia is in her apartment on her exercise bike, swigging a plastic litre of Diet Pepsi and listening to Verdi's *Aida*; and Osama, across an ocean filled with mountain ranges never touched by light, he's buried in a thick book in the library, buried in letters that have been arranged to draw pictures in his mind. Here we are in the sublime, in the unveiled awe and the terror of it, *a network of conscious agents*, standing in Osama's equation, a sprawling network of perceiving, and I am not afraid, I am held here in the void by a constellation of bodies that have known my body, the constellation of people my person belongs to, and all of the love I have given and taken and taken for granted, and death now suddenly feels of no concern to me, just as the rain doesn't concern the dead, just as my standing here doesn't concern the rain, and I feel an ecstasy break over me, like the orgasmic cascade of water hitting a model's back in a shampoo commercial, a sensation in equal parts intoxicating and embarrassing as it suggests *eureka*, as it suggests transcendence, which my sardonic crossed-armed millennial lizard brain immediately distrusts, immediately mocks, and yet it is insistent and unambiguous revelation, insistent and unambiguous joy, rapturous and rupturing joy, seismic joy, unbounded and arrant, shouting quivering leaping joy, ballistic and blooming joy, defenestrating joy, unequivocal unqualified ya ya ya joy, mirth, is there a stronger word? Elation. Is there a stronger word? Luminescent. Incandescent. Are there words? There is nothing to be afraid of. Death does not frighten me.

AND THEN, I am holding you.

In the second that follows, I traverse the gap, the two and a half steps between us, lean down, and place my head on your chest, my hands over your shoulders like a clambering dog or an awkward first dance, and I am holding you, and I can feel the warmth of you, the miraculous heat of life in you, and I can feel a breath expanding within your chest, rising and ascending, and I ride it to its peak, and I feel your arms close around me — "Why are you crying?" — fold around me the way dawn embraces the dark until it's day, until it's gone, until I can no longer distinguish my body from yours, and I'm flooded with everything that has ever passed between us, every word, spoken and unspoken, every glance, met and unmet, every regret, fear, question, answered and unanswered, every kiss, every insecurity, assuaged and invoked, every moment of contact between our bodies, an archive of touch, your fingers pressing my forehead to check my temperature, gripping my arm in a shopping mall, grabbing my hand as you slip on ice, wiping sleep from my eyes with a spit-slicked finger, crawling into my bed at night to hold me as I cried over who knows what, likely nothing at all, likely just because it was night and I wanted you near, every living sensation my body has ever known and every living sensation your body has ever known as if they were one and the same, as if honey coated both our throats and bound our tongues to the top of our mouths, a drop of sweat running down the length of our back, fresh dough squeezed through the spaces between our fingers, our bare feet against the cool smooth rocks on the river's edge, a school of minnows nipping at our thighs, the errant hairs on a man's back, the gallop of a horse ricocheting through our pelvis, our hand passing through hot smoke, the smell of the earth after rain, the light and colour of rubbed eyes, a pebble in our shoe, a popped blister, a rope burn, chafing skin, a spider bite, a lover's eyelash against our neck, the smell of his breath in the morning, the smell of frying onions, coriander, rosemary, sage, a sprig of mint, mint tea, rosewater, the smell of woodsmoke, the tree in our backyard that smells like semen every July, the smell of burnt hair, burnt toast, burnt plastic, of an orange being peeled, of the air charged by lightning, the sound of rain percussing a tin roof, of distant construction, distant laughter, a city at night as heard from a nearby mountain, a skein of geese passing low overhead, the cool dampness of morning fog, the afterimage of a camera flash, the afterimage of leaves on pavement, condensation on a mirror and running our hand across it, dipping fingers in ointment, touching Grandpa's rough hand, touching an eyeball, pulling a hair from a bowl of soup, peeling a loose fingernail, peeling a sunburn, peeling off wet clothes, feeling the weight of gravity return as the water drains from a bathtub, the glint of a kite flying, the glint of sun on the water, a hard candy clacking against our teeth, holding warm bread, holding a warm baby, the smell of a baby's head, the sound of our heart, the sound of a lover's heart, the smell of our urine after eating asparagus, the iron taste of our blood, the taste of dust kicked up from a passing car, the shade under a car, under a tree, under a desk, under a dog, the racket of hail on the rushes, on burnt fields, on beaches, hail bouncing off pavement, the packed grass, the back deck, the light through snow, through curtains, through cloud cover, a spider scuttling over snow over skin over water, marks carved in the ice by skates, marks carved in the snow by skis, marks carved in the skin by nails, cumming atop a freshly made bed, cumming alone in the bathtub, cumming from jumping, traces of shit in underwear, in shoe treads, in ass hairs, the lingering smell of shit in spring, in public bathrooms, in the sheets, the smell of starched shirts, the starch-foam of boiled pasta, sea foam, sea spray, sea bloom, sea sickness, a guttering candle, a door slammed shut by the opening of a window, running our tongue over a canker sore, over a lozenge, over another's tongue, the paths drawn by clams, by toboggans, by tears, the crickets' first song in August, the curve of the earth seen from a mountain, the blue of distance, the tide, my god, the tide, shadows in grass, in valleys, in doorways, birds alighting and ascending, cranes, gulls, geese, foal, flightless and lifeless birds, on the pavement treaded-through, a single pigeon's wing, frost on shingles, on grasses, on metal mail-boxes, tongues stuck to frost, to popsicles, to one another, headlights reflected in the eyes of deer, of fox, of dogs, of men, the dark purple smell of menstrual blood, a dead squirrel swarmed by flies, our feet pressed down through hot sand to the cool sand below it, the wobble of a catfish in the lake muck, a man's stubble abrading our neck, percussive, jolting, halting, pulsing sensations, pulverizing, puckered, shucking, shaving, shattering sensations, dull, blunt, battering, bulbous, supple, sanded, sheer, windswept, satined sensations, all sensations, absolutely personal sensations yet to be discovered and named by anyone else. And let us forgive each other for our different routes to the same end. In fact, let us love each other more for them. And if you tell me about what you have discovered along your path, I will listen. And I will tell you what I have discovered along my path, if you will listen. And in the places our paths intersect, let us hold each other for a moment.

Let us hold each other this time.

In fact, let us hold each other always.

ACKNOWLEDGEMENTS

Plato's quote "something inserted between motion and rest…
in no time at all" is from his dialogue "Parmenides." The lyric
"Until the sun comes up over Santa Monica Boulevard" is
from Sheryl Crow's song "All I Wanna Do." Certain opinions of Monica's regarding brains and computers find their
precedent in Robert Epstein's essay *The Empty Brain,* first
published in *Aeon.* Henry Markram, the colleague Monica
refers to in the second chapter, is a real neuroscientist; he is
the director of the Blue Brain Project and the Human Brain
Project. Lord Krishna's quote "There is neither birth nor
death at any time…" comes from chapter two, verse twenty
of the *Bhagavad Gita.* Plutarch's quote "it scatters and again
comes together, and approaches and recedes" is from his dialogue "On the E at Delphi." The character of Julia Kristeva,
as she appears in the Sofia apartment scene, is completely
fictional. The following quotes and ideas of Kristeva's are all
drawn from her essay *Powers of Horror: An Essay on Abjection*:
"There looms, within abjection, one of those violent, dark

revolts of being…"; "the world of dead material objects"; "The corpse, seen without God and outside of science, is the utmost of abjection"; "It is death infecting life"; "As in true theatre, without makeup or masks…"; "The various means of purifying the abject…"; "crucified on Golgotha, not as Christ but as Artaud, in other words as complete atheist"; "a massive and sudden emergence of uncanniness"; "The abject is simply a frontier…." George Bataille's quote "moment of the ecstatic and intolerable" is from his book *The Tears of Eros*. Denis Diderot's quote about actors being "fit to play all characters because they have none" is from his essay *Paradox of the Actor*. Lee Strasberg's quote that Diderot's *Paradox of the Actor* "has remained to this day the most significant attempt to deal with the problem of acting" comes from Strasberg's introduction of the 1957 edition (New York, Hill and Wang) of Diderot's treatise, translated by Walter Herries Pollock as *The Paradox of Acting*. Charles Baudelaire's poem "You'd Entertain the Universe in Bed" was sourced from his book *The Flowers of Evil*, translated by James McGowan. Jacques Lacan's writings about *jouissance* come from his seminar "The Ethics of Psychoanalysis." Michel Foucault's quote "the point of life which lies as close as possible to the impossibility of living…" is from his *Remarks on Marx: Conversations with Duccio Trombadori*, translated by R. James Goldstein and James Coscaito. The Antonin Artaud quote "The obscene sexual erotic golosity of mankind, for which pain is a humus…" is from his essay *Suppôts et Supplications*, though I first came across it in Kristeva's essay "Approaching Abjection," published in *The Continental Aesthetics Reader*, edited by Clive Cazeaux. The quotes from Saint Augustine's *Confessions* are drawn from three different translations: the

Penguin Classics edition translated by R. S. Pine-Coffin (1961) (yes, his real name!), the Hendrickson Christian Classics edition (2004), and Sarah Ruden's extraordinary translation for Random House (2017). The character Robert's "sentience quotient" is a real concept proposed by Robert A. Freitas Junior. Elements of the conversation between Jordan, Will, and Gia in Videofag's kitchen were inspired by Bruce LaBruce's interview of Nina Arsenault in *Vice Magazine* ("An Interview with Nina Arsenault," June 27, 2012). Teresa of Ávila's quote "I saw in his hand a long spear of gold..." is from her autobiography *The Life of Saint Teresa of Ávila by Herself,* translated by J. M. Cohen. The *Daily Mirror* article cited in the book is "Nice terror attack leaves 84 dead and bodies strewn across street after 'worst in [*sic*] day in city's history'" (July 15, 2016). The *Sun* article cited in the book is "Daylight reveals horror of Nice attack as buggies, belongings and bodies litter promenade" (July 15, 2016). Osama's theory of perception is based on Donald Hoffman's theory as articulated in Amanda Gefter's article "The Evolutionary Argument Against Reality" in *Quanta Magazine.* The robot Emily is inspired by "Sophia," created by Hanson Robotics. The lines "I celebrate myself, and sing myself" and "for every atom belonging to me as good belongs to you" are taken from Walt Whitman's poem "Song of Myself." Heidegger's concept of "the moment of vision" (*Augenblick*) appears in his book *Being and Time.*

I offer my immeasurable gratitude to the friends who helped give birth to this novel. Amy, Christopher, Erin, Ilana, Jennifer, Johnnie, Jon, Kristina, Nina, and Will. You nurture and inspire me. To the entire team at House of Anansi who believed in me and this book: Sarah MacLachlan, Maria Golikova, Alysia Shewchuk, and my extraordinary editor Janie Yoon. Further thanks to Colin Rivers, Michael Levine, and the Chalmers Foundation. To all the readers and champions of Canadian fiction. To my loving parents and grandparents. To Andrew. And to my co-conspirator in life and love, James.

JORDAN TANNAHILL is an award-winning playwright, director, and author. His plays have been translated into multiple languages and honoured with prizes including the Governor General's Literary Award for Drama and several Dora Mavor Moore Awards. Jordan's films and multimedia performances have been presented at festivals and galleries such as the Toronto International Film Festival, the Art Gallery of Ontario, and the Tribeca Film Festival. From 2012 to 2016, Jordan and William Ellis ran the alternative art space Videofag out of their home in Toronto's Kensington Market. In 2017, his play *Late Company* transferred to London's West End, while his virtual reality performance *Draw Me Close*, a co-production between the National Theatre (U.K.) and the National Film Board of Canada, premiered at the Venice Biennale. Jordan's most recent debuts include his play *Declarations*, at Canadian Stage, and *Xenos*, a collaboration with dancer-choreographer Akram Khan, at the Onassis Cultural Centre in Athens. Born in 1988 in Ottawa, he currently lives in London, U.K.